James Baldwin

Choice English Lyrics

James Baldwin

Choice English Lyrics

ISBN/EAN: 9783744788304

Printed in Europe, USA, Canada, Australia, Japan

Cover: Foto ©Andreas Hilbeck / pixelio.de

More available books at **www.hansebooks.com**

CHOICE ENGLISH LYRICS

SELECTED AND ARRANGED

BY

JAMES BALDWIN

AUTHOR OF " THE BOOK OF ELEGIES," " THE FAMOUS ALLEGORIES,"
" SIX CENTURIES OF ENGLISH POETRY," ETC.

SILVER, BURDETT & COMPANY

NEW YORK   BOSTON   CHICAGO

1894

Norwood Press:
J. S. Cushing & Co. — Berwick & Smith.
Boston, Mass., U.S.A.

PUBLISHERS' NOTE.

This is the fourth volume of a series of Select English Classics which the publishers have in course of preparation. The series will include an extensive variety of selections chosen from the different departments of English literature, and arranged and annotated for the use of classes in schools. It will embrace, among other things, representative specimens from all the best English writers, whether of poetry or of prose; selections from English dramatic literature, especially of the eighteenth and nineteenth centuries; choice extracts from the writings of the great essayists; selections from famous English allegories; a volume of elegies and elegiacal poetry; studies of English prose fiction, with illustrative specimens, etc. Each volume will contain copious notes, critical, explanatory, and biographical, besides the necessary vocabularies, glossaries, and indexes; and the series when complete will present a varied and comprehensive view of all that is best in English literature. For supplementary reading, as well as for systematic class instruction, the books will possess many peculiarly valuable as well as novel features; while their attractive appearance, combined with the sterling quality of their contents, will commend them for general reading and make them desirable acquisitions for every library.

CONTENTS.

PAGE

SONGS OF BATTLE, BRAVERY, AND PATRIOTISM:

SONNETS:

LYRICS OF LIFE:

Songs of Nature and the Seasons.

So goeth the poet hand in hand with nature, not enclosed within the narrow warrant of her gifts, but freely ranging within the zodiac of his own wit. Nature never set forth the earth in so rich tapestry as divers poets have done; neither with pleasant rivers, fruitful trees, sweet-smelling flowers, nor whatever else may make the too-much-loved earth more lovely; her world is brazen, the poets only deliver a golden. —SIR PHILIP SIDNEY.

I.

A MORNING SONG.

HARK, hark ! the lark at heaven's gate sings,
  And Phœbus 'gins arise,
His steeds to water at those springs
  On chaliced flowers that lies ;
And winking Mary-buds begin
  To ope their golden eyes :
With every thing that pretty is,
  My lady sweet, arise :
    Arise, arise.
              —WILLIAM SHAKESPEARE.

2.

DAWN-SONG.

THE lark now leaves his watery nest
    And, climbing, shakes his dewy wings ;
He takes this window for the East,
    And to implore your light, he sings.
        Awake ! awake ! the morn will never rise
        Till she can dress her beauty at your eyes.

The merchant bows unto the seaman's star ;
    The ploughman from the sun his season takes,
But still the lover wonders what they are
    Who look for day before his mistress wakes.
        Awake ! awake ! break through your veils of lawn !
        Then draw your curtains, and begin the dawn.
                            —SIR WILLIAM DAVENANT.

3.

MORNING.

WHAT tongue the melodies of morn can tell ?
The wild-brook babbling down the mountain side ;
The lowing herd ; the sheepfold's simple bell ;
The pipe of early shepherd dim descried
In the lone valley ; echoing far and wide
The clamorous horn along the cliffs above ;
The hollow murmur of the ocean-tide ;
The hum of bees, and linnet's lay of love,
And the full choir that wakes the universal grove.

The cottage-curs at early pilgrim bark ;
Crown'd with her pail, the tripping milkmaid sings ;

The whistling ploughman stalks afield ; and, hark !
Down the rough slope the ponderous wagon rings ;
Thro' rustling corn the hare astonish'd springs ;
Slow tolls the village-clock the drowsy hour ;
The partridge bursts away on whirring wings ;
Deep mourns the turtle in sequester'd bower,
And shrill lark carols clear from her aerial tower.

—JAMES BEATTIE.

4.

A GREETING.

PACK clouds, away, and welcome day,
　　With night we banish sorrow ;
Sweet air blow soft, mount larks aloft
　　To give my Love good-morrow ;
Wings from the wind to please her mind
　　Notes from the lark I'll borrow ;
Bird prune thy wing, nightingale sing,
　　To give my Love good-morrow ;
　　　　To give my Love good-morrow,
　　　　Notes from them both I'll borrow.

Wake from thy nest, Robin Redbreast,
　　Sing birds in every furrow ;
And from each hill let music shrill
　　Give my fair Love good-morrow !
Blackbird and thrush in every bush,
　　Stare, linnet, and cock-sparrow !
You pretty Elves, amongst yourselves
　　Sing my fair Love good-morrow :
　　　　To give my Love good-morrow
　　　　Sing birds in every furrow !

—THOMAS HEYWOOD.

5.

MAY MORNING.

Now the bright morning star, day's harbinger,
Comes dancing from the East, and leads with her
The flow'ry May, who from her green lap throws
The yellow cowslip, and the pale primrose.
    Hail, bounteous May! that dost inspire
    Mirth, and youth, and warm desire;
    Woods and groves are of thy dressing,
    Hill and dale doth boast thy blessing.
Thus we salute thee with our early song,
And welcome thee and wish thee long.

                 —JOHN MILTON.

6.

HUNTING SONG.

    WAKEN, lords and ladies gay,
  On the mountain dawns the day,
  All the jolly chase is here,
  With hawk, and horse, and hunting-spear!
  Hounds are in their couples yelling,
  Hawks are whistling, horns are knelling,
  Merrily, merrily, mingle they,
  "Waken, lords and ladies gay."

  Waken, lords and ladies gay,
  The mist has left the mountain gray,
  Springlets in the dawn are steaming,
  Diamonds on the brake are gleaming:

And foresters have busy been,
To track the buck in thickest green :
Now we come to chant our lay,
" Waken, lords and ladies gay."

Waken, lords and ladies gay,
To the green-wood haste away ;
We can show you where he lies,
Fleet of foot, and tall of size ;
We can show the marks he made,
When 'gainst the oak his antlers frayed ;
You shall see him brought to bay,
" Waken, lords and ladies gay."

Louder, louder chant the lay,
Waken, lords and ladies gay!
Tell them youth, and mirth, and glee,
Run a course as well as we ;
Time, stern huntsman! who can balk,
Stanch as hound, and fleet as hawk ;
Think of this, and rise with day,
Gentle lords and ladies gay.

—SIR WALTER SCOTT.

7.

MAY–DAY.

GET up, get up for shame! the blooming morn
Upon her wings presents the god unshorn.
    See how Aurora throws her fair
    Fresh-quilted colours through the air :

B

Get up, sweet-slug-a-bed, and see
The dew bespangling herb and tree.
Each flower has wept, and bowed toward the east,
Above an hour since ; yet you not drest,
     Nay ! not so much as out of bed ?
     When all the birds have matins said,
     And sung their thankful hymns : 'tis sin,
     Nay, profanation, to keep in, —
Whenas a thousand virgins on this day,
Spring, sooner than the lark, to fetch in May.

Rise ; and put on your foliage, and be seen
To come forth, like the Spring-time, fresh and green,
     And sweet as Flora.   Take no care
     For jewels for your gown or hair :
     Fear not ; the leaves will strew
     Gems in abundance upon you :
Besides, the childhood of the day has kept,
Against you come, some orient pearls unwept :
     Come, and receive them while the light
     Hangs on the dew-locks of the night :
     And Titan on the eastern hill
     Retires himself, or else stands still
Till you come forth.   Wash, dress, be brief in praying :
Few beads are best, when once we go a Maying.

Come, my Corinna, come ; and coming, mark
How each field turns a street ; each street a park
     Made green, and trimmed with trees : see how
     Devotion gives each house a bough
     Or branch : each porch, each door, ere this,
     An ark, a tabernacle is

Made up of white-thorn neatly interwove;
As if here were those cooler shades of love.
    Can such delights be in the street,
    And open fields, and we not see't?
    Come, we'll abroad: and let's obey
    The proclamation made for May:
And sin no more, as we have done, by staying;
But, my Corinna, come, let's go a Maying.

There's not a budding boy or girl, this day,
But is got up, and gone to bring in May.
    A deal of youth, ere this, is come
    Back, and with white-thorn laden home.
    Some have dispatched their cakes and cream,
    Before that we have left to dream:
And some have wept, and woo'd, and plighted troth,
And chose their priest, ere we can cast off sloth:
    Many a green-gown has been given;
    Many a kiss, both odd and even:
    Many a glance, too, has been sent
    From out the eye, love's firmament:
Many a jest told of the keys betraying
This night, and locks picked:—yet we're not a Maying.

—Come, let us go, while we are in our prime;
And take the harmless folly of the time!
    We shall grow old apace, and die
    Before we know our liberty.
    Our life is short; and our days run
    As fast away as does the sun:—
And as a vapour, or a drop of rain
Once lost, can ne'er be found again:

So when or you or I are made
A fable, song, or fleeting shade :
All love, all liking, all delight
Lies drowned with us in endless night.
—— Then while time serves, and we are but decaying,
Come, my Corinna! come, let's go a Maying.

—ROBERT HERRICK.

———◆———

8.

THE STORY OF A SUMMER DAY.

O PERFECT Light, which shaid away
The darkness from the light,
And set a ruler o'er the day,
Another o'er the night;

Thy glory, when the day forth flies,
More vively does appear,
Than at midday unto our eyes
The shining sun is clear.

The shadow of the earth anon
Removes and drawès by,
While in the east, when it is gone,
Appears a clearer sky.

Which soon perceive the little larks,
The lapwing and the snipe,
And tune their songs, like Nature's clerks,
O'er meadow, muir, and stripe.

Our hemisphere is polished clean,
And lightened more and more ;
While everything is clearly seen,
Which seemèd dim before :

Except the glistering astres bright,
Which all the night were clear,
Offuskèd with a greater light
No longer do appear.

The golden globe incontinent
Sets up his shining head,
And o'er the earth and firmament
Displays his beams abread.

For joy the birds with boulden throats
Against his visage sheen
Take up their kindly music notes
In woods and gardens green.

The dew upon the tender crops,
Like pearls white and round,
Or like to melted silver drops,
Refreshes all the ground.

The misty reek, the clouds of rain
From tops of mountains skails,
Clear are the highest hills and plain,
The vapours take the vales.

The ample heaven, of fabric sure,
In cleanness does surpass
The crystal and the silver pure,
Or clearest polished glàss.

The time so tranquil is and still,
That no where shall ye find,
Save on a high and barren hill,
An air of peeping wind.

All trees and simples, great and small,
That balmy leaf do bear,
Than they were painted on a wall,
No more they move or steir.

Calm is the deep and purple sea,
Yea, smoother than the sand;
The waves, that weltering wont to be,
Are stable like the land.

So silent is the cessile air,
That every cry and call,
The hills and dales and forest fair
Again repeats them all.

The flourishes and fragrant flowers,
Through Phœbus' fostering heat,
Refreshed with dew and silver showers,
Cast up an odour sweet.

The cloggèd busy humming bees,
That never think to drone,
On flowers and flourishes of trees,
Collect their liquor brown.

The sun, most like a speedy post,
With ardent course ascends;
The beauty of the heavenly host
Up to our zenith tends;

Not guided by a Phaëthon,
Not trainèd in a chair,
But by the high and holy One,
Who does all where empire.

The burning beams down from his face
So fervently can beat,
That man and beast now seek a place
To save them from the heat.

The herds beneath some leafy tree,
Amidst the flowers they lie;
The stable ships upon the sea
Tend up their sails to dry.

With gilded eyes and open wings,
The cock his courage shows;
With claps of joy his breast he dings,
And twenty times he crows.

The dove with whistling wings so blue
The winds can fast collect,
Her purple pens turn many a hue
Against the sun direct.

Now noon is went; gone is midday,
The heat does slake at last,
The sun descends down west away,
For three of clock is past.

The rayons of the sun we see
Diminish in their strength,
The shade of every tower and tree
Extended is in length.

Great is the calm, for everywhere
The wind is setting down,
The reek throws right up in the air
From every tower and town.

The gloaming comes, the day is spent,
The sun goes out of sight,
And painted is the occident
With purple sanguine bright.

The scarlet nor the golden thread,
Who would their beauty try,
Are nothing like the colour red
And beauty of the sky.

Our west horizon circular,
From time the sun be set,
Is all with rubies, as it were,
Or roses red o'erfret.

What pleasure were to walk and see,
Endlong a river clear,
The perfect form of every tree
Within the deep appear.

Oh, then it were a seemly thing,
While all is still and calm,
The praise of God to play and sing
With cornet and with shalm!

All labourers draw home at even,
And can to other say,
Thanks to the gracious God of heaven,
Which sent this summer day.

—ALEXANDER HUME.

9.

HOLIDAY IN ARCADIA.

WOODMEN, shepherds, come away,
This is Pan's great holiday;
    Throw off cares,
With your heaven-aspiring airs
    Help us to sing,
While valleys with your echoes ring.

Nymphs that dwell within these groves,
Leave your arbours, bring your loves,
    Gather posies,
Crown your golden hair with roses;
    As you pass,
Foot like fairies on the grass.

Joy crown our bowers!   Philomel,
Leave of Tereus' rape to tell.
    Let trees dance,
As they at Thracian lyre did once;
    Mountains play,
This is the shepherds' holiday.

—JAMES SHIRLEY.

10.

AFTER RAIN.

THE cock is crowing,
The stream is flowing,
The small birds twitter,
The lake doth glitter,

The green field sleeps in the sun;
　The oldest and youngest
　Are at work with the strongest;
　The cattle are grazing,
　Their heads never raising;
There are forty feeding like one!

　Like an army defeated
　The snow hath retreated,
　And now doth fare ill
　On the top of the bare hill;
The plough-boy is whooping — anon — anon;
　There's joy in the mountains;
　There's life in the fountains;
　Small clouds are sailing;
　Blue sky prevailing;
The rain is over and gone!

　　　　　— WILLIAM WORDSWORTH.

II.

UNDER THE GREENWOOD TREE.

　UNDER the greenwood tree
　Who loves to lie with me,
　And turn his merry note
　Unto the sweet bird's throat,
Come hither, come hither, come hither:
　　Here shall he see
　　No enemy
But winter and rough weather.

Who doth ambition shun
And loves to live i' the sun,
Seeking the food he eats
And pleased with what he gets,
Come hither, come hither, come hither:
Here shall he see
No enemy
But winter and rough weather.

— WILLIAM SHAKESPEARE.

12.

EVENING.

IF aught of oaten stop or pastoral song
May hope, chaste Eve, to soothe thy modest ear
Like thy own solemn springs,
Thy springs, and dying gales;

O Nymph reserved,—while now the bright-hair'd sun
Sits in yon western tent, whose cloudy skirts
With brede ethereal wove,
O'erhang his wavy bed,

Now air is hush'd, save where the weak-eyed bat
With short shrill shriek flits by on leathern wing,
Or where the beetle winds
His small but sullen horn,

As oft he rises midst the twilight path,
Against the pilgrim borne in heedless hum,—
Now teach me, maid composed,
To breathe some soften'd strain

Whose numbers, stealing through thy dark'ning vale,
May not unseemly with its stillness suit;
As musing slow I hail
Thy genial love return.

For when thy folding-star arising shows
His paly circlet, at his warning lamp
The fragrant Hours, and Elves
Who slept in buds the day,

And many a Nymph who wreathes her brows with
    sedge
And sheds the freshening dew, and lovelier still
The pensive Pleasures sweet,
Prepare thy shadowy car.

Then let me rove some wild and heathy scene;
Or find some ruin midst its dreary dells,
Whose walls more awful nod
By thy religious gleams.

Or if chill blustering winds or driving rain
Prevent my willing feet, be mine the hut
That, from the mountain's side,
Views wilds and swelling floods,

And hamlets brown, and dim-discover'd spires;
And hears their simple bell; and marks o'er all
Thy dewy fingers draw
The gradual dusky veil.

While Spring shall pour his showers, as oft he wont,
And bathe thy breathing tresses, meekest Eve!
While Summer loves to sport
Beneath thy lingering light;

While sallow Autumn fills thy lap with leaves;
Or Winter, yelling through the troublous air,
Affrights thy shrinking train
And rudely rends thy robes;

So long, regardful of thy quiet rule,
Shall Fancy, Friendship, Science, smiling Peace,
Thy gentlest influence own,
And love thy favorite name!

—WILLIAM COLLINS.

13.

EVENING SONG.

SHEPHERDS all, and maidens fair,
Fold your flocks up, for the air
'Gins to thicken, and the sun
Already his great course hath run.
See the dew-drops how they kiss
Every little flower that is,
Hanging on their velvet heads,
Like a rope of crystal beads:
See the heavy clouds low falling,
And bright Hesperus down calling
The dead Night from under ground;
At whose rising, mists unsound,
Damps and vapors fly apace,
Hovering o'er the wanton face
Of these pastures, where they come,
Striking dead both bud and bloom:
Therefore, from such danger lock
Every one his lovèd flock;

And let your dogs lie loose without,
Lest the wolf come as a scout
From the mountain, and, ere day,
Bear a lamb or kid away ;
Or the crafty thievish fox
Break upon your simple flocks.
To secure yourselves from these,
Be not too secure in ease ;
Let one eye his watches keep,
Whilst the other eye doth sleep ;
So you shall good shepherds prove,
And for ever hold the love
Of our great god.   Sweetest slumbers,
And soft silence, fall in numbers
On your eyelids !   So, farewell !
Thus I end my evening's knell.

—John Fletcher.

14.

TO DIANA.

Hail, beauteous Dian, queen of shades,
That dwell'st beneath these shadowy glades,
Mistress of all those beauteous maids
    That are by her allowed.
Virginity we all profess,
Abjure the worldly vain excess,
And will to Dian yield no less
    Than we to her have vowed.
The shepherds, satyrs, nymphs, and fawns,
For thee will trip it o'er the lawns.

Come, to the forest let us go,
And trip it like the barren doe;
The fawns and satyrs still do so,
    And freely thus they may.
The fairies dance and satyrs sing,
And on the grass tread many a ring,
And to their caves their ven'son bring;
    And we will do as they.
        The shepherds, satyrs, &c., &c.

Our food is honey from the bees,
And mellow fruits that drop from trees;
In chace we climb the high degrees
    Of every steepy mountain.
And when the weary day is past,
We at the evening hie us fast,
And after this, our field repast,
    We drink the pleasant fountain.
        The shepherds, satyrs, &c., &c.
                    —THOMAS HEYWOOD.

15.

EVENING HYMN.

THE night is come, like to the day;
Depart not Thou, great God, away.
Let not my sins, black as the night,
Eclipse the lustre of thy light.
Keep still in my horizon; for to me
The sun makes not the day, but Thee.
Thou whose nature cannot sleep,
On my temples sentry keep!

Guard me 'gainst those watchful foes,
Whose eyes are open while mine close;
Let no dreams my head infest,
But such as Jacob's temples blest.
While I do rest, my soul advance;
Make my sleep a holy trance,
That I may, my rest being wrought,
Awake into some holy thought;
And with as active vigour run
My course as doth the nimble sun.
Sleep is a death; oh! make me try,
By sleeping, what it is to die;
And as gently lay my head
On my grave, as now my bed.
Howe'er I rest, great God, let me
Awake again at last with Thee.
And thus assured, behold I lie
Securely, or to wake or die.
These are my drowsy days; in vain
I do now wake to sleep again:
Oh! come that hour, when I shall never
Sleep again, but wake for ever.

— SIR THOMAS BROWNE.

16.

SERENADE.

THE day is down into his bower;
 In languid lights his feet he steeps;
The flush'd sky darkens, low and lower,
 And closes on the glowing deeps.

In creeping curves of yellow foam
  Up shallow sands the waters slide;
And warmly blow what whispers roam
  From isle to isle the lullëd tide;

The boats are drawn; the nets drip bright;
  Dark casements gleam; old songs are sung;
And out upon the verge of night
  Green lights from lonely rocks are hung.

O winds of eve that somewhere rove
  Where darkest sleeps the distant sea,
Seek out where haply dreams my love,
  And whisper all her dreams to me!
        —OWEN MEREDITH (LORD LYTTON).

17.

SLUMBER–SONG.

CARE-CHARMING Sleep, thou easer of all woes,—
Brother to Death, sweetly thyself dispose
On this afflicted prince; fall like a cloud
In gentle showers; give nothing that is loud
Or painful to his slumbers;—easy, sweet,
And as a purling stream, thou son of Night,
Pass by his troubled senses:—sing his pain
Like hollow murmuring wind, or silver rain.
  Into this prince gently, oh, gently slide,
  And kiss him into slumbers like a bride!
        —JOHN FLETCHER.

C

18.

INVOCATION TO SLEEP.

Come, Sleep, and with thy sweet deceiving
    Lock me in delight awhile ;
    Let some pleasing dreams beguile
    All my fancies ; that from thence
    I may feel an influence,
All my powers of care bereaving !

Though but a shadow, but a sliding,
    Let me know some little joy !
    We that suffer long annoy
    Are contented with a thought,
    Through an idle fancy wrought ;
Oh, let my joys have some abiding !

—Beaumont and Fletcher.

19.

THE YOUNG MAY MOON.

The young May moon is beaming, love,
The glow-worm's lamp is gleaming, love,
    How sweet to rove
    Through Morna's grove,
When the drowsy world is dreaming, love !
Then awake ! — the heavens look bright, my dear,
'Tis never too late for delight, my dear,

And the best of all ways
To lengthen our days
Is to steal a few hours from the night, my dear.

Now all the world is sleeping, love,
But the Sage, his star-watch keeping, love,
    And I whose star,
    More glorious far,
Is the eye from that casement peeping, love.
Then awake!—till rise of sun, my dear,
The Sage's glass we'll shun, my dear,
    Or, in watching the flight
    Of bodies of light,
He might happen to take thee for one, my dear.

—THOMAS MOORE.

20.

NIGHT IN THE DESERT.

How beautiful is night!
A dewy freshness fills the silent air;
No mist obscures, nor cloud, nor speck, nor stain,
    Breaks the serene of heaven:
In full-orbed glory yonder moon divine
    Rolls through the dark blue depths.
        Beneath her steady ray
        The desert-circle spreads,
    Like the round ocean, girdled with the sky.
        How beautiful is night!

—ROBERT SOUTHEY.

21.

THE WORLD'S WANDERERS.

Tell me, thou star, whose wings of light
Speed thee in thy fiery flight,
In what cavern of the night
    Will thy pinions close now?

Tell me, moon, thou pale and gray
Pilgrim of heaven's homeless way,
In what depth of night or day
    Seekest thou repose now?

Weary wind, who wanderest
Like the world's rejected guest,
Hast thou still some secret nest
    On the tree or billow?

—Percy Bysshe Shelley.

22.

TO THE MOON — A FRAGMENT.

Art thou pale for weariness
Of climbing heaven, and gazing on the earth,
Wandering companionless
Among the stars that have a different birth,—
And ever changing, like a joyless eye
That finds no object worth its constancy?
Thou chosen sister of the spirit,
That gazes on thee till in thee it pities. . . .

—Percy Bysshe Shelley.

23.

THE COMING OF SPRING.

SUMMER is i-cumen in,
Lhude sing, cuccu;
Groweth sed, and bloweth med,
And springeth the wde nu.
  Sing, cuccu, cuccu!
Awe bleteth after lamb,
Louth after calve cu,
Bulluc sterteth, bucke verteth,
  Murie sing, cuccu.
  Well sings the cuccu,
Ne swik thou never nu.
  Sing, cuccu, nu,
  Sing, cuccu.
          —ANON. (*13th Century*).

24.

SPRING.

SPRING, the sweet Spring, is the year's pleasant king;
Then blooms each thing, then maids dance in a ring,
Cold doth not sting, the pretty birds do sing,
  Cuckoo, jug-jug, pu-we, to-witta-woo!

The palm and May make country houses gay;
Lambs frisk and play, the shepherds pipe all day,
And we hear aye birds tune this merry lay,
  Cuckoo, jug-jug, pu-we, to-witta-woo!

The fields breathe sweet, the daisies kiss our feet,
Young lovers meet, old wives a sunning sit,
In every street these tunes our ears do greet,
  Cuckoo, jug-jug, pu-we, to-witta-woo!
    Spring! the sweet Spring!

          —THOMAS NASH.

25.

TO BLOSSOMS.

FAIR pledges of a fruitful tree,
  Why do ye fall so fast?
  Your date is not so past,
But you may stay yet here awhile
  To blush and gently smile,
    And go at last.

What, were ye born to be,
  An hour or half's delight,
  And so to bid good-night?
'Twas pity Nature brought ye forth
  Merely to show your worth,
    And lose you quite.

But you are lovely leaves, where we
  May read how soon things have
  Their end, though ne'er so brave;
And after they have shown their pride,
  Like you, awhile, they glide
    Into the grave.

         —ROBERT HERRICK.

26.

A SPRING IDYLL.

THIS day, Dame Nature seem'd in love!
The lusty sap began to move;
Fresh juice did stir th' embracing vines;
And birds had drawn their valentines.
Already were the eaves possess'd
With the swift pilgrim's daubèd nest;
The groves already did rejoice
In Philomel's triumphing voice;
The show'rs were short; the weather mild;
The morning fresh; the evening smil'd.
   Joan takes her neat-rubbed pail, and now
She trips to milk the sand-red cow,
Where, for some sturdy foot-ball swain,
She strokes a syllabub or twain.
The fields and gardens were beset
With tulip, crocus, violet;
And now, though late, the modest rose
Did more than half a blush disclose.
   Thus all looks gay and full of cheer,
   To welcome the new-liveried year.

—SIR HENRY WOTTON.

27.

TO DAFFADILS.

FAIR Daffadils, we weep to see
   You haste away so soon;
As yet the early-rising sun
   Has not attain'd his noon.

Stay, stay,
Until the hasting day
Has run
But to the even-song;
And, having pray'd together, we
Will go with you along.

We have short time to stay, as you;
We have as short a spring;
As quick a growth to meet decay,
As you, or anything.
We die
As your hours do, and dry
Away,
Like to the summer's rain;
Or as the pearls of morning's dew,
Ne'er to be found again.

—ROBERT HERRICK.

28.

TO THE LARK.

GOOD speed, for I this day
Betimes my matins say,
Because I do
Begin to woo.
Sweet singing Lark,
Be thou the clerk,
And know thy when
To say Amen.

And if I prove
Blest in my love,
Then thou shalt be
High Priest to me,
At my return
To incense burn,
And so to solemnise
Love's and my sacrifice.

—ROBERT HERRICK.

29.

ODE TO THE CUCKOO.

HAIL, beauteous stranger of the grove!
Thou messenger of spring!
Now Heaven repairs thy rural seat,
And woods thy welcome sing.

What time the daisy decks the green,
Thy certain voice we hear;
Hast thou a star to guide thy path,
Or mark the rolling year?

Delightful visitant! with thee
I hail the time of flowers,
And hear the sound of music sweet
From birds among the bowers.

The schoolboy, wandering through the wood
To pull the primrose gay,
Starts, the new voice of spring to hear,
And imitates thy lay.

What time the pea puts on the bloom,
Thou fliest thy vocal vale,
An annual guest in other lands,
Another spring to hail.

Sweet bird! thy bower is ever green,
Thy sky is ever clear;
Thou hast no sorrow in thy song,
No winter in thy year!

Oh, could I fly, I'd fly with thee!
We'd make, with joyful wing,
Our annual visit o'er the globe,
Companions of the spring.

—Michael Bruce.

———◆———

30.

TO THE CUCKOO.

O blithe new-comer! I have heard,
I hear thee and rejoice:
O Cuckoo! shall I call thee bird,
Or but a wandering Voice?

While I am lying on the grass,
Thy twofold shout I hear;
From hill to hill it seems to pass,
At once far off and near.

Though babbling only to the vale
Of sunshine and of flowers,
Thou bringest unto me a tale
Of visionary hours.

Thrice welcome, darling of the Spring!
Even yet thou art to me
No bird, but an invisible thing,
A voice, a mystery;

The same whom in my school-boy days
I listened to; that Cry
Which made me look a thousand ways
In bush, and tree, and sky.

To seek thee did I often rove
Through woods and on the green;
And thou wert still a hope, a love;
Still longed for, never seen!

And I can listen to thee yet;
Can lie upon the plain
And listen, till I do beget
That golden time again.

O blessèd bird! the earth we pace
Again appears to be
An unsubstantial, fairy place
That is fit home for thee!

—WILLIAM WORDSWORTH.

———◆———

31.

TO THE DAISY.

WITH little here to do or see
Of things that in the great world be,
Sweet Daisy! oft I talk to thee
    For thou art worthy,

Thou unassuming commonplace
Of Nature, with that homely face,
And yet with something of a grace
      Which love makes for thee!

Oft on the dappled turf at ease
I sit and play with similes,
Loose types of things through all degrees,
      Thoughts of thy raising;
And many a fond and idle name
I give to thee, for praise or blame
As is the humor of the game,
      While I am gazing.

A nun demure, of lowly port;
Or sprightly maiden, of love's court,
In thy simplicity the sport
      Of all temptations;
A queen in crown of rubies drest;
A starveling in a scanty vest;
Are all, as seems to suit thee best,
      Thy appellations.

A little Cyclops, with one eye
Staring to threaten and defy,
That thought comes next — and instantly
      The freak is over,
The shape will vanish, and behold!
A silver shield with boss of gold
That spreads itself, some fairy bold
      In fight to cover.

I see thee glittering from afar —
And then thou art a pretty star,

Not quite so fair as many are
    In heaven above thee!
Yet like a star, with glittering crest,
Self-poised in air thou seem'st to rest; —
May peace come never to his nest
    Who shall reprove thee!

Sweet Flower! for by that name at last
When all my reveries are past
I call thee, and to that cleave fast,
    Sweet silent Creature!
That breath'st with me in sun and air,
Do thou, as thou art wont, repair
My heart with gladness, and a share
    Of thy meek nature!

—William Wordsworth.

32.

ALMOND BLOSSOM.

Blossom of the almond trees,
April's gift to April's bees,
Birthday ornament of spring,
Flora's fairest daughterling;
Coming when no flowerets dare
Trust the cruel outer air;
When the royal kingcup bold
Dares not don his coat of gold;
And the sturdy black-thorn spray
Keeps his silver for the May; —
Coming when no flowerets would,
Save thy lowly sisterhood,

Early violets, blue and white,
Dying for their love of light.
Almond blossom, sent to teach us
That the spring-days soon will reach us,
Lest, with longing over-tried,
We die as the violets died —
Blossom, clouding all the tree
With thy crimson broidery,
Long before a leaf of green
O'er the bravest bough is seen ;
Ah ! when winter winds are swinging
All thy red bells into ringing,
With a bee in every bell,
Almond blossom, we greet thee well.

— EDWIN ARNOLD.

33.

THE FLY.

BUSY, curious, thirsty fly,
Drink with me, and drink as I ;
Freely welcome to my cup,
Couldst thou sip, and sip it up.
Make the most of life you may ;
Life is short, and wears away.

Both alike are mine and thine,
Hastening quick to their decline ;
Thine's a summer, mine's no more,
Though repeated to threescore ;
Threescore summers, when they're gone,
Will appear as short as one.

— WILLIAM OLDYS.

34.

THE TIGER.

TIGER! Tiger! burning bright
In the forests of the night,
What immortal hand or eye
Fram'd thy fearful symmetry?

In what distant deeps or skies
Burn'd the fervor of thine eyes?
On what wings dar'd he aspire —
What the hand dar'd seize the fire?

And what shoulder and what art
Could twist the sinews of thy heart?
When thy heart began to beat,
What dread hand form'd thy dread feet?

What the hammer, what the chain
Formed thy strength and forged thy brain?
What the anvil?　What dread grasp
Dar'd thy deadly terrors clasp?

When the stars threw down their spears,
And sprinkled heav'n with shining tears,
Did He smile, his work to see?
Did He who made the lamb make thee?

—WILLIAM BLAKE.

35.

THE NIGHTINGALE.

As it fell upon the day
In the merry month of May,
Sitting in a pleasant shade
Which a grove of myrtles made,

Beasts did leap and birds did sing,
Trees did grow and plants did spring,
Everything did banish moan
Save the nightingale alone.
She, poor bird, as all forlorn,
Lean'd her breast against a thorn,
And there sung the dolefullest ditty
That to hear it was great pity.
Fie, fie, fie, now would she cry;
Tereu, tereu, by and by:
That to hear her so complain
Scarce I could from tears refrain;
For her griefs so lively shown
Made me think upon mine own.
— Ah, thought I, thou mournst in vain,
None takes pity on thy pain:
Senseless trees, they cannot hear thee,
Ruthless beasts, they will not cheer thee;
King Pandion, he is dead,
All thy friends are lapp'd in lead:
All thy fellow birds do sing
Careless of thy sorrowing:
Even so, poor bird, like thee
None alive will pity me.

— RICHARD BARNFIELD.

36.

TO A WATERFOWL.

WHITHER, midst falling dew,
While glow the heavens with the last steps of day,
Far, through their rosy depths, dost thou pursue
Thy solitary way?

Vainly the fowler's eye
Might mark thy distant flight to do thee wrong,
As, darkly seen against the crimson sky,
    Thy figure floats along.

Seek'st thou the plashy brink
Of weedy lake, or marge of river wide,
Or where the rocking billows rise and sink
    On the chafed ocean-side?

There is a Power whose care
Teaches thy way along that pathless coast —
The desert and illimitable air —
    Lone-wandering, but not lost.

All day thy wings have fanned,
At that far height, the cold thin atmosphere,
Yet stoop not, weary, to the welcome land,
    Though the dark night is near.

And soon that toil shall end,
Soon shall thou find a summer home, and rest
And scream among thy fellows; reeds shall bend
    Soon o'er thy sheltered nest.

Thou art gone — the abyss of heaven
Hath swallowed up thy form; yet on my heart
Deeply hath sunk the lesson thou hast given,
    And shall not soon depart.

He who, from zone to zone,
Guides through the boundless sky thy certain flight,
In the long way that I must tread alone,
    Will lead my steps aright.

— WILLIAM CULLEN BRYANT.

D

37.

THE CHOUGH AND CROW.

THE chough and crow to roost are gone,
  The owl sits on the tree,
The hush'd wind wails with feeble moan,
  Like infant charity.
The wild fire dances on the fen,
  The red star sheds its ray;
Uprouse ye, then, my merry men!
  It is our opening day.

Both child and nurse are fast asleep,
  And closed is every flower,
The winking tapers faintly peep
  High from my lady's bower;
Bewildered hinds with shortened ken
  Shrink in their murky way;
Uprouse ye, then, my merry men!
  It is our opening day.

Nor board nor garner own we now,
  Nor roof nor latched door,
Nor kind mate bound by holy vow
  To bless a good man's store;
Noon lulls us in a gloomy den,
  And night is grown our day;
Uprouse ye, then, my merry men!
  It is our opening day.

—JOANNA BAILLIE.

38.

AUTUMN.

A DIRGE.

The warm sun is failing, the bleak wind is wailing,
The bare boughs are sighing, the pale flowers are
     dying,
          And the Year
On the earth her death-bed, in a shroud of leaves dead,
          Is lying.
     Come, Months, come away,
     From November to May,
     In your saddest array ;
     Follow the bier
     Of the dead cold Year,
And like dim shadows watch by her sepulchre.

The chill rain is falling, the nipped worm is crawling,
The rivers are swelling, the thunder is knelling
          For the Year ;
The blithe swallows are flown, and the lizards each
     gone
          To his dwelling.
     Come, Months, come away ;
     Put on white, black, and gray ;
     Let your light sisters play —
     Ye, follow the bier
     Of the dead cold Year,
And make her grave green with tear on tear.
                    — Percy Bysshe Shelley.

39.

ODE TO AUTUMN.

I saw old Autumn in the misty morn
Stand shadowless like Silence listening
To silence, for no lonely bird would sing
Into his hollow ear from woods forlorn,
Nor lowly hedge, nor solitary thorn;
Shaking his languid locks all dewy bright
With tangled gossamer that fell by night,
　　Pearling his coronet of golden corn.

Where are the songs of Summer? — With the sun,
Oping the dusky eyelids of the south,
Till shade and silence waken up as one,
And Morning sings with a warm odorous mouth.
Where are the merry birds? — Away, away,
On panting wings through the inclement skies,
　　　Lest owls should prey
　　　Undazzled at noon-day,
And tear with horny beak their lustrous eyes.

Where are the blooms of Summer? — In the west,
Blushing their last to the last sunny hours,
When the mild Eve by sudden Night is prest
Like tearful Proserpine, snatch'd from her flow'rs
　　　To a most gloomy breast.
Where is the pride of Summer, — the green prime, —
The many, many leaves all twinkling? — Three
On the moss'd elm; three on the naked lime
Trembling, — and one upon the old oak tree!
　　Where is the Dryad's immortality? —

Gone into mournful cypress and dark yew,
Or wearing the long gloomy Winter through
  In the smooth holly's green eternity.

The squirrel gloats o'er his accomplish'd hoard,
The ants have brimm'd their garners with ripe grain,
    And honey bees have stored
The sweets of Summer in their luscious cells;
And swallows all have wing'd across the main;
But here the Autumn melancholy dwells,
    And sighs her tearful spells
Amongst the sunless shadows of the plain.
      Alone, alone,
      Upon a mossy stone,
She sits and reckons up the dead and gone,
With the last leaves for a love-rosary;
Whilst all the wither'd world looks drearily,
Like a dim picture of the drownëd past
In the hush'd mind's mysterious far-away,
Doubtful what ghostly thing would steal the last
Into that distance, gray upon the gray.

O go and sit with her, and be o'ershaded
Under the languid downfall of her hair;
She wears a coronal of flowers faded
Upon her forehead, and a face of care;—
There is enough of wither'd everywhere
To make her bower,— and enough of gloom;
There is enough of sadness to invite,
If only for the rose that died, whose doom
Is Beauty's, —she that with the living bloom
Of conscious cheeks most beautifies the light;
There is enough of sorrowing, and quite

Enough of bitter fruits the earth doth bear, —
Enough of chilly droppings from her bowl;
Enough of fear and shadowy despair,
To frame her cloudy prison for the soul!

—THOMAS HOOD.

—————◆—————

40.

TO AUTUMN.

SEASON of mists and mellow fruitfulness!
 Close bosom-friend of the maturing sun;
Conspiring with him how to load and bless
 With fruit the vines that round the thatch-eaves run;
To bend with apples the mossed cottage-trees,
 And fill all fruit with ripeness to the core;
  To swell the gourd, and plump the hazel shells
 With a sweet kernel; to set budding more,
And still more, later flowers for the bees,
Until they think warm days will never cease,
  For Summer has o'erbrimmed their clammy cells.

Who hath not seen thee oft amid thy store?
 Sometimes whoever seeks abroad may find
Thee sitting careless on a granary floor,
 Thy hair soft-lifted by the winnowing wind;
Or on a half-reaped furrow sound asleep,
 Drowsed with the fume of poppies, while thy hook
  Spares the next swath and all its twined flowers;
And sometimes like a gleaner thou dost keep
 Steady thy laden head across a brook;
 Or by a cider-press, with patient look,
  Thou watchest the last oozings, hours by hours.

Where are the songs of Spring?   Ay, where are they?
  Think not of them, thou hast thy music too,
While barred clouds bloom the soft-dying day,
  And touch the stubble-plains with rosy hue;
Then in a wailful choir the small gnats mourn
    Among the river sallows, borne aloft
      Or sinking as the light wind lives or dies;
And full-grown lambs loud bleat from hilly bourn;
    Hedge-crickets sing; and now with treble soft
    The redbreast whistles from the garden-croft,
      And gathering swallows twitter in the skies.

— JOHN KEATS.

41.

ODE TO THE WEST WIND.

I.

O WILD West Wind, thou breath of Autumn's being,
Thou, from whose unseen presence the leaves dead
Are driven, like ghosts from an enchanter fleeing,

Yellow, and black, and pale, and hectic red,
Pestilence-stricken multitudes : O thou,
Who chariotest to their dark wintry bed

The wingèd seeds, where they lie cold and low,
Each like a corpse within its grave, until
Thine azure sister of the spring shall blow

Her clarion o'er the dreaming earth, and fill
(Driving sweet buds like flocks to feed in air),
With living hues and odors, plain and hill:

Wild Spirit, which art moving everywhere;
Destroyer and Preserver: hear, O hear!

II.

Thou on whose stream, 'mid the steep sky's commotion,
Loose clouds like earth's decaying leaves are shed,
Shook from the tangled boughs of heaven and ocean,

Angels of rain and lightning; there are spread
On the blue surface of thine airy surge,
Like the bright hair uplifted from the head

Of some fierce Mænad, ev'n from the dim verge
Of the horizon to the zenith's height —
The locks of the approaching storm.   Thou dirge

Of the dying year, to which this closing night
Will be the dome of a vast sepulchre,
Vaulted with all thy congregated might

Of vapours, from whose solid atmosphere
Black rain, and fire, and hail, will burst: O hear!

III.

Thou who didst waken from his summer-dreams
The blue Mediterranean, where he lay,
Lulled by the coil of his crystalline streams,

Beside a pumice isle in Baiæ's bay,
And saw in sleep old palaces and towers
Quivering within the wave's intenser day,

All overgrown with azure moss and flowers
So sweet, the sense faints picturing them!   Thou
For whose path the Atlantic's level powers

Cleave themselves into chasms, while far below
The sea-blooms and the oozy woods which wear
The sapless foliage of the ocean, know

Thy voice, and suddenly grow gray with fear,
And tremble and despoil themselves: O hear!

IV.

If I were a dead leaf thou mightest bear;
If I were a swift cloud to fly with thee;
A wave to pant beneath thy power, and share

The impulse of thy strength, only less free
Than thou, O uncontrollable! If even
I were as in my boyhood, and could be

The comrade of thy wanderings over heaven,
As then, when to outstrip thy skyey speed
Scarce seemed a vision, I would ne'er have striven

As thus with thee in prayer in my sore need.
O lift me as a wave, a leaf, a cloud!
I fall upon the thorns of life! I bleed!

A heavy weight of hours has chained and bowed
One too like thee, tameless, and swift, and proud.

V.

Make me thy lyre, ev'n as the forest is:
What if my leaves are falling like its own!
The tumult of thy mighty harmonies

Will take from both a deep autumnal tone,
Sweet though in sadness. Be thou, Spirit fierce,
My spirit! be thou me, impetuous One!

Drive my dead thoughts over the universe
Like withered leaves to quicken a new birth;
And, by the incantation of this verse,

Scatter, as from an unextinguished hearth,
Ashes and sparks, my words among mankind!
Be through my lips to unawakened earth

The trumpet of a prophecy! O Wind,
If winter comes, can spring be far behind?

—PERCY BYSSHE SHELLEY.

42.

THE SEA.

THE Sea! the Sea! the open Sea!
The blue, the fresh, the ever free!
Without a mark, without a bound,
It runneth the earth's wide regions 'round;
It plays with the clouds; it mocks the skies;
Or like a cradled creature lies.

I'm on the Sea! I'm on the Sea!
I am where I would ever be;
With the blue above, and the blue below,
And silence wheresoe'er I go;
If a storm should come and awake the deep,
What matter? *I* shall ride and sleep.

I love (oh! *how* I love) to ride
On the fierce foaming bursting tide,
When every mad wave drowns the moon,
Or whistles aloft his tempest tune,

And tells how goeth the world below,
And why the south-west blasts do blow.

I never was on the dull tame shore,
But I lov'd the great Sea more and more,
And backwards flew to her billowy breast,
Like a bird that seeketh its mother's nest;
And a mother she *was*, and *is* to me;
For I was born on the open Sea!

The waves were white, and red the moon,
In the noisy hour when I was born;
And the whale it whistled, the porpoise rolled,
And the dolphins bared their backs of gold;
And never was heard such an outcry wild
As welcomed to life the Ocean-child!

I've lived since then, in calm and strife,
Full fifty summers a sailor's life,
With wealth to spend and a power to range,
But never have sought, nor sighed for change;
And Death, whenever he come to me,
Shall come on the wide unbounded Sea!

—BRYAN WALLER PROCTER.

———◆———

43.

WINTER.

WHEN icicles hang by the wall
  And Dick the shepherd blows his nail,
And Tom bears logs into the hall,
  And milk comes frozen home in pail;

When blood is nipt, and ways be foul,
Then nightly sings the staring owl,
  Tuwhoo!
Tuwhit! tuwhoo!   A merry note!
While greasy Joan doth keel the pot.

When all around the wind doth blow,
 And coughing drowns the parson's saw,
And birds sit brooding in the snow,
 And Marian's nose looks red and raw;
When roasted crabs hiss in the bowl—
Then nightly sings the staring owl,
  Tuwhoo!
Tuwhit! tuwhoo!   A merry note!
While greasy Joan doth keel the pot.

     —WILLIAM SHAKESPEARE.

44.

CHRISTMAS CAROL.

OUTLANDERS, whence come ye last?
 The snow in the street and the wind on the door.
Through what green seas and great have ye past?
 Minstrels and maids, stand forth on the floor.

From far away, O masters mine,
 The snow in the street and the wind on the door.
We come to bear you goodly wine,
 Minstrels and maids, stand forth on the floor.

From far away we come to you,
  The snow in the street and the wind on the door.
To tell of great tidings strange and true,
  Minstrels and maids, stand forth on the floor.

News, news of the Trinity,
  The snow in the street and the wind on the door.
And Mary and Joseph from over the sea!
  Minstrels and maids, stand forth on the floor.

For as we wandered far and wide,
  The snow in the street and the wind on the door.
What hap do ye deem there should us betide!
  Minstrels and maids, stand forth on the floor.

Under a bent when the night was deep,
  The snow in the street and the wind on the door.
There lay three shepherds tending their sheep.
  Minstrels and maids, stand forth on the floor.

"O ye shepherds, what have ye seen,
  The snow in the street and the wind on the door.
To slay your sorrow, and heal your teen?"
  Minstrels and maids, stand forth on the floor.

"In an ox-stall this night we saw,
  The snow in the street and the wind on the door.
A babe and a maid without a flaw.
  Minstrels and maids, stand forth on the floor.

"There was an old man there beside,
  The snow in the street and the wind on the door.
His hair was white and his hood was wide.
  Minstrels and maids, stand forth on the floor.

" And as we gazed this thing upon,
  The snow in the street and the wind on the door.
Those twain knelt down to the Little One.
  Minstrels and maids, stand forth on the floor.

" And a marvellous song we straight did hear,
  The snow in the street and the wind on the door.
That slew our sorrow and healed our care."
  Minstrels and maids, stand forth on the floor.

News of a fair and marvellous thing,
  The snow in the street and the wind on the door.
Nowell, nowell, nowell, we sing!
  Minstrels and maids, stand forth on the floor.

—WILLIAM MORRIS.

45.

DIRGE FOR THE YEAR.

" ORPHAN Hours, the Year is dead!
  Come and sigh, come and weep!"—
" Merry Hours, smile instead,
  For the Year is but asleep;
See, it smiles as it is sleeping,
Mocking your untimely weeping."—

" As an earthquake rocks a corse
  In its coffin in the clay,
So white Winter, that rough nurse,
  Rocks the dead-cold Year to-day;
Solemn Hours! wail aloud
For your Mother in her shroud."—

"As the wild air stirs and sways
   The tree-swung cradle of a child,
So the breath of these rude Days
   Rocks the Year.   Be calm and mild,
Trembling Hours; she will arise
With new love within her eyes.

"January grey is here,
   Like a sexton by her grave;
February bears the bier;
   March with grief doth howl and rave;
And April weeps:—but O ye Hours!
Follow with May's fairest flowers."

—Percy Bysshe Shelley.

NOTES.

No. 1. Morning Song. This is from *Cymbeline*, act ii., scene 2. Cloten, in whose mouth it is put, describes it as "a very excellent good conceited thing, after a wonderful sweet air, with admirable rich words to it."

l. 2. **Phœbus.** The sun-god. See Classical Dictionary.

l. 4. **lies.** "The disagreement in number between 'lies' and its nominative is not' worth all that has been written about it," says Richard Grant White.   "A relic of an old usage, it was common enough in Shakespeare's day."   See *Romeo and Juliet*, ii., 4:—

> "Both our remedies
> Within thy help and holy physic lies."

No. 6. Hunting Song. This song is included in the continuation of *Queenhoo Hall*, an unfinished romance by Joseph Strutt, published by Sir Walter Scott in 1808. It was this novel that first inspired Scott with the idea of writing a historical romance like his *Waverley*, which, however, was not completed until six years later.

No. 7. May-Day. From *Hesperides : or, the Works both Humane and Divine of Robert Herrick*, 1648. This poem possesses a double interest on account of its allusions to ancient May-day customs in England. " Bourne tells us that in his time, in the villages in the north of England, the juvenile part of both sexes were wont to rise a little after midnight on the morning of that day, and walk to some neighboring wood, accompanied with music and the blowing of horns, where they broke down branches from the trees and adorned them with nosegays and crowns of flowers. This done they returned homewards with their booty about the time of sunrise, and made their doors and windows triumph in the flowery spoil." — *Brande's Popular Antiquities.*

An old ballad, called *The Milkmaid's Life*, published about 1630, says : —

> " Upon the first of May,
> With garlands fresh and gay,
> With mirth and musick sweet,
> For such a season meet,
> They passe their time away.
> They dance away sorrow,
> And all the day thorow
> Their legs doe never fayle.
> They nimbly their feet doe ply,
> And bravely try the victory
> In honour o' th' milking paile."

l. 28. beads. From Old English *bede*, or Anglo-Saxon *bed*, prayer. When round balls with holes through them came to be used for counting prayers, the name was transferred to them.

No. 8. THE STORY OF A SUMMER DAY. Alexander Hume was a minister of the Scotch Kirk and a contemporary of Shakespeare's. His poems were first published in 1599 in a black-letter volume entitled *Hymnes, or Sacred Songs.* Thomas Campbell, who includes a portion of this poem in his *Specimens of the British Poets*, describes it as containing " a train of images that seem peculiarly pleasing and unborrowed, — the pictures of a poetical mind, humble but genuine in its cast."

l. 1. shaid. Perfect tense of the verb *shed* in its now obsolete meaning of to separate — from A.-S. *sceadan*, to divide, to part. See *Genesis*, i., 4.

l. 6. vively. In a lively manner.

l. 16. muir and stripe. Moor and rill.

l. 21. glistering astres. Glittering stars.

l. 23. offuskèd. Obfuscated, eclipsed.

l. 29. boulden. Inflated.

l. 38. skails. Disperses.

l. 52. steir. Stir.

l. 57. **cessile.** "This must, I think, be intended the yielding, or buxom air." — *Trench.*

l. 60. **repeats.** See note on "lies," No. 1, above.

l. 74. **trainèd in a chair.** Drawn in a chariot.

l. 93. **is went.** Is wended. **slake.** Abate.

No. 9. HOLIDAY IN ARCADIA. Arcadia is the typical home of wood-men, shepherds, and country pleasures. Pan was the god of flocks, herds, the woods and the fields.

l. 13. **Philomel.** See *The Nightingale* by Richard Barnfield, page 47; also *Itylus*, by Swinburne, page 354. Tereus was king of Daulis. His wife was Procne, the sister of Philomela. Wishing to marry Philo-mela, he had Procne removed to a secret place, and gave out that she was dead. Philomela became his wife, and afterwards, fearing that she had discovered and would publish his falsehood, he cut out her tongue. But she contrived to weave the story into the pattern of a peplum, which she sent to Procne. Tereus thereupon attempted to slay both the sisters with an axe. They, however, prayed the gods to change them into birds, and Procne thereupon was transformed into a swallow and Philomela into a nightingale. Tereus himself became a hoopoe. The story is told some-what differently by different writers, but the main facts remain the same. The cry " *Tereu, tereu!* " of the nightingale seems to have suggested the name Tereus.

l. 16. **Thracian lyre.** The reference is to the music of Orpheus, a Thracian poet, who is said to have played so sweetly on his lyre that even inanimate things were charmed by it. See Pope's *Ode on St. Cecilia's Day.*

No. 11. UNDER THE GREENWOOD TREE. A song from *As You Like It*, ii., 5.

No. 12. EVENING. 7. **brede ethereal.** Heavenly braid. Keats uses the word *brede* in quite a different sense. See *Ode on a Grecian Urn*, page 343 : —

> " With brede of marble men and maidens overwrought."

l. 11. **beetle, etc.** Compare with —

> " Where the beetle wheels his droning flight." — *Gray's Elegy*, 7.

l. 21. **folding-star.** The evening star. See Milton's *Comus*, 93 : —

> " The star that bids the shepherd fold,
> Now the top of heaven doth hold."

E

Also Shakespeare, *Measure for Measure*, iv., 2: —

> " Look, th' unfolding star calls up the shepherd."

NO. 14. TO DIANA. Compare this poem with Ben Jonson's *To Cynthia* (See *Six Centuries of English Poetry*, p. 209). Diana is the moon.

NO. 17. SLUMBER-SONG. This song occurs in *Valentinian*, a drama by Beaumont and Fletcher. Leigh Hunt shows that a portion of it is repeated in the play *An Honest Man's Fortune*, by Fletcher, and gives other evidence that the lines are Fletcher's own.

l. 2. brother to death. So Shelley, in *Queen Mab:* —

> " Death and his brother Sleep."

NO. 19. THE YOUNG MAY MOON. From *Irish Melodies*.

l. 4. Morna. Morna is the name of a heroine in Ossian's *Fingal*. She was the daughter of Cormac, an Irish king.

l. 12. Sage. Astrologer. Compare the second stanza with the *Dawn-Song*, by Davenant, No. 2, page 1.

NO. 22. TO THE MOON. This fragment was never completed by the poet. The last two lines were first printed by Rossetti (1870), from Shelley's own manuscript.

NO. 23. THE COMING OF SPRING. This is the oldest English song in existence that has come down to us with its musical setting. It is supposed to have been written about the year 1226, by John of Fonsete, a monk of Reading Abbey. The MS. is now in the Harleian Library, with its accompanying music, which is arranged for six voices.

Lhude, loudly.	**awe,** ewe.	**murie,** merrily.
sed, seed.	**louth,** cow.	**swik,** such.
med, meadow.	**sterteth,** leaps.	**ne,** not.
wde, wood.	**verteth,** skips.	**nu,** new.

NO. 26. A SPRING IDYLL. Written in 1638. " I do easily believe that peace and patience, and a calm content, did cohabit in the cheerful heart of Sir Henry Wotton, because I know that when he was beyond seventy years of age he made this description of a part of the present pleasure that possessed him as he sat quietly, in a summer's evening, on a bank a-fishing." — *Izaak Walton.*

NO. 30. THE CUCKOO. " This poem has an exaltation and a glory, joined with an exquisiteness of expression, which place it in the highest rank among the many masterpieces of its illustrious author." — *Palgrave.* It was written in 1804, and published in 1807.

No. 31. To the Daisy. Written in 1802; published in 1807.

l. 3. **Sweet Daisy ! oft I talk to thee.** This is the original reading in the first edition. Later editions have it : —

> " Daisy, again I talk to thee."

Wordsworth had written two other poems addressed to the same flower.

No. 35. The Nightingale. See note on *Philomel*, page 65. King Pandion, according to the old Greek legend, related in Ovid's *Metamorphoses*, was the father of Philomel and Procne. He gave the latter in marriage to Tereus, king of Daulis, in return for military aid rendered him in time of need.

No. 39. Ode to Autumn.

l. 21. **Proserpine.** Persephone. See Classical Dictionary; also the poem *The Garden of Proserpine*, page 351.

l. 27. **Dryad.** A wood-nymph. Her life was believed to be coexistent with that of the tree in which she dwelt.

No. 41. Ode to the West Wind. Written in 1819.

" This poem was conceived and chiefly written in a wood that skirts the Arno, near Florence, and on a day when that tempestuous wind, whose temperature is at once mild and animating, was collecting the vapors which pour down the autumnal rains. They began, as I foresaw, at sunset, with a violent tempest of hail and rain, attended by that magnificent thunder and lightning peculiar to the Cisalpine regions. The phenomenon alluded to at the conclusion of the third stanza is well known to naturalists. The vegetation at the bottom of the sea, of rivers, and of lakes, sympathizes with that of the land in the change of seasons, and is consequently influenced by the winds which announce it." — *Shelley.*

" Had Shelley left nothing but this magnificent Ode, it would have been enough to vindicate his claim to the rank of a great poet." — *Amelia B. Edwards.*

No. 42. The Sea. It is curious to note that the writer of this rapturous eulogy of the sea was never able, during the course of a long life, to cross even the English Channel. The shortest voyages in the most favorable weather were undertaken only with the certainty of the severest attacks of sea-sickness.

No. 43. Winter. From *Love's Labour's Lost*, v., 2.

l. 2. **nail.** A cow-horn.

l. 9. **keel.** To keel the pot is to cool its contents by stirring with a ladle.

No. 44. Christmas Carol.
l. 21. **bent.** Shed, rude shelter.
l. 27. **teen.** Trouble, pain.
l. 47. **Nowell.** A cry of joy — joy for the birth of the Saviour — uttered at Christmas-time.

No. 45. Dirge for the Year. Written January 1, 1821. "This lyric must be conceived as spoken by 'Two Voices,' one of them condoling the death of the year, and the other predicting her return to life." — *W. M. Rossetti.*

Songs of Battle, Bravery, and Patriotism.

—∘∘⦂⦂∘∘—

Patriots have toiled, and in their country's cause
Bled nobly; and their deeds, as they deserve,
Receive proud recompense.   We give in charge
Their names to the sweet lyre.   The historic Mu:
Proud of the treasure, marches with it down
To latest times; and Sculpture, in her turn,
Gives bond in stone and ever-during brass
To guard them, and to immortalize her trust.

—WILLIAM COWPER.

I.

THE BATTLE OF AGINCOURT.

FAIR stood the wind for France,
When we our sails advance,
Nor now to prove our chance
    Longer will tarry;
But putting to the main,
At Caux, the mouth of Seine,
With all his martial train,
    Landed King Harry.

And taking many a fort,
Furnished in warlike sort,

Marcheth towards Agincourt,
    In happy hour;
Skirmishing day by day
With those that stopped his way,
Where the French general lay
    With all his power.

Which in his height of pride,
King Henry to deride,
His ransom to provide
    To the king sending.
Which he neglects the while,
As from a nation vile,
Yet with an angry smile
    Their fall portending.

And turning to his men,
Quoth our brave Henry then,
"Though they be one to ten,
    Be not amazèd;
Yet have we well begun,
Battles so bravely won
Have ever to the sun
    By fame been raisèd.

"And for myself," quoth he,
"This my full rest shall be,
England ne'er mourn for me,
    Nor more esteem me.
Victor I will remain,
Or on this earth lie slain,
Never shall she sustain
    Loss to redeem me.

" Poitiers and Cressy tell,
When most their pride did swell,
Under our swords they fell.
    No less our skill is,
That when our grandsire great,
Claiming the regal seat,
By many a warlike feat
    Lopped the French lilies."

The Duke of York so dread
The eager va'ward led ;
With the main Henry sped,
    Amongst his henchmen.
Exeter had the rear,
A braver man not there :
Heavens ! how hot they were
    On the false Frenchmen !

They now to fight are gone,
Armor on armor shone,
Drum now to drum did groan,
    To hear was wonder :
That with the cries they make,
The very earth did shake ;
Trumpet to trumpet spake,
    Thunder to thunder.

Well it thine age became,
O noble Erpingham,
Which didst the signal aim
    To our hid forces ;
When from a meadow by,
Like a storm suddenly,
The English archery
    Struck the French horses.

With Spanish yew so strong,
Arrows a cloth-yard long,
That like to serpents stung,
　Piercing the weather;
None from his fellow starts,
But playing manly parts,
And like true English hearts,
　Stuck close together.

When down their bows they threw,
And forth their bilbos drew,
And on the French they flew,
　Not one was tardy;
Arms were from shoulders sent,
Scalps to the teeth were rent,
Down the French peasants went,
　Our men were hardy.

This while our noble King,
His broad sword brandishing,
Down the French host did ding,
　As to o'erwhelm it;
And many a deep wound lent,
His arms with blood besprent,
And many a cruel dent
　Bruisèd his helmet.

Gloucester, that duke so good,
Next of the royal blood,
For famous England stood,
　With his brave brother,
Clarence, in steel so bright,
Though but a maiden knight,
Yet in that furious fight
　Scarce such another.

Warwick in blood did wade,
Oxford the foe invade,
And cruel slaughter made,
   Still as they ran up;
Suffolk his axe did ply,
Beaumont and Willoughby
Bare them right doughtily,
    Ferrers and Fanhope.

Upon Saint Crispin's day
Fought was this noble fray,
Which fame did not delay
   To England to carry;
Oh, when shall English men
With such acts fill a pen,
Or England breed again
    Such a King Harry?

        — MICHAEL DRAYTON.

2.

THE CHARGE OF THE LIGHT BRIGADE.

HALF a league, half a league,
Half a league onward,
All in the valley of Death,
  Rode the six hundred.
" Forward, the Light Brigade!
Charge for the guns!" he said:
Into the valley of Death
  Rode the six hundred.

" Forward, the Light Brigade ! "
Was there a man dismayed ?
Not though the soldiers knew
  Some one had blundered :
Theirs not to make reply,
Theirs not to reason why,
Theirs but to do and die,
Into the valley of Death
  Rode the six hundred.

Cannon to right of them,
Cannon to left of them,
Cannon in front of them
  Volleyed and thundered ;
Stormed at with shot and shell,
Boldly they rode and well,
Into the jaws of Death,
Into the mouth of Hell,
  Rode the six hundred.

Flashed all their sabres bare,
Flashed as they turned in air,
Sab'ring the gunners there,
Charging an army, while
  All the world wondered :
Plunged in the battery-smoke,
Right through the line they broke ;
  Cossack and Russian
Reeled from the sabre-stroke,
  Shattered and sundered.
Then they rode back, but not —
  Not the six hundred.

Cannon to right of them,
Cannon to left of them,
Cannon behind them
   Volleyed and thundered ;
Stormed at with shot and shell,
While horse and hero fell,
They that had fought so well
Came through the jaws of Death
Back from the mouth of Hell,
All that was left of them,
   Left of six hundred.

When can their glory fade ?
Oh the wild charge they made !
   All the world wondered.
Honor the charge they made !
Honor the Light Brigade,
   Noble six hundred !

                    — ALFRED TENNYSON.

3.

COMING OF CHARLEMAGNE.

To Oggier spake king Didier:
   "When cometh Charlemagne ?
We looked for him in harvest,
   We looked for him in rain.
Crops are reaped, and floods are past,
   And still he is not here.
Some token show, that we may know
   That Charlemagne is near."

Then to the king made answer
    Oggier, the christened Dane :
" When stands the iron harvest
    Ripe on the Lombard plain,
That stiff harvest which is reaped
    With sword of knight and peer,
Then by that sign ye may divine
    That Charlemagne is near.

" When round the Lombard cities
    The iron flood shall flow,
A swifter flood than Ticin,
    A broader flood than Po,
Frothing white with many a plume,
    Dark blue with many a spear,
Then by that sign ye may divine
    That Charlemagne is near."

—Lord Macaulay.

———◆———

4.

THE BATTLE OF BANNOCKBURN.

BRUCE'S ADDRESS TO HIS MEN.

Scots, wha hae wi' Wallace bled,
Scots, wham Bruce has aften led ;
Welcome to your gory bed,
    Or to glorious liberty !

Now's the day and now's the hour :
See the front o' battle lour :
See approach proud Edward's power —
    Edward ! chains and slavery !

Wha will be a traitor knave?
Wha can fill a coward's grave?
Wha sae base as be a slave?
　　Traitor! coward! turn, and flee!

Wha for Scotland's king and law
Freedom's sword will strongly draw,
Freemen stand, or freemen fa',
　　Caledonian! on wi' me!

By oppression's woes and pains!
By your sons in servile chains!
We will drain our dearest veins,
　　But they shall be — shall be free!

Lay the proud usurpers low!
Tyrants fall in every foe!
Liberty's in every blow! —
　　Forward! let us do or die!

　　　　　　　　　— ROBERT BURNS.

5.

GATHERING SONG OF DONUIL DHU.

PIBROCH of Donuil Dhu,
　　Pibroch of Donuil,
Wake thy wild voice anew,
　　Summon Clan Conuil.
Come away, come away,
　　Hark to the summons!
Come in your war-array,
　　Gentles and commons.

Come from deep glen, and
 From mountain so rocky;
The war-pipe and pennon
 Are at Inverlocky.
Come every hill-plaid, and
 True heart that wears one,
Come every steel blade, and
 Strong hand that bears one.

Leave untended the herd,
 The flock without shelter;
Leave the corpse uninterr'd,
 The bride at the altar;
Leave the deer, leave the steer,
 Leave nets and barges:
Come with your fighting gear,
 Broadswords and targes.

Come as the winds come, when
 Forests are rended,
Come as the waves come, when
 Navies are stranded:
Faster come, faster come,
 Faster and faster,
Chief, vassal, page and groom,
 Tenant and master.

Fast they come, fast they come;
 See how they gather!
Wide waves the eagle plume
 Blended with heather.
Cast your plaids, draw your blades,
 Forward each man set!
Pibroch of Donuil Dhu
 Knell for the onset!

       — SIR WALTER SCOTT.

6.

KILLIECRANKIE.

(The Burial-March of Dundee.)

On the heights of Killiecrankie
    Yester-morn our army lay:
Slowly rose the mist in columns
    From the river's broken way;
Hoarsely roared the swollen torrent,
    And the Pass was wrapt in gloom,
When the clansmen rose together
    From their lair amidst the broom.
Then we belted on our tartans,
    And our bonnets down we drew,
And we felt our broadsword's edges,
    And we proved them to be true;
And we prayed the prayer of soldiers,
    And we cried the gathering-cry,
And we clasped the hands of kinsmen,
    And we swore to do or die!
Then our leader rode before us
    On his war-horse black as night —
Well the Cameronian rebels
    Knew that charger in the fight! —
And a cry of exultation
    From the bearded warriors rose;
For we loved the house of Claver'se,
    And we thought of good Montrose,
But he raised his hand for silence —
    "Soldiers! I have sworn a vow:
Ere the evening star shall glisten
    On Schehallion's lofty brow,

Either we shall rest in triumph,
  Or another of the Græmes
Shall have died in battle-harness
  For his country and King James!
Think upon the Royal Martyr —
  Think of what his race endure —
Think of him whom butchers murdered
  On the field of Magus Muir : —
By his sacred blood I charge ye,
  By the ruined hearth and shrine —
By the blighted hopes of Scotland,
  By your injuries and mine —
Strike this day as if the anvil
  Lay beneath your blows the while,
Be they covenanting traitors,
  Or the brood of false Argyle!
Strike! and drive the trembling rebels
  Backwards o'er the stormy Forth ;
Let them tell their pale Convention
  How they fared within the North.
Let them tell that Highland honor
  Is not to be bought or sold,
That we scorn their prince's anger
  As we loathe his foreign gold.
Strike! and when the fight is over,
  If ye look in vain for me,
Where the dead are lying thickest,
  Search for him that was Dundee!"

Loudly then the hills re-echoed
  With our answer to his call,
But a deeper echo sounded
  In the bosoms of us all.

For the lands of wide Breadelbane
  Not a man who heard him speak
Would that day have left the battle.
  Burning eye and flushing cheek
Told the clansmen's fierce emotion,
  And they harder drew their breath;
For their souls were strong within them,
  Stronger than the grasp of death.
Soon we heard a challenge-trumpet
  Sounding in the Pass below,
And the distant tramp of horses,
  And the voices of the foe:
Down we crouched amid the brachen,
  Till the Lowland ranks drew near,
Panting like the hounds in summer,
  When they scent the stately deer.
From the dark defile emerging,
  Next we saw the squadrons come,
Leslie's foot and Leven's troopers
  Marching to the tuck of drum;
Through the scattered wood of birches,
  O'er the broken ground and heath,
Wound the long battalion slowly,
  Till they gained the plain beneath;
Then we bounded from our covert. —
  Judge how looked the Saxons then,
When they saw the rugged mountain
  Start to life with armèd men!
Like a tempest down the ridges
  Swept the hurricane of steel,
Rose the slogan of Macdonald, —
  Flashed the broadsword of Lochiell!

F

Vainly sped the withering volley
   'Mongst the foremost of our band —
On we poured until we met them,
   Foot to foot, and hand to hand.
Horse and man went down like drift-wood
   When the floods are black at Yule,
And their carcasses are whirling
   In the Garry's deepest pool.
Horse and man went down before us —
   Living foe there tarried none
On the field of Killiecrankie,
   When that stubborn fight was done!

And the evening star was shining
   On Schehallion's distant head,
When we wiped our bloody broadswords,
   And returned to count the dead.
There we found him gashed and gory,
   Stretched upon the cumbered plain,
As he told us where to seek him,
   In the thickest of the slain.
And a smile was on his visage,
   For within his dying ear
Pealed the joyful note of triumph,
   And the clansmen's clamorous cheer:
So, amidst the battle's thunder,
   Shot, and steel, and scorching flame,
In the glory of his manhood
   Passed the spirit of the Græme!

—W. E. Aytoun.

7.

LAMENT FOR FLODDEN.

I've heard them lilting at our ewe-milking,
  Lasses a' lilting before dawn. o' day ;
But now they are moaning on ilka green loaning —
  The Flowers of the Forest are a' wede away.

At bughts, in the morning, nae blythe lads are scorning,
  Lasses are lonely and dowie and wae;
Nae daffin', nae gabbin', but sighing and sabbing,
  Ilk ane lifts her leglin, and hies her away.

In har'st, at the shearing, nae youths now are jeering,
  Bandsters are lyart, and runkled, and grey;
At fair or at preaching, nae wooing, nae fleeching —
  The Flowers of the Forest are a' wede away.

At e'en, in the gloaming, nae younkers are roaming
  'Bout stacks wi' the lasses at bogle to play;
But ilk ane sits drearie, lamenting her dearie —
  The Flowers of the Forest are a' wede away.

Dool and wae for the order, sent our lads to the Border!
  The English, for ance, by guile wan the day ;
The Flowers of the Forest, that fought aye the foremost,
  The prime of our land, are cauld in the clay.

We'll hear nae mair lilting at the ewe-milking ;
  Women and bairns are heartless and wae;
Sighing and moaning on ilka green loaning —
  The Flowers of the Forest are a' wede away.

— Jane Elliott.

BONNIE GEORGE CAMPBELL.

SCOTTISH BALLAD.

HIGH upon Highlands,
　　And low upon Tay,
Bonnie George Campbell
　　Rode out on a day,
Saddled and bridled,
　　And gallant to see:
Hame cam' his gude horse,
　　But hame came not he.

Out ran his auld mither,
　　Greeting full sair;
Out ran his bonnie bride
　　Reaving her hair.
He rode saddled and bridled,
　　Wi' boots to the knee:
Hame cam' his gude horse,
　　But never cam' he.

" My meadow lies green,
　　And my corn is unshorn,
My barn is unbuilt,
　　And my babe is unborn ! "
He rode saddled and bridled,
　　Careless and free:
Hame cam' his gude horse,
　　And never cam' he.

9.

THE BATTLE OF IVRY.

Now glory to the Lord of hosts, from whom all glories
are!
And glory to our Sovereign Liege, King Henry of
Navarre!
Now let there be the merry sound of music and of dance,
Through thy corn-fields green, and sunny vines, oh
pleasant land of France!
And thou, Rochelle, our own Rochelle, proud city of the
waters,
Again let rapture light the eyes of all thy mourning
daughters.
As thou wert constant in our ills, be joyous in our joy,
For cold, and stiff, and still are they who wrought thy
walls annoy.
Hurrah! hurrah! a single field hath turned the chance of
war,
Hurrah! hurrah! for Ivry, and King Henry of Navarre.

Oh! how our hearts were beating, when at the dawn of
day
We saw the army of the League drawn out in long
array;
With all its priest-led citizens, and all its rebel peers,
And Appenzel's stout infantry, and Egmont's Flemish
spears.
There rode the brood of false Lorraine, the curses of our
land!
And dark Mayenne was in the midst, a truncheon in his
hand!

And as we looked on them, we thought of Seine's em-
        purpled flood,
And good Coligni's hoary hair all dabbled with his
        blood ;
And we cried unto the living God, who rules the fate of
        war,
To fight for his own holy name, and Henry of Navarre.

The King is come to marshal us, in all his armor
        drest,
And he has bound a snow-white plume upon his gallant
        crest.
He looked upon his people, and a tear was in his eye ;
He looked upon the traitors, and his glance was stern and
        high.
Right graciously he smiled on us, as rolled from wing to
        wing,
Down all our line, a deafening shout, "God save our
        Lord the King!"
"And if my standard-bearer fall, as fall full well he
        may,
For never saw I promise yet of such a bloody fray,
Press where ye see my white plume shine, amidst the
        ranks of war,
And be your oriflamme to-day the helmet of Navarre."

Hurrah ! the foes are moving.   Hark to the mingled din
Of fife, and steed, and trump and drum, and roaring
        culverin !
The fiery Duke is pricking fast across Saint André's
        plain,
With all the hireling chivalry of Guelders and Almayne.

Now by the lips of those ye love, fair gentlemen of
    France,
Charge for the Golden Lilies now — upon them with the
    lance !
A thousand spurs are striking deep, a thousand spears in
    rest,
A thousand knights are pressing close behind the snow-
    white crest ;
And in they burst, and on they rushed, while, like a
    guiding star,
Amidst the thickest carnage blazed the helmet of
    Navarre.

Now, God be praised, the day is ours ! Mayenne hath
    turned his rein.
D'Aumale hath cried for quarter.   The Flemish Count
    is slain.
Their ranks are breaking like thin clouds before a Bis-
    cay gale ;
The field is heaped with bleeding steeds, and flags, and
    cloven mail ;
And then, we thought on vengeance, and, all along our
    van,
" Remember St. Bartholomew," was passed from man to
    man ;
But out spake gentle Henry, " No Frenchman is my
    foe :
Down, down with every foreigner, but let your brethren
    go. "
Oh ! was there ever such a knight, in friendship or in
    war,
As our Sovereign Lord King Henry, the soldier of
    Navarre !

Ho! maidens of Vienna!   Ho! matrons of Lucerne!
Weep, weep, and rend your hair for those who never
　　　shall return.
Ho! Philip, send, for charity, thy Mexican pistoles,
That Antwerp monks may sing a mass for thy poor
　　　spearmen's souls!
Ho! gallant nobles of the League, look that your arms
　　　be bright!
Ho! burghers of Saint Genevieve, keep watch and ward
　　　to-night!
For our God hath crushed the tyrant, our God hath
　　　raised the slave,
And mocked the counsel of the wise, and the valor of
　　　the brave.
Then glory to His holy name, from whom all glories
　　　are ;
And glory to our Sovereign Lord, King Henry of
　　　Navarre.

— Lord Macaulay.

10.

THE ARMADA.

Attend, all ye who list to hear our noble England's
　　　praise ;
I sing of the thrice famous deeds she wrought in
　　　ancient days,
When that great fleet invincible against her bore, in
　　　vain
The richest spoils of Mexico, the stoutest hearts in
　　　Spain.

It was about the lovely close of a warm summer's
    day,
There came a gallant merchant-ship full sail to Ply-
    mouth bay;
The crew had seen Castile's black fleet, beyond Au-
    rigny's isle,
At earliest twilight, on the waves lie heaving many a
    mile.
At sunrise she escaped their van, by God's especial
    grace;
And the tall Pinta, till the noon, had held her close in
    chase.
Forthwith a guard at every gun was placed along the
    wall;
The beacon blazed upon the roof of Edgecumbe's lofty
    hall;
Many a light fishing-bark put out to pry along the
    coast;
And with loose rein and bloody spur rode inland many
    a post.

With his white hair unbonneted, the stout old sheriff
    comes;
Behind him march the halberdiers; before him sound
    the drums:
The yeomen round the market cross make clear an
    ample space;
For there behoves him to set up the standard of Her
    Grace:
And haughtily the trumpets peal, and gaily dance the
    bells,
As slow upon the laboring wind the royal blazon
    swells.

Look how the Lion of the sea lifts up his ancient
      crown,
And underneath his deadly paw treads the gay lilies
      down !
So stalked he when he turned to flight, on that famed
      Picard field,
Bohemia's plume, and Genoa's bow, and Cæsar's eagle
      shield.
So glared he went at Agincourt in wrath he turned to
      bay,
And crushed, and torn beneath his claws the princely
      hunters lay.
Ho ! strike the flagstaff deep, Sir Knight : ho ! scatter
      flowers, fair maids !
Ho, gunners ! fire a loud salute : ho ! gallants, draw your
      blades :
Thou sun, shine on her joyously ; ye breezes, waft her
      wide ;
Our glorious SEMPER EADEM ! the banner of our pride.

The fresh'ning breeze of eve unfurled that banner's
      massy fold —
The parting gleam of sunshine kissed that haughty
      scroll of gold :
Night sank upon the dusky beach, and on the purple
      sea ;
Such night in England ne'er had been, nor e'er again
      shall be.
From Eddystone to Berwick bounds, from Lynn to Mil-
      ford Bay,
That time of slumber was as bright and busy as the
      day ;

For swift to east and swift to west the ghastly war-
    flame spread —
High on St. Michael's Mount it shone — it shone on
    Beachy Head:
Far o'er the deep the Spaniard saw, along each south-
    ern shire,
Cape beyond cape, in endless range, those twinkling
    points of fire.
The fisher left his skiff to rock on Tamar's glittering
    waves,
The rugged miners poured to war from Mendip's sun-
    less caves;
O'er Longleat's towers, o'er Cranbourne's oaks, the
    fiery herald flew:
He roused the shepherds of Stonehenge — the rangers
    of Beaulieu.
Right sharp and quick the bells rang out all night from
    Bristol town,
And, ere the day, three hundred horse had met on
    Clifton Down.

The sentinel on Whitehall gate looked forth into the
    night,
And saw, o'erhanging Richmond Hill, that streak of
    blood-red light:
The bugle's note and cannon's roar the death-like
    silence broke,
And with one start, and with one cry, the royal city
    woke.
At once on all her stately gates arose the answering
    fires;
At once the wild alarum clashed from all her reeling
    spires;

From all the batteries of the Tower pealed loud the
　　　voice of fear;
And all the thousand masts of Thames sent back a
　　　louder cheer:
And from the furthest wards was heard the rush of
　　　hurrying feet,
And the broad streams of pikes and flags rushed down
　　　each roaring street;
And broader still became the blaze, and louder still
　　　the din,
As fast from every village round the horse came spur-
　　　ring in;
And eastward straight from wild Blackheath the war-
　　　like errand went,
And roused in many an ancient hall the gallant squires
　　　of Kent:
Southward from Surrey's pleasant hills flew those bright
　　　couriers forth;
High on bleak Hampstead's swarthy moor they started
　　　for the north;
And on, and on, without a pause, untired they bounded
　　　still;
All night from tower to tower they sprang; they sprang
　　　from hill to hill;
Till the proud peak unfurled the flag o'er Darwin's
　　　rocky dales;
Till like volcanoes flared to heaven the stormy hills of
　　　Wales;
Till twelve fair counties saw the blaze on Malvern's
　　　lonely height;
Till streamed in crimson on the wind the Wrekin's
　　　crest of light;

Till broad and fierce the star came forth, on Ely's stately
     fane,
And tower and hamlet rose in arms o'er all the bound-
     less plain ;
Till Belvoir's lordly terraces the sign to Lincoln sent,
And Lincoln sped the message on o'er the wide vale of
     Trent :
Till Skiddaw saw the fire that burnt on Gaunt's em-
     battled pile,
And the red glare on Skiddaw roused the burghers of
     Carlisle.
                           —LORD MACAULAY.

II.

YE MARINERS OF ENGLAND.

I.

YE Mariners of England!
That guard our native seas ;
Whose flag has braved, a thousand years,
The battle and the breeze !
Your glorious standard launch again
To match another foe !
And sweep through the deep,
While the stormy winds do blow ;
While the battle rages loud and long,
And the stormy winds do blow.

II.

The spirits of your fathers
Shall start from every wave !—
For the deck it was their field of fame,

And Ocean was their grave:
Where Blake and mighty Nelson fell,
Your manly hearts shall glow,
As ye sweep through the deep,
While the stormy winds do blow;
While the battle rages loud and long,
And the stormy winds do blow.

III.

Britannia needs no bulwarks,
No towers along the steep;
Her march is o'er the mountain-waves,
Her home is on the deep.
With thunders from her native oak,
She quells the floods below, —
As they roar on the shore,
When the stormy winds do blow;
When the battle rages loud and long,
And the stormy winds do blow.

IV.

The meteor flag of England
Shall yet terrific burn;
Till danger's troubled night depart,
And the star of peace return.
Then, then, ye ocean-warriors!
Our song and feast shall flow
To the fame of your name,
When the storm has ceased to blow;
When the fiery fight is heard no more,
And the storm has ceased to blow.

— THOMAS CAMPBELL.

12.

THE BATTLE OF NASEBY.

BY OBADIAH BIND - THEIR - KINGS - IN - CHAINS - AND - THEIR -
NOBLES - WITH - LINKS - OF - IRON, SERGEANT IN IRETON'S
REGIMENT.

OH! wherefore come ye forth, in triumph from the
 North,
 With your hands, and your feet, and your raiment all
  red?
And wherefore doth your rout send forth a joyous
 shout?
 And whence be the grapes of the wine-press which
  ye tread?

Oh evil was the root, and bitter was the fruit,
 And crimson was the juice of the vintage that we
  trod;
For we trampled on the throng of the haughty and the
 strong,
 Who sate in the high places and slew the saints of
  God.

It was about the noon of a glorious day of June,
 That we saw their banners dance, and their cuirasses
  shine,
And the Man of Blood was there, with his long essenced
 hair,
 And Astley, and Sir Marmaduke, and Rupert of the
  Rhine.

Like a servant of the Lord, with his Bible and his
        sword,
The General rode along us to form us for the fight,
When a murmuring sound broke out, and swelled into a
        shout,
    Among the godless horsemen upon the tyrant's
        right.

And hark! like the roar of the billows on the shore,
    The cry of battle rises along their charging line!
For God! for the Cause! for the Church! for the
        Laws!
    For Charles King of England and Rupert of the
        Rhine!

The furious German comes, with his clarions and his
        drums,
    His bravoes of Alsatia, and pages of Whitehall;
They are bursting on our flanks. Grasp your pikes,
        close your ranks;
    For Rupert never comes but to conquer or to fall.

They are here! They rush on! We are broken! We
        are gone!
    Our left is borne before them like stubble on the
        blast.
O Lord, put forth thy might! O Lord, defend the
        right!
    Stand back to back, in God's name, and fight it to the
        last.

Stout Skippon hath a wound; the centre hath given
    ground :
  Hark! hark! — what means the trampling of horse-
    men on our rear?
Whose banner do I see, boys? 'Tis he, thank God, 'tis
    he, boys,
  Bear up another minute : brave Oliver is here.

Their heads all stooping low, their points all in a row,
  Like a whirlwind on the trees, like a deluge on the
    dykes,
Our cuirassiers have burst on the ranks of the Ac-
    curst,
  And at a shock have scattered the forest of his
    pikes.

Fast, fast, the gallants ride, in some safe nook to hide
  Their coward heads, predestined to rot on Temple
    Bar ;
And he — he turns, he flies : — shame on those cruel
    eyes
  That bore to look on torture, and dare not look on
    war.

Ho! comrades, scour the plain ; and, ere ye strip the
    slain,
  First give another stab to make your search secure,
Then shake from sleeves and pockets their broad-pieces
    and lockets,
  The tokens of the wanton, the plunder of the poor.

G

Fools! your doublets shone with gold, and your hearts
        were gay and bold,
  When you kissed your lily hands to your lemans
        to-day ;
And to-morrow shall the fox, from her chambers in the
        rocks,
  Lead forth her tawny cubs to howl above the prey.

Where be your tongues that late mocked at heaven
        and hell and fate,
  And the fingers that once were so busy with your
        blades,
Your perfumed satin clothes, your catches and your
        oaths,
  Your stage-plays and your sonnets, your diamonds
        and your spades ?

Down, down, for ever down with the mitre and the
        crown,
  With the Belial of the Court and the Mammon of the
        Pope !
There is woe in Oxford halls ; there is wail in Durham's
        Stalls ;
  The Jesuit smites his bosom ; the Bishop rends his
        cope.

And She of the seven hills shall mourn her children's ills,
  And tremble when she thinks on the edge of Eng-
        land's sword ;
And the Kings of earth in fear shall shudder when they
        hear
What the hand of God hath wrought for the Houses
        and the Word.   — LORD MACAULAY.

13.

THE BATTLE OF THE BALTIC.

I.

Of Nelson and the North,
Sing the glorious day's renown,
When to battle fierce came forth
All the might of Denmark's crown,
And her arms along the deep proudly shone;
By each gun the lighted brand,
In a bold determined hand,
And the Prince of all the land
Led them on. —

II.

Like leviathans afloat,
Lay their bulwarks on the brine;
While the sign of battle flew
On the lofty British line;
It was ten of April morn by the chime:
As they drifted on their path,
There was silence deep as death;
And the boldest held his breath,
For a time. —

III.

But the might of England flushed
To anticipate the scene;
And her van the fleeter rushed
O'er the deadly space between.
" Hearts of oak ! " our captains cried; when each gun
From its adamantine lips

Spread a death-shade round the ships,
Like the hurricane eclipse
Of the sun.

IV.

Again! again! again!
And the havoc did not slack,
Till a feeble cheer the Dane
To our cheering sent us back; —
Their shots along the deep slowly boom : —
Then ceased — and all is wail,
As they strike the shattered sail,
Or, in conflagration pale,
Light the gloom. —

V.

Out spoke the victor then,
As he hailed them o'er the wave;
"Ye are brothers! ye are men!
And we conquer but to save : —
So peace instead of death let us bring;
But yield, proud foe, thy fleet,
With the crews, at England's feet,
And make submission meet
To our King." —

VI.

Then Denmark blest our chief,
That he gave her wounds repose;
And the sounds of joy and grief
From her people wildly rose,
As death withdrew his shades from the day.
While the sun looked smiling bright

O'er a wide and woeful sight,
Where the fires of funeral light
Died away.

VII.

Now joy, old England, raise!
For the tidings of thy might,
By the festal cities' blaze,
While the wine-cup shines in light;
And yet amidst that joy and uproar,
Let us think of them that sleep,
Full many a fathom deep,
By thy wild and stormy steep,
Elsinore!

VIII.

Brave hearts! to Britain's pride
Once so faithful and so true,
On the deck of fame that died;—
With the gallant good Riou:
Soft sigh the winds of Heaven o'er their grave!
While the billow mournful rolls
And the mermaid's song condoles,
Singing glory to the souls
Of the brave!—

— THOMAS CAMPBELL.

14.

HOHENLINDEN.

On Linden, when the sun was low,
All bloodless lay the untrodden snow;
And dark as winter was the flow
    Of Iser, rolling rapidly.

But Linden saw another sight,
When the drum beat at dead of night,
Commanding fires of death to light
    The darkness of her scenery.

By torch and trumpet fast arrayed,
Each horseman drew his battle-blade,
And furious every charger neighed
    To join the dreadful revelry.

Then shook the hills, with thunder riven;
Then rushed the steed, to battle driven;
And louder than the bolts of Heaven
    Far flashed the red artillery.

But redder yet that light shall glow
On Linden's hills of stainèd snow,
And bloodier yet the torrent flow
    Of Iser, rolling rapidly.

'Tis morn; but scarce yon level sun
Can pierce the war-clouds, rolling dun,
Where furious Frank and fiery Hun
    Shout in their sulphurous canopy.

The combat deepens.   On, ye brave,
Who rush to glory, or the grave!
Wave, Munich, all thy banners wave,
    And charge with all thy chivalry!

Few, few shall part, where many meet;
The snow shall be their winding-sheet;
And every turf beneath their feet
    Shall be a soldier's sepulchre.

—THOMAS CAMPBELL.

15.

THE BATTLE.

I. BEFORE.

By the hope within us springing,
  Herald of to-morrow's strife;
By that sun whose light is bringing
  Chains or freedom, death or life—
Oh! remember life can be
No charm for him who lives not free!
  Like the day-star in the wave
  Sinks a hero in his grave,
'Midst the dew-fall of a nation's tears.

  Happy is he o'er whose decline
  The smiles of home may soothing shine,
And light him down the steep of years —
  But oh! how blessed they sink to rest,
  Who close their eyes on victory's breast!

O'er his watch-fire's fading embers
  Now the foeman's cheek turns white,
When his heart that field remembers,
  Where we tamed his tyrant might!

Never let him bind again
A chain, like that we broke from then.
  Hark! the horn of combat calls —
  Ere the golden evening falls,
May we pledge that horn in triumph round!

  Many a heart that now beats high,
  In slumber cold at night shall lie,
Nor waken even at victory's sound —

But oh! how blessed that hero's sleep,
O'er whom a wondering world shall weep.

II. AFTER.

Night closed around the conqueror's way
  And lightnings showed the distant hill,
Where those who lost that dreadful day,
  Stood few and faint, but fearless still.

The soldier's hope, the patriot's zeal,
  Forever dimmed, forever crost —
Oh! who shall say what heroes feel,
  When all but life and honor's lost?

The last sad hour of freedom's dream,
  And valor's task, moved slowly by,
While mute they watched, till morning's beam
  Should rise and give them light to die.

There's yet a world, where souls are free,
  Where tyrants taint not nature's bliss; —
If death that world's bright opening be,
  Oh! who would live a slave in this?

— THOMAS MOORE.

16.

THE END OF THE SIEGE.

THEY have fetched the steed with care, in the harness
    he did wear,
        Toll slowly.

Past the court and through the doors, across the rushes
    of the floors,
        But they goad him up the stair.

Then from out her bower chambère, did the Duchess
    May repair:
        Toll slowly.

"Tell me now what is your need," said the lady, "of
    this steed,
        That ye goad him up the stair?"

Calm she stood; unbodkined through, fell her dark hair
    to her shoe;
        Toll slowly.

And the smile upon her face, ere she left the tiring-glass,
    Had not time enough to go.

"Get thee back, sweet Duchess May! hope is gone like
    yesterday.
        Toll slowly.

"One half-hour completes the breach: and thy lord
    grows wild of speech —
        Get thee in, sweet lady, and pray!

"In the east tower, highest of all, loud he cries for steed
    from stall:
        Toll slowly.

"He would ride as far," quoth he, "as for love and
    victory,
        Though he rides the castle wall.

"And we fetch the steed from stall, up where never a
    hoof did fall —
        Toll slowly.

"Wifely prayer meets deathly need: may the sweet
    Heavens hear thee plead
        If he rides the castle wall!"

Low she dropt her head, and lower, till her hair coiled
    on the floor,
        Toll slowly.

And tear after tear you heard fall distinct as any word
    Which you might be listening for.

"Get thee in, thou soft ladye! here is never a place for
    thee!
        Toll slowly.

"Braid thine hair and clasp thy gown, that thy beauty
    in its moan
    May find grace with Leigh of Leigh."

She stood up in bitter case, with a pale yet steady face,

        Toll slowly.

Like a statue thunderstruck, which, though quivering,
    seems to look
    Right against the thunder-place.

And her foot trod in, with pride, her own tears i' the
    stone beside, —
        Toll slowly.

"Go to, faithful friends, go to! judge no more what
    ladies do,
    No, nor how their lords may ride!"

Then the good steed's rein she took, and his neck did
    kiss and stroke:
        Toll slowly.

Soft he neighed to answer her, and then followed up
    the stair
    For the love of her sweet look:

Oh, and steeply, steeply wound up the narrow stair around,
>> *Toll slowly.*

Oh, and closely, closely speeding, step by step beside her treading,
>> Did he follow, meek as hound.

On the east tower highest of all, — there, where never a hoof did fall, —
>> *Toll slowly.*

Out they swept, a vision steady, noble steed and lovely lady,
>> Calm as if in bower or stall.

Down she knelt at her lord's knee, and she looked up silently,
>> *Toll slowly.*

And he kissed her twice and thrice, for that look within her eyes
>> Which he could not bear to see.

Quoth he, " Get thee from this strife, and the sweet saints bless thy life !
>> *Toll slowly.*

" In this hour I stand in need of my noble red-roan steed,
>> But no more of my noble wife."

Quoth she, " Meekly have I done all thy biddings under sun ;
>> *Toll slowly.*

" But by all my womanhood, which is proved so, true and good,
>> I will never do this one.

"Now by womanhood's degree and by wifehood's
      verity,
                Toll slowly.

"In this hour if thou hast need of thy noble roan
      steed,
            Thou hast also need of *me.*

"By this golden ring ye see on this lifted hand pardié,
                Toll slowly.

"If this hour, on castle wall can be room for steed from
      stall,
            Shall be also room for *me.*

"So the sweet saints with me be," (did she utter
      solemnly),
                Toll slowly.

"If a man, this eventide, on this castle wall will ride,
            He shall ride the same with *me.*"

Oh, he sprang up in the selle and he laughed out bitter-
      well, —
                Toll slowly.

"Wouldst thou ride among the leaves, as we used on
      other eves,
            To hear chime a vesper-bell?"

She clung closer to his knee — "Ay, beneath the cypress
      tree!
                Toll slowly.

"Mock me not, for otherwhere than along the greenwood
      fair
            Have I ridden fast with thee.

" Fast I rode with new-made vows from my angry kins-
man's house :

> *Toll slowly.*

"What, and would you men should reck that I dared
more for love's sake
As a bride than as a spouse ?

" What, and would you it should fall, as a proverb, before
all,
> *Toll slowly.*

" That a bride may keep your side while through castle-
gate you ride,
Yet eschew the castle-wall ? "

Ho ! the breach yawns into ruin and roars up against
her suing,
> *Toll slowly.*

With the inarticulate din and the dreadful falling in —
Shrieks of doing and undoing.

Twice he wrung her hands in twain, but the small hands
closed again.
> *Toll slowly.*

Back he reined the steed — back, back ! but she trailed
along his track
With a frantic clasp and strain.

Evermore the foemen pour through the crash of window
and door,
> *Toll slowly.*

And the shouts of Leigh and Leigh, and the shrieks of
" kill ! " and " flee ! "
Strike up clear amid the roar.

Thrice he wrung her hands in twain, but they closed and
    clung again,
        Toll slowly.

While she clung, as one, withstood, clasps a Christ upon
    the rood,
        In a spasm of deathly pain.

She clung wild and she clung mute with her shuddering
    lips half-shut;

        Toll slowly.

Her head fallen as half in swound, hair and knee swept
    on the ground,
        She clung wild to stirrup and foot.

Back he reined his steed back-thrown on the slippery
    coping-stone;
        Toll slowly.

Back the iron hoofs did grind on the battlement behind
    Whence a hundred feet went down:

And his heel did press and goad on the quivering flank
    bestrode, —
        Toll slowly.

"Friends and brothers, save my wife! Pardon, Sweet, in
    change for life, —
        But I ride alone to God."

Straight as if the holy name had upbreathed her like a
    flame,
        Toll slowly.

She upsprang, she rose upright, in his selle she sat in
    sight,
        By her love she overcame.

And her head was on his breast where she smiled as one
    at rest, —
               Toll slowly.

" Ring, " she cried, " O vesper-bell in the beechwood's
    old chapelle, —
        But the passing-bell rings best ! "

They have caught out at the rein which Sir Guy threw
    loose — in vain,
             Toll slowly.

For the horse in stark despair, with his front hoofs poised
    in air
        On the last verge rears amain.

Now he hangs, he rocks between, and his nostrils curdle
    in,
             Toll slowly.

Now he shivers head and hoof, and the flakes of foam
    fall off,
        And his face grows fierce and thin :

And a look of human woe from his staring eyes did go,

             Toll slowly.

And a sharp cry uttered he, in a foretold agony
        Of the headlong death below, —

And, " Ring, ring, thou passing-bell, " still she cried, " i'
    the old chapelle ! "

             Toll slowly.

Then back-toppling, crashing back — a dead weight flung
    out to wrack,
        Horse and riders overfell.
                — E. B. BROWNING.

17.

THE BURIAL OF SIR JOHN MOORE AT CORUNNA.

Not a drum was heard, not a funeral note,
  As his corpse to the ramparts we hurried;
Not a soldier discharged his farewell shot
  O'er the grave where our hero we buried.

We buried him darkly at dead of night,
  The sods with our bayonets turning;
By the struggling moonbeam's misty light,
  And the lantern dimly burning.

No useless coffin enclosed his breast,
  Not in sheet nor in shroud we wound him;
But he lay like a warrior taking his rest
  With his martial cloak around him.

Few and short were the prayers we said,
  And we spoke not a word of sorrow,
But we steadfastly gazed on the face that was dead,
  And we bitterly thought of the morrow.

We thought as we hollowed his narrow bed,
  And smoothed down his lonely pillow,
That the foe and the stranger would tread o'er his head,
  And we far away on the billow!

Lightly they'll talk of the spirit that's gone,
  And o'er his cold ashes upbraid him,—
But little he'll reck, if they let him sleep on
  In the grave where a Briton has laid him.

But half of our heavy task was done
  When the clock struck the hour for retiring :
And we heard the distant and random gun
  That the foe was sullenly firing.

Slowly and sadly we laid him down,
  From the field of his fame fresh and gory ;
We carved not a line, and we raised not a stone —
  But we left him alone with his glory.

—CHARLES WOLFE.

18.

BATTLE SONG.

DAY, like our souls, is fiercely dark ;
  What then ? 'Tis day !
We sleep no more ; the cock crows — hark !
  To arms ! away !
They come ! they come ! the knell is rung
  Of us or them ;
Wide o'er their march the pomp is flung
  Of gold and gem.
What collared hound of lawless sway,
  To famine dear —
What pensioned slave of Attila,
  Leads in the rear ?
Come they from Scythian wilds afar,
  Our blood to spill ?
Wear they the livery of the Czar ?
  They do his will.
Nor tasselled silk, nor epaulette,
  Nor plume, nor torse —

No splendor gilds, all sternly met,
    Our foot and horse.
But, dark and still, we inly glow,
    Condensed in ire !

Strike, tawdry slaves, and ye shall know
    Our gloom is fire.
In vain your pomp, ye evil powers,
    Insults the land ;
Wrongs, vengeance, and *the cause* are ours,
    And God's right hand !
Madmen ! they trample into snakes
    The wormy clod !
Like fire, beneath their feet awakes
    The sword of God !
Behind, before, above, below,
    They rouse the brave ;
Where'er they go, they make a foe,
    Or find a grave.
        —EBENEZER ELLIOTT.

19.

THE WAR-SONG OF DINAS VAWR.

THE mountain sheep are sweeter,
But the valley sheep are fatter ;
We therefore deemed it meeter
To carry off the latter.
We made an expedition ;
We met an host and quelled it ;
We forced a strong position,
And killed the men who held it.

On Dyfed's richest valley,
Where herds of kine were browsing,
We made a mighty sally,
To furnish our carousing.
Fierce warriors rushed to meet us;
We met them, and o'erthrew them:
They struggled hard to beat us;
But we conquered them, and slew them.

As we drove our prize at leisure,
The king marched forth to catch us:
His rage surpassed all measure,
But his people could not match us.
He fled to his hall-pillars;
And, ere our force we led off,
Some sacked his house and cellars,
While others cut his head off.

We there, in strife bewildering,
Spilt blood enough to swim in:
We orphaned many children,
And widowed many women.
The eagles and the ravens
We glutted with our foemen:
The heroes and the cravens,
The spearmen and the bowmen.

And much their land bemoaned them,
Two thousand head of cattle,
And the head of him who owned them:
Ednyfed, King of Dyfed,
His head was borne before us;
His wine and beasts supplied our feasts,
And his overthrow, our chorus.

— THOMAS LOVE PEACOCK.

THE DESTRUCTION OF SENNACHERIB.

THE Assyrian came down like a wolf on the fold,
And his cohorts were gleaming in purple and gold;
And the sheen of their spears was like stars on the sea,
When the blue wave rolls nightly on deep Galilee.

Like the leaves of the forest when Summer is green,
That host with their banners at sunset were seen;
Like the leaves of the forest when Autumn hath blown,
That host on the morrow lay withered and strown.

For the Angel of Death spread his wings on the blast,
And breathed in the face of the foe as he passed;
And the eyes of the sleepers waxed deadly and chill,
And their hearts but once heaved, and forever grew
    still!

And there lay the steed with his nostril all wide,
But through it there rolled not the breath of his pride;
And the foam of his gasping lay white on the turf,
And cold as the spray of the rock-beating surf.

And there lay the rider distorted and pale,
With the dew on his brow, and the rust on his mail;
And the tents were all silent, the banners alone,
The lances unlifted, the trumpet unblown.

And the widows of Ashur are loud in their wail,
And the idols are broke in the temple of Baal;
And the might of the Gentile, unsmote by the sword,
Hath melted like snow in the glance of the Lord!

—LORD BYRON.

21.

THE SOLDIER'S DREAM.

Our bugles sang truce; for the night-cloud had lowered,
　And the sentinel stars set their watch in the sky;
And thousands had sunk on the ground overpowered —
　The weary to sleep, and the wounded to die.

When reposing that night on my pallet of straw,
　By the wolf-scaring fagot that guarded the slain,
At the dead of the night a sweet vision I saw,
　And thrice ere the morning I dreamt it again.

Methought from the battle-field's dreadful array,
　Far, far I had roamed on a desolate track;
'Twas autumn — and sunshine arose on the way
　To the home of my fathers, that welcomed me back.

I flew to the pleasant fields traversed so oft
　In life's morning march, when my bosom was young;
I heard my own mountain-goats bleating aloft,
　And knew the sweet strain that the corn-reapers sung.

Then pledged we the wine-cup, and fondly I swore
　From my home and my weeping friends never to part;
My little ones kissed me a thousand times o'er,
　And my wife sobbed aloud in her fulness of heart.

"Stay, stay with us! — rest; thou art weary and worn!"
　And fain was their war-broken soldier to stay;
But sorrow returned with the dawning of morn,
　And the voice in my dreaming ear melted away!

— Thomas Campbell.

22.

THE MINSTREL-BOY.

THE Minstrel-boy to the war is gone,
   In the ranks of death you'll find him;
His father's sword he has girded on,
   And his wild harp slung behind him. —
" Land of song ! " said the warrior-bard,
   " Though all the world betrays thee,
One sword, at least, thy rights shall guard,
   One faithful harp shall praise thee ! "

The Minstrel fell ! — but the foeman's chain
   Could not bring his proud soul under;
The harp he loved ne'er spoke again,
   For he tore its chords asunder;
And said, " No chains shall sully thee,
   Thou soul of love and bravery !
Thy songs were made for the brave and free,
   They shall never sound in slavery ! "

— THOMAS MOORE.

23.

THE LAST BUCCANIER.

OH England is a pleasant place for them that's rich and
   · high,
But England is a cruel place for such poor folks as I;
And such a port for mariners I shall ne'er see again
As the pleasant Isle of Avès, beside the Spanish main.

There were forty craft in Avès that were both swift and
    stout,
All furnished well with small arms and cannons round
    about;
And a thousand men in Avès made laws so fair and
    free
To choose their valiant captains and obey them loyally.

Thence we sailed against the Spaniard with his hoards
    of plate and gold,
Which he wrung with cruel tortures from Indian folk
    of old ;
Likewise the merchant captains, with hearts as hard as
    stone,
Who flog men and keel-haul them, and starve them to
    the bone.

Oh the palms grew high in Avès, and fruits that shone
    like gold ;
And the colibris and parrots they were gorgeous to be-
    hold ;
And the negro maids to Avès from bondage fast did
    flee,
To welcome gallant sailors, a-sweeping in from sea.

Oh sweet it was in Avès to hear the landward breeze
A-swing with good tobacco in a net between the trees,
With a negro lass to fan you, while you listened to the
    roar
Of the breakers on the reef outside, that never touched
    the shore.

But Scripture saith, an ending to all fine things must be;
So the King's ships sailed on Avès, and quite put down
   were we.
All day we fought like bulldogs, but they burst the
   booms at night;
And I fled in a piragua, sore wounded, from the fight.

Nine days I floated starving, and a negro lass beside,
Till for all I tried to cheer her, the poor young thing
   she died;
But as I lay a-gasping, a Bristol sail came by,
And brought me home to England here, to beg until
   I die.

And now I'm old and going—I'm sure I can't tell
   where;
One comfort is, this world's so hard, I can't be worse
   off there:
If I might but be a sea-dove, I'd fly across the main,
To the pleasant Isle of Avès, to look at it once again.

       —CHARLES KINGSLEY.

24.

MY NATIVE VALE.

DEAR is my little native vale,
The ring-dove builds and murmurs there;
Close by my cot she tells her tale
To every passing villager.
The squirrel leaps from tree to tree
And shells his nuts at liberty.

In orange-groves and myrtle-bow'rs,
That breathe a gale of fragrance round,
I charm the fairy-footed hours
With my loved lute's romantic sound;
Or crowns of living laurel weave,
For those that win the race at eve.

The shepherd's horn at break of day,
The ballet danced in twilight glade,
The canzonet and roundelay
Sung in the silent green-wood shade;
These simple joys, that never fail,
Shall bind me to my native vale.

—SAMUEL ROGERS.

25.

"I TRAVELLED AMONG UNKNOWN MEN."

I TRAVELLED among unknown men,
  In lands beyond the sea;
Nor, England, did I know till then
  What love I bore to thee.

'Tis past, that melancholy dream!
  Nor will I quit thy shore
A second time; for still I seem
  To love thee more and more.

Among thy mountains did I feel
  The joy of my desire;
And she I cherished turned her wheel
  Beside an English fire.

Thy mornings showed, thy nights concealed
 The bowers where Lucy played ;
And thine is too the last green field
 That Lucy's eyes surveyed.

     —WILLIAM WORDSWORTH.

26.

THE ISLES OF GREECE.

THE isles of Greece, the isles of Greece !
 Where burning Sappho loved and sung,
Where grew the arts of war and peace, —
 Where Delos rose, and Phœbus sprung !
Eternal summer gilds them yet,
But all, except their sun, is set.

The Scian and the Teian muse,
 The hero's harp, the lover's lute,
Have found the fame your shores refuse ;
 Their place of birth alone is mute
To sounds which echo further west
Than your sires' " Islands of the Blest."

The mountains look on Marathon —
 And Marathon looks on the sea ;
And musing there an hour alone,
 I dreamed that Greece might still be free ;
For standing on the Persians' grave,
I could not deem myself a slave.

A king sat on the rocky brow
  Which looks o'er sea-born Salamis;
And ships by thousands lay below,
  And men in nations;—all were his!
He counted them at break of day—
And when the sun set, where were they?

And where are they? and where art thou,
  My country? On thy voiceless shore
The heroic lay is tuneless now—
  The heroic bosom beats no more!
And must thy lyre, so long divine,
Degenerate into hands like mine?

'Tis something, in the dearth of fame,
  Though linked among a fettered race,
To feel at least a patriot's shame,
  Even as I sing, suffuse my face;
For what is left the poet here?
For Greeks a blush—for Greece a tear.

Must we but weep o'er days more blest?
  Must we but blush?—Our fathers bled.
Earth! render back from out thy breast
  A remnant of our Spartan dead!
Of the three hundred grant but three,
To make a new Thermopylæ!

What, silent still? and silent all?
  Ah! no;—the voices of the dead
Sound like a distant torrent's fall,
  And answer, "Let one living head,
But one arise,—we come, we come!"
'Tis but the living who are dumb.

In vain — in vain; strike other chords;
  Fill high the cup with Samian wine!
Leave battles to the Turkish hordes,
  And shed the blood of Scio's vine!
Hark! rising to the ignoble call,
How answers each bold Bacchanal!

You have the Pyrrhic dance as yet —
  Where is the Pyrrhic phalanx gone?
Of two such lessons, why forget
  The nobler and the manlier one?
You have the letters Cadmus gave —
Think ye he meant them for a slave?

Fill high the bowl with Samian wine!
  We will not think of themes like these!
It made Anacreon's song divine:
  He served — but served Polycrates —
A tyrant; but our masters then
Were still, at least, our countrymen.

The tyrant of the Chersonese
  Was freedom's best and bravest friend;
That tyrant was Miltiades!
  Oh! that the present hour would lend
Another despot of the kind!
Such chains as his were sure to bind.

Fill high the bowl with Samian wine!
  On Suli's rock, and Parga's shore,
Exists the remnant of a line
  Such as the Doric mothers bore;
And there, perhaps, some seed is sown,
The Heracleidan blood might own.

Trust not for freedom to the Franks —
  They have a king who buys and sells:
In native swords, and native ranks,
  The only hope of courage dwells;
But Turkish force and Latin fraud
Would break your shield, however broad.

Fill high the bowl with Samian wine!
  Our virgins dance beneath the shade —
I see their glorious black eyes shine;
  But gazing on each glowing maid,
My own the burning tear-drop laves,
To think such breasts must suckle slaves.

Place me on Sunium's marbled steep,
  Where nothing, save the waves and I,
May hear our mutual murmurs sweep;
  There, swan-like, let me sing and die.
A land of slaves shall ne'er be mine —
Dash down yon cup of Samian wine!

— LORD BYRON.

NOTES.

No. 1. THE BATTLE OF AGINCOURT. The battle of Agincourt was fought on the 25th of October (St. Crispin's Day), 1415, between a small army of English, under Henry V., and a much larger French force, led by the Dauphin. The skill and prowess of the English bowmen won the day, and more than ten thousand French knights and soldiers were left dead on the field. The best account of the battle is that contained in Shakespeare's epic drama, *Henry the Fifth;* but there is a military and patriotic spirit in this martial lyric by Drayton which is seldom found in any of our later battle-songs. This poem was published in 1627. It is plainly imitated by Thomas Heywood in the following little song, included in his drama of *King Edward IV.*, written very soon afterward: —

> " Agincourt, Agincourt! Know ye not Agincourt?
> Where the English slew and hurt
>   All the French foemen?
> With our guns and bills brown,
>   Oh, the French were beaten down,
>   Morris pikes and bowmen!"

l. 41. Poitiers and Cressy. The battle of Poitiers was fought September 19, 1356, and that of Crecy August 26, 1346. The English were led in both battles by Edward the Black Prince, and in both were victorious.

No. 2. THE CHARGE OF THE LIGHT BRIGADE AT BALAKLAVA. This poem was written, as its author tells us, " after reading the first report of the *Times* correspondent, where only 607 sabres are mentioned as having taken part in the charge." It was first published in the London *Examiner*, December 9, 1854. The charge upon the Russian cavalry which the lines commemorate was the result of a misconceived order by Lord Raglan, and occurred October 25, 1854. Of the 607 British horsemen who rode into the " valley of Death," only 198 returned.

The resemblance in versification between this poem and Drayton's ballad of *Agincourt* will be observed at once.

No. 3. THE COMING OF CHARLEMAGNE. This poem is founded on a passage in the chronicle entitled *Des Gestes de Charlemagne*, written by a monk of St. Gaul about the end of the ninth century. King Didier of Pavia had asked Oggier to show him some sign of the coming of Charlemagne into Lombardy. "Then they saw Carl himself, the Iron King, crested with an iron helmet, his arms protected with iron bracelets, an iron hauberk sheltering his iron chest and his huge shoulders, in his left hand a lance of iron lifted upright. . . . Iron filled the fields and the streets; the sun's rays fell upon naught but iron; so that the people of Pavia, more *glacé* by terror than by the iron itself, fell down before the *glacé* iron. 'O iron! Alas, iron!' such was the confused clamor which filled the city. Oggier saw all these things at a glance, and said to Didier, ' Behold that which thou hast so much wished to see!'"

No. 4. THE BATTLE OF BANNOCKBURN. The battle of Bannockburn, in Stirling, Scotland, was fought June 24, 1314. The English army, led by Edward II., was totally defeated by the Scots under Robert Bruce, and Scotland regained its freedom.

> " Departed spirits of the mighty dead!
> Oh! once again to Freedom's cause return
> The patriot Tell, the Bruce of Bannockburn."
>
> — *Campbell, Pleasures of Hope.*

In another version of this song, "to the tune of *Hey, Tuttie Taitie,*" the fourth line of each stanza is shortened to five syllables, as follows: —

    (1) Or to victory!
    (2) Chains and slavery!
    (3) Let him turn and flee!
    (4) Let him follow me!
    (5) But they shall be free!
    (6) Let us do or die!

No. 5. PIBROCH OF DONUIL DHU. The Gathering Song of Donuil Dhu, or Donald the Black, is founded on a very ancient pibroch belonging to Clan McDonald. "It is supposed," says Sir Walter Scott, "to refer to the expedition of Donald Balloch, who, in 1431, launched from the Isles with a considerable force, invaded Lochaber, and at Inverlochy defeated and put to flight the Earls of Mar and Caithness, though at the head of an army superior to his own." This song was published in 1816, in the romance of *Guy Mannering.*

pibroch. The pipe-summons peculiar to any clan. "The connoisseurs in pipe-music affect to discover in a well-composed pibroch the imitative sounds of march, conflict, flight, pursuit, and all the ' current of a heady fight.' "

No. 6. KILLIECRANKIE. John Græme of Claverhouse, whose title of Viscount Dundee had been given him in reward for his cruelties to the Western Covenanters, was the instigator and leader of a revolt of the Highland clans against the government of William III. in Scotland. General Mackay, with his loyal Scotch regiments, was sent out to suppress the uprising. But as they climbed the pass of Killiecrankie, on the 27th of July, 1689, Dundee charged them at the head of three thousand clansmen, and swept them in headlong rout down the glen. His death in the moment of victory broke, however, the only bond which held the Highlanders together, and in a few weeks the host which had spread terror through the Lowlands melted helplessly away.

The Græmes, or Grahams, were among the most noted of Scottish families, and included among them some of the most distinguished men of the country. Among them were Sir John the Græme, the faithful aid of Sir William Wallace, who fell in the battle of Falkirk, 1298, and the celebrated Marquis of Montrose, who died in 1650, and whose exploits are immortalized in Scott's *Legend of Montrose.*

No. 7. LAMENT FOR FLODDEN. The battle of Flodden Field was fought September 9, 1513, between the English, under the Earl of Surrey, and the Scotch, led by King James the Fourth. The latter were defeated with great loss, and the king himself was slain. See Sir Walter Scott's description of the battle in the last canto of *Marmion*.

This poem was for a long time supposed to be an ancient ballad, and it has in fact some portions of a much older song worked into it. Its original title was *The Flowers of the Forest*.

l. 1. **lilting.** Singing merrily.

l. 3. **ilka.** Every. **loaning.** Broad lane.

l. 4. **wede.** Gone, departed.

l. 5. **scorning.** Rallying.

l. 6. **dowie and wae.** Dreary and sad.

l. 8. **leglin.** Milk-pail.

l. 9. **shearing.** Reaping.

l. 10. **bandsters.** Binders. **lyart.** Grizzled. **runkled.** Wrinkled.

l. 11. **fleeching.** Coaxing.

l. 14. **bogle.** Ghost.

l. 17. **Dool and wae.** Sorrow and woe.

No. 8. Bonnie George Campbell. This little Scottish song vividly describes an incident all too common in the romantic days of Border warfare.

l. 10. **Greeting.** Lamenting.

l. 12. **Reaving.** Tearing, rending.

No. 9. The Battle of Ivry. At Ivry, in northwestern France, Henry IV., of Navarre, totally defeated the army of the League, March 14, 1590. This poem was written in 1842.

No. 10. The Armada. A fragment. The Invincible Armada, consisting of one hundred and thirty ships of war, and carrying over twenty thousand soldiers, under the command of the Duke of Medina Sidonia, was sent out by Philip II. for the conquest of England. It arrived in the English Channel July 19, 1588, and was defeated next day by Drake and Howard with a far inferior fleet. A running fight continued for a week, and the Armada was obliged to sail around Scotland and Ireland in order to return to Spain. The English lost but one ship, while more than two-thirds of the Armada was destroyed.

l. 7. **Aurigny's isle.** The island of Alderney.

l. 21. **Lion of the sea.** England as represented in the royal colors.

l. 23. **Picard field.** Crecy, in Picardy.

l. 30. **semper eadem.** Always the same.

No. 11. Ye Mariners of England. Written at Altona, in 1800. Its original title was " Alteration of the Old Ballad, *Ye Gentlemen of England*, composed on the prospect of a Russian War."

l. 3. **a thousand years.** A good example of hyperbole. Although a small armed fleet was organized by King Alfred as early as 890, the English navy had no real existence until the reign of Henry VII., when the first war-ship, " The Great Harry," was launched. The " thousand years " of the poet, if reduced to a mere matter of fact, would, therefore, become three hundred years.

l. 15. Admiral Blake did not fall in battle, as would be inferred from this line. He died peacefully on shipboard as he was entering Plymouth Harbor, 1657. If the poem was written in 1800, this line must have been altered later, as Admiral Nelson's death in the battle of Trafalgar did not occur until October 21, 1805.

NO. 12. THE BATTLE OF NASEBY. The battle of Naseby, between the Parliamentary forces, under Cromwell and Fairfax, and the Royalist army, under King Charles I., occurred June 14, 1645. The Royalists were defeated with great loss. The poem purports to have been written by a Puritan officer in the Parliamentary army.

l. 11. **Man of blood.** Charles I., so called by the Puritans because he made war on his parliament. See 2 *Samuel*, xvi. 7. **Astley.** Lord Jacob Astley, who commanded the infantry. **Sir Marmaduke.** Sir Marmaduke Langdale, the leader of the left wing of the King's army. **Sir Rupert.** Prince Rupert, third son of Frederick V., Elector Palatine, and Elizabeth, daughter of James I. During the war against Parliament he had command of the Royalist cavalry.

l. 14. **The General.** Lord Fairfax, the commander of the "New Model Army."

l. 57. **She of the seven hills.** Rome — but particularly the Roman Catholic Church, with which King Charles was accused of being in league.

NO. 13. THE BATTLE OF THE BALTIC. The battle here referred to is known in history as the battle of Copenhagen, and was fought off Copenhagen, April 2, 1801. The action was between a fleet of British war-ships, under Lord Nelson, and a Danish force of nineteen vessels, protected by both floating and land batteries. The result of the battle was the breaking up of the northern coalition against England, which had been one of Napoleon's most cherished schemes.

The poem was written in 1809. The first stanza originally read : —

> " Of Nelson and the North
>   Sing the day,
> When, their haughty powers to vex,
> He engaged the Danish decks,
> And with twenty floating wrecks
>   Crowned the fray."

l. 54. **Elsinore.** Shakespeare, in *Hamlet*, makes Elsinore the capital of Denmark. The name is here used for Copenhagen.

l. 58. **Riou.** Captain Riou was killed while directing a fierce attack upon the Crown batteries. The title of "the gallant and good" was bestowed upon him by Nelson in his despatches.

No. 14. Hohenlinden. The battle of Hohenlinden was fought December 3, 1800, between the Austrians under Archduke John and the French and Bavarians, commanded by General Moreau. The former were defeated.

This poem was written soon after the battle, and was published in 1802.

No. 15. The Battle. From *Irish Melodies*, written about 1820.

No. 16. The End of the Siege. Part of a longer poem, entitled *The Rhyme of the Duchess May*, published in 1844.

No. 17. The Burial of Sir John Moore. The battle of Corunna, Spain, between the English and French, was fought January 16, 1809. The English army, which was on a retreat from Madrid, gained a decided victory, and the embarkation of the troops was safely effected. The commander, Sir John Moore, was killed in the action, however, and his men buried him secretly while the embarkation was going on.

No. 19. The War-Song of Dinas Vawr. From a romance entitled *The Misfortunes of Elphin*, published in 1829.

No. 20. The Destruction of Sennacherib. See 2 *Kings*, xix. 35. Sennacherib is called King Moussal by the Orientals. This poem is one of the series of *Hebrew Melodies* which Lord Byron published in 1815. The series was written at the request of a friend for a selection of Hebrew melodies arranged by Braham and Nathan, and includes twenty-two pieces.

No. 25. "I travelled among Unknown Men." This poem was written in Germany, in 1799, and was published in 1807.

Stanza 4. "A friend, a true poet himself, to whom I owe some new insight into the merits of Mr. Wordsworth's poetry, and who showed me, to my surprise, that there were nooks in that rich and varied region some of the shy treasures of which I was not perfectly acquainted with, first made me feel the great beauty of this stanza; in which the poet, as it were, *spreads day and night* over the object of his affections, and seems, under the influence of his passionate feeling, to think of England, whether in light or darkness, only as her play-place and verdant home." — *Sara Coleridge.*

No. 26. THE ISLES OF GREECE. A song from *Don Juan*, canto iii., supposed to have been sung by a minstrel in the suite of the hero of that poem.

l. 7. **The Scian and the Teian muse.** The epic and the lyric poets as represented by Homer and Anacreon.

l. 12. **"Islands of the Blest."** Described by Homer as lying far in the western seas, where men

> " Lead easiest lives. No snow, no bitter cold,
> No beating rains are there; the ocean-deeps
> With murmuring breezes from the west refresh
> The dwellers." — *Odyssey,* iv., 562.

l. 17. **Persians' grave.** Marathon, where the Persians were defeated by the Greeks, B.C. 490.

l. 19. **A king.** Xerxes, before the battle of Salamis, B.C. 480.

l. 35. **Thermopylæ.** The famous defence of Thermopylæ by three hundred Spartans under Leonidas, in the summer of 480 B.C., is referred to.

l. 55. **Pyrrhic dance.** An ancient war-dance, named after Pyrrhicus, its inventor.

l. 67. **Chersonese.** The Chersonesus, a narrow strip of land between the Hellespont and the Gulf of Melas, was colonized by a body of Athenians under the elder Mithridates, about 108 B.C.

l. 74. **Suli and Parga.** Towns in Epirus.

l. 78. **Heracleidan blood.** The race of Heracles, or of the heroes.

l. 91. **Sunium's marbled steep.** The promontory of Sunium forms the southern extremity of Attica. It is crowned by the ruins of a magnificent marble temple to Athena.

---

*" I knew a very wise man of Sir Christopher Musgrave's senti-
ment. He believed, if a man were permitted to make all the ballads,
he need not care who should make the laws."*

—Andrew Fletcher (1703).

*" Ballads are the resource which in peace amuses leisure, and in
war stimulates courage."*

—Henry Thomas Buckle.

I.

ROBIN HOOD'S DEATH AND BURIAL.

When Robin Hood and Little John
    Went o'er yon bank of broom,
Said Robin Hood to Little John,
    We have shot for many a pound:

But I am not able to shoot one shot more,
    My arrows will not flee;
But I have a cousin lives down below,
    Please God, she will bleed me.

Now Robin is to fair Kirkley gone,
    As fast as he can win;
But before he came there, as we do hear,
    He was taken very ill.

And when that he came to fair Kirkley-hall,
  He knock'd all at the ring,
But none was so ready as his cousin herself
  For to let bold Robin in.

"Will you please to sit down, Cousin Robin,"
      she said,
  "And drink some beer with me?"
" No, I will neither eat nor drink,
  Till I am blooded by thee."

"Well, I have a room, Cousin Robin," she said,
  "Which you did never see,
And if you please to walk therein,
  You blooded by me shall be."

She took him by the lily-white hand,
  And led him to a private room,
And there she blooded bold Robin Hood,
  Whilst one drop of blood would run.

She blooded him in the vein of the arm,
  And locked him up in the room;
There did he bleed all the live-long day,
  Until the next day at noon.

He then bethought him of a casement door,
  Thinking for to be gone,
He was so weak he could not leap,
  Nor he could not get down.

He then bethought him of his bugle-horn,
  Which hung low down to his knee,
He set his horn unto his mouth,
  And blew out weak blasts three.

Then Little John, when hearing him,
   As he sat under the tree,
" I fear my master is near dead,
   He blows so wearily."

Then Little John to fair Kirkley is gone,
   As fast as he can dree ;
But when he came to Kirkley-hall,
   He broke locks two or three :

Until he came bold Robin to,
   Then he fell on his knee ;
" A boon, a boon," cries Little John,
   " Master, I beg of thee."

" What is that boon," quoth Robin Hood,
   " Little John thou begs of me ? "
" It is to burn fair Kirkley-hall,
   And all thy nunnery."

" Now nay, now nay," quoth Robin Hood,
   " That boon I'll not grant thee ;
I never hurt woman in all my life,
   Nor man in woman's company.

" I never hurt fair maid in all my time,
   Nor at my end shall it be :
But give me my bent bow in my hand,
   And a broad arrow I'll let flee ;
And where this arrow is taken up,
   There shall my grave digg'd be.

" Lay me a green sod under my head,
    And another at my feet ;
And lay my bent bow by my side,
    Which was my music sweet ;
And make my grave of gravel and green,
    Which is most right and meet.

" Let me have length and breadth enough,
    With a green sod under my head ;
That they may say, when I am dead,
    Here lies bold Robin Hood."

These words they readily promis'd him,
    Which did bold Robin please :
And there they buried bold Robin Hood,
    Near to the fair Kirklèys.

2.

THE WIFE OF USHER'S WELL.

There lived a wife at Usher's Well,
    And a wealthy wife was she ;
She had three sons and stalwart sons,
    And sent them o'er the sea.

They hadna been a week from her,
    A week but barely ane,
When word came to the carline wife,
    That her three sons were gane.

They hadna been a week from her,
    A week but barely three,
When word came to the carline wife,
    That her sons she'd never see.

"I wish the wind may never cease,
    Nor fish be in the flood,
Till my three sons come home to me,
    In earthly flesh and blood!"

It fell about the Martinmas,
    When nights are lang and mirk,
The carline wife's three sons came home,
    And their hats were o' the birk.

It neither grew in dyke nor ditch,
    Nor yet in any sheugh;
But at the gates o' Paradise,
    That birk grew fair eneugh.

.   .   .   .   .   .

"Blow up the fire, my maidens!
    Bring water from the well!
For a' my house shall feast this night,
    Since my three sons are well."

And she has made to them a bed,
    She's made it large and wide;
And she's ta'en her mantle her about,
    Sate down at the bedside.

.   .   .   .   .   .

Up then crew the red, red cock,
    And up and crew the gray;
The eldest to the youngest said,
    "'Tis time we were away."

The cock he hadna crawed but once,
    And clapped his wings at a',
When the youngest to the oldest said,
    "Brother, we must awa.

"The cock doth craw, the day doth daw
    The channerin' worm doth chide;
'Gin we be mist out o' our place
    A sair pain we maun bide.

"Fare ye well, my mother dear!
    Farewell to barn and byre!
And fare ye well, the bonny lass,
    That kindles my mother's fire!"

3.

KING JOHN AND THE ABBOT.

An ancient story Ile tell you anon
Of a notable prince, that was called King John;
And he ruled England with maine and with might,
For he did great wrong, and maintein'd little right.

And Ile tell you a story, a story so merrye,
Concerning the Abbot of Canterbùrye;
How for his house-keeping, and high renowne,
They rode poste for him to fair London towne.

An hundred men, the king did heare say,
The abbot kept in his house every day;
And fifty golde chaynes, without any doubt,
In velvet coates waited the abbot about.

How now, father abbot, I heare it of thee,
Thou keepest a farre better house than mee,
And for thy house-keeping and high renowne,
I feare thou work'st treason against my crown.

My liege, quo' the abbot, I would it were knowne,
I never spend nothing but what is my owne;
And I trust your grace will doe me no deere
For spending of my owne true-gotten geere.

Yes, yes, father abbot, thy fault is highe,
And now for the same thou needest must dye;
For except thou canst answer me questions three,
Thy head shall be smitten from thy bodie.

And first, quo' the king, when I'm in this stead,
With my crowne of golde so faire on my head,
Among all my liege-men, so noble of birthe,
Thou must tell me to one penny what I am worthe.

Secondlye, tell me, without any doubt,
How soone I may ride the whole world about,
And at the third question thou must not shrink,
But tell me here truly what I do think.

Oh, these are hard questions for my shallow witt,
Nor I cannot answer your grace as yet;
But if you will give me but three weekes space,
Ile do my endeavour to answer your grace.

Now three days space to thee will I give,
And that is the longest time thou hast to live;
For if thou dost not answer my questions three,
Thy lands and thy livings are forfeit to mee.

Away rode the abbot, all sad at that word,
And he rode to Cambridge and Oxenford;
But never a doctor there was so wise,
That could with his learning an answer devise.

Then home rode the abbot, of comfort so cold,
And he mett his shepheard agoing to fold:
How now, my lord abbot, you are welcome home,
What newes do you bring us from good King John?

Sad newes, sad newes, shepheard, I must give:
That I have but three days more to live;
For if I do not answer him questions three,
My head will be smitten from my bodie.

The first is to tell him there in that stead,
With his crowne of golde so fair on his head,
Among all his liege-men so noble of birth,
To within one penny of what he is worth.

The seconde, to tell him, without any doubt,
How soone he may ride this whole world about:
And at the third question I must not shrinke,
But tell him there truly what he does thinke.

Now cheare up, sire abbot, did you never hear yet,
That a fool he may learne a wise man witt?
Lend me horse, and serving-men, and your apparel,
And I'll ride to London to answere your quarrel.

Nay frowne not, if it hath bin told unto mee,
I am like your lordship, as ever may bee:
And if you will but lend me your gowne,
There is none shall knowe us in fair London towne.

Now horses and serving-men thou shalt have,
With sumptuous array most gallant and brave;
With crozier, and mitre, and rochet, and cope,
Fit to appeare 'fore our fader the pope.

Now welcome, sire abbot, the king he did say,
'Tis well thou'rt come back to keepe thy day;
For and if thou canst answer my questions three,
Thy life and thy living both saved shall bee.

And first, when thou seest me here in this stead,
With my crown of golde so fair on my head,
Among all my liege-men so noble of birthe,
Tell me to one penny what I am worth.

For thirty pence our Saviour was sold
Among the false Jewes, as I have bin told:
And twenty-nine is the worth of thee,
For I thinke, thou art one penny worser than hee.

The king he laughed, and swore by St. Bittel,
I did not think I had been worth so littel!
— Now secondly tell me, without any doubt,
How soone I may ride this whole world about.

You must rise with the sun, and ride with the same,
Until the next morning he riseth againe;
And then your grace need not make any doubt
But in twenty-four hours you'll ride it about.

The king he laughed, and swore by St. Jone,
I did not think it could be gone so soone!
— Now from the third question thou must not shrinke,
But tell me here truly what I do thinke.

Yea, that shall I do, and make your grace merry :
You thinke I'm the Abbot of Canterbùry ;
But I'm his poor shepheard, as plain you may see,
That am come to beg pardon for him and for mee.

The king he laughed, and swore by the masse,
Ile make thee lord abbot this day in his place !
Now naye, my liege, be not in such speede,
For alacke I can neither write, ne reade.

Four nobles a week, then, I will give thee,
For this merry jest thou hast showne unto mee :
And tell the old abbot, when thou comest home,
Thou hast brought him a pardon from good King John.

4.

THE DOUGLAS TRAGEDY.

" Rise up, rise up, now, Lord Douglas," she says,
  "And put on your armour so bright;
Let it never be said, that a daughter of thine
  Was married to a lord under night.

" Rise up, rise up, my seven bold sons,
  And put on your armour so bright,
And take better care of your youngest sister,
  For your eldest's awa the last night."

He's mounted her on a milk-white steed,
　And himself on a dapple grey,
With a bugelet horn hung down by his side,
　And lightly they rode away.

Lord William lookit o'er his left shoulder,
　To see what he could see,
And there he spy'd her seven brethren bold,
　Come riding over the lee.

"Light down, light down, Lady Marg'ret," he said,
　"And hold my steed in your hand,
Until that against your seven brothers bold,
　And your father, I mak a stand."

She held his steed in her milk-white hand,
　And never shed one tear,
Until that she saw her seven brethren fa',
　And her father hard fighting, who loved her so dear.

"O hold your hand, Lord William!" she said,
　"For your strokes they are wondrous sair;
True lovers I can get many a ane,
　But a father I can never get mair."

O she's ta'en out her handkerchief,
　It was o' the holland sae fine,
And aye she dighted her father's bloody wounds,
　That were redder than the wine.

"O chuse, O chuse, Lady Marg'ret," he said,
　"O whether will ye gang or bide?"
"I'll gang, I'll gang, Lord William," she said,
　"For ye have left me no other guide."

He's lifted her on a milk-white steed,
   And himself on a dapple grey,
With a bugelet horn hung down by his side,
   And slowly they baith rade away.

O they rade on, and on they rade,
   And a' by the light of the moon,
Until they came to yon wan water,
   And there they lighted down.

They lighted down to tak a drink
   Of the spring that ran sae clear;
And down the stream ran his gude heart's blood,
   And sair she gan to fear.

" Hold up, hold up, Lord William," she says,
   " For I fear that you are slain!"
"'Tis naething but the shadow of my scarlet cloak,
   That shines in the water sae plain."

O they rade on, and on they rade,
   And a' by the light of the moon,
Until they cam' to his mother's ha' door,
   And there they lighted down.

" Get up, get up, lady mother," he says,
   " Get up, and let me in!—
Get up, get up, lady mother," he says,
   " For this night my fair ladye I've win.

" O mak my bed, lady mother," he says,
   " O mak it braid and deep!
And lay Lady Marg'ret close at my back,
   And the sounder I will sleep."

Lord William was dead lang ere midnight,
   Lady Marg'ret lang ere day —
And all true lovers that go thegither,
   May they have mair luck than they!

Lord William was buried in St. Mary's kirk,
   Lady Margaret in Mary's quire;
Out o' the lady's grave grew a bonny red rose,
   And out o' the knight's a brier.

And they twa met, and they twa plat,
   And fain they wad be near;
And a' the warld might ken right weel,
   They were twa lovers dear.

But bye and rade the Black Douglas,
   And wow but he was rough!
For he pull'd up the bonny brier,
   And flang'd in St. Mary's loch.

5.

THE TWA CORBIES.

As I was walking all alane,
I heard twa corbies making a mane;
The tane unto the t'other say,
"Where sall we gang and dine to-day?"

"In behint yon auld fail dyke,
I wot there lies a new-slain knight;
And naebody kens that he lies there,
But his hawk, his hound, and lady fair.

" His hound is to the hunting gane,
His hawk to fetch the wild-fowl hame,
His lady's ta'en another mate,
So we may make our dinner sweet.

"'Ye'll sit on his white hause bane,
And I'll pike out his bonny blue een :
Wi' ae lock o' his gowden hair,
We'll theek our nest when it grows bare.

" Mony a one for him makes mane,
But nane sall ken whare he is gane ;
O'er his white banes, when they are bare,
The wind sall blaw for evermair."

———◆———

6.

EDWARD OF THE BLOODY BRAND.

" WHY does your brand so drop with blood ?
Edward ! Edward !
Why does your brand so drop with blood,
  And why so sad go ye, O ? "

" O ! I have killed my hawk so good,
Mother ! Mother !
O ! I have killed my hawk so good,
  And I have no more but he, O ! "

" Your hawk's blood was never so red,
Edward ! Edward !
Your hawk's blood was never so red,
  My dear son, I tell thee, O ! "

K

"O! I have killed my red roan steed,
　　　　　Mother! Mother!
O! I have killed my red roan steed,
　That once was fair and free, O!"

"Your steed was old and ye have got more,
　　　　　Edward! Edward!
Your steed was old and ye have got more,
　Some other dule you drie, O!"

"O! I have killed my father dear,
　　　　　Mother! Mother!
O! I have killed my father dear,
　Alas, and woe is me, O!"

"And what penance will ye drie for that?
　　　　　Edward! Edward!
And what penance will ye drie for that?
　My dear son, now tell me, O!"

"I'll set my feet in yonder boat,
　　　　　Mother! Mother!
I'll set my feet in yonder boat,
　And I'll fare over the sea, O!"

"And what will you do with your towers and your hall?
　　　　　Edward! Edward!
And what will you do with your towers and your hall,
　That were so fair to see, O?"

"I'll let them stand till they down fall,
　　　　　Mother! Mother!
I'll let them stand till they down fall,
　For here never more must I be, O!"

" And what will you leave to your bairns and your wife?
       Edward! Edward!
And what will you leave to your bairns and your wife,
  When you go over the sea, O ? "

" The world's room, let them beg through life,
       Mother! Mother!
The world's room, let them beg through life,
  For them never more will I see, O ! "

" And what will you leave to your own mother dear?
       Edward! Edward!
And what will you leave to your own mother dear?
  My dear son, now tell me, O ! "

" The curse of hell from me shall you bear,
       Mother! Mother!
The curse of hell from me shall you bear,
  Such counsels you gave to me, O ! "
          —SIR DAVID DALRYMPLE (*Lord Hailes*).

7.

BARBARA ALLEN'S CRUELTY.

IN Scarlet towne, where I was borne,
  There was a faire maid dwellin,
Made every youth crye, Wel-awaye!
  Her name was Barbara Allen.

All in the merrye month of May,
  When greene buds they were swellin,
Young Jemmye Grove on his death-bed lay,
  For love of Barbara Allen.

He sent his man unto her then,
  To the towne where shee was dwellin;
You must come to my master deare,
  Giff your name be Barbara Allen.

For death is printed on his face,
  And ore his hart is stealin:
Then haste away to comfort him,
  O lovelye Barbara Allen.

Though death be printed on his face,
  And ore his hart is stealin,
Yet little better shall he bee
  For bonny Barbara Allen.

So slowly, slowly, she came up,
  And slowly she came nye him;
And all she sayd, when there she came,
  Yong man, I think y'are dying.

He turned his face unto her strait,
  With deadlye sorrow sighing;
O lovely maid, come pity mee,
  Ime on my deth-bed lying.

If on your death-bed you doe lye,
  What needs the tale you are tellin;
I cannot keep you from your death;
  Farewell, sayd Barbara Allen.

He turned his face unto the wall,
  As deadlye pangs he fell in:
Adieu! adieu! adieu to you all,
  Adieu to Barbara Allen.

As she was walking ore the fields,
  She heard the bell a knellin ;
And every stroke did seem to saye,
  Unworthye Barbara Allen.

She turned her bodye round about,
  And spied the corps a coming :
Laye down, laye down the corps, she sayd,
  That I may look upon him.

With scornful eye she looked downe,
  Her cheeke with laughter swellin :
Whilst all her friends cryd out amaine ;
  Unworthye Barbara Allen.

When he was dead, and laid in grave,
  Her harte was struck with sorrowe,
O mother, mother, make my bed,
  For I shall dye to-morrowe.

Hard-harted creature him to slight,
  Who loved me so dearlye :
O that I had beene more kind to him,
  When he was alive and neare me !

She, on her death-bed as she laye,
  Beg'd to be buried by him ;
And sore repented of the daye,
  That she did ere denye him.

Farewell, she sayd, ye virgins all,
  And shun the fault I fell in :
Henceforth take warning by the fall
  Of cruel Barbara Allen.

8.

BURD HELEN.

I wish I were where Helen lies;
Night and day on me she cries;
Oh, that I were where Helen lies
    On fair Kirconnell lea!

Curst be the heart that thought the thought,
And curst the hand that fired the shot,
When in my arms burd Helen dropt,
    And died to succor me!

Oh, think na but my heart was sair,
When my Love dropt down and spak nae mair!
I laid her down wi' meikle care
    On fair Kirconnell lea.

As I went down the water-side,
None but my foe to be my guide,
None but my foe to be my guide,
    On fair Kirconnell lea;

I lighted down my sword to draw,
I hackèd him in pieces sma',
I hackèd him in pieces sma',
    For her sake that died for me.

O Helen fair, beyond compare!
I'll make a garland of thy hair
Shall bind my heart for evermair
    Until the day I die.

Oh, that I were where Helen lies!
Night and day on me she cries;
Out of my bed she bids me rise,
    Says, " Haste and come to me!"

O Helen fair! O Helen chaste!
If I were with thee, I were blest,
Where thou lies low and takes thy rest
    On fair Kirconnell lea.

I wish my grave were growing green,
A winding-sheet drawn o'er my een,
And I in Helen's arms lying,
    On fair Kirconnell lea.

I wish I were where Helen lies:
Night and day on me she cries;
And I am weary of the skies,
    Since my Love died for me.

                      — ANON.

9.

THE TWA SISTERS.

THERE were twa sisters lived in a bouir;
  Binnoric, O Binnoric ;
The youngest o' them, oh, she was a flouir!
  By the bonnie mill-dams o' Binnoric.

There came a squire frae the west;
He lo'ed them baith, but the youngest best;

He gied the eldest a gay gowd ring;
But he lo'ed the youngest abune a' thing.

He courted the eldest wi' broach and knife;
But he lo'ed the youngest as his life.

The eldest she was vexèd sair,
And sore envied her sister fair.

And it fell once upon a day,
The eldest to the youngest did say:

"Oh, sister, come to the sea-strand,
And see our father's ships come to land."

She's ta'en her by the milk-white hand,
And led her down to the sea-strand.

The youngest sat upon a stane;
The eldest came and pushed her in.

"Oh, sister, sister, lend me your hand,
And you shall be heir of half my land."

"Oh, sister, I'll not reach my hand,
And I'll be heir of all your land.

"Shame fa' the hand that I should take!
It twinned me and my world's maik."

"Oh, sister, reach me but your glove,
And you shall be sweet William's love."

"Sink on, nor hope for hand or glove,
And sweet William shall better be my love.

"Your cherry cheeks and yellow hair
Had gar'd me gang maiden evermair."

First she sank, and syne she swam,
Until she cam to Tweed mill-dam.

The miller's dauchter was baking breid,
And gaed for water as she had need.

"Oh, father, father, in our mill-dam
There's either a mermaid or a milk-white swan."

The miller quickly drew his dam;
And there he fand a drown'd woman.

You couldna see her yellow hair,
For gowd and pearls that were sae rare.

You couldna see her middle sma',
Her gowden girdle was sae braw.

You couldna see her lilie feet,
Her gowden fringes were sae deep.

You couldna see her fingers sma',
Wi' diamond rings they were covered a'.

"Sair will they be, whae'er they be,
The hearts that live to weep for thee!"

Then by there cam a harper fine,
That harpèd to the king at dine:

And, when he looked that lady on,
He sighed, and made a heavy moan:

He has ta'en three locks o' her yellow hair,
And wi' them strung his harp sae fair.

And he brought the harp to her father's hall,
And there the court was assembled all.

He laid his harp upon a stone,
And straight it began to play alone.

"O yonder sits my father, the king!
And yonder sits my mother, the queen!

"And yonder stands my brother Hugh,
And by him my William sweet and true!"

But the last tune that the harp played then,
  Binnorie, O Binnorie,
Was, "Woe to my sister, false Helen!"
  By the bonny mill-dams o' Binnorie.

—ANON.

10.

THE TWA BROTHERS.

THERE were twa brothers at the scule,
  And when they got awa'—
"It's will ye play at the stane-chucking,
  Or will ye play at the ba',
Or will ye gae up to yon hill head,
  And there we'll warsell a fa'?"

"I winna play at the stane-chucking,
  Nor will I play at the ba',
But I'll gae up to yon bonnie green hill,
  And there we'll warsell a fa'."

They warsled up, they warsled down,
  Till John fell to the ground;
A dirk fell out of Willie's pouch,
  And gave him a deadly wound.

"Oh, Billie, lift me on your back,
  Take me to yon well fair,
And wash the bluid frac aff my wound,
  And it will bleed nae mair."

He's lifted his brother upon his back,
  Ta'en him to yon well fair;
He's washed the bluid fra aff his wound,
  But ay it bled mair and mair.

"Tak ye aff my Holland sark,
  And rive it gair by gair,
And stap it in my bluidy wound,
  And syne 'twill bleed nae mair."

He's taken aff his Holland sark,
  And torn it gair by gair;
He's stappit it in his bluidy wound,
  But aye it bled mair and mair.

"Tak now aff my green sleiding,
  And row me saftly in :
And tak me up to yon kirk style,
  Where the grass grows fair and green."

He's taken aff the green sleiding,
  And rowd him saftly in ;
He's laid him down by yon kirk style,
  Where the grass grows fair and green.

"What will ye say to your father dear
  When ye gae hame at e'en ? "
"I'll say ye're lying at yon kirk style,
  Where the grass grows fair and green."

"O no, O no, my brother dear,
  O you must not say so:
But say that I'm gane to a foreign land,
  Where nae man does me know."

When he sat in his father's chair
  He grew baith pale and wan.
"O what blude's that upon your brow?
  O dear son, tell to me."
"It is the blude o' my gude grey steed,
  He wadna ride wi' me."

"O thy steed's blude was ne'er sae red,
  Nor e'er sae dear to me:
O what blude's this upon your cheek?
  O dear son, tell to me."
"It is the blude of my greyhound,
  He wadna hunt for me."

"O thy hound's blude was ne'er sae red,
  Nor e'er sae dear to me:
O what blude's this upon your hand?
  O dear son, tell to me."
"It is the blude of my gay gosshawk,
  He wadna flee for me."

"O thy hawk's blude was ne'er sae red,
  Nor e'er sae dear to me:
O what blude's this upon your dirk?
  Dear Willie, tell to me."
"It is the blude of my ae brother,
  O dule and wae is me!"

"O what will ye say to your father,
  Dear Willie, tell to me?"
"I'll saddle my steed, and awa' I'll ride
  To dwell in some far countrie."

"O when will ye come hame again,
  Dear Willie, tell to me?"
"When the sun and the mune dance on yon green,
  And that will never be."

She turned hersel' right round about,
  And her heart burst into three:
"My ae best son is deid and gane,
  And my 'tother ane I'll ne'er see."

II.

LOCHINVAR.

OH, young Lochinvar is come out of the west,
Through all the wide Border his steed was the best,
And save his good broad-sword he weapons had none;
He rode all unarmed, and he rode all alone.
So faithful in love, and so dauntless in war,
There never was knight like the young Lochinvar.

He stayed not for brake, and he stopped not for stone,
He swam the Eske river where ford there was none;
But, ere he alighted at Netherby gate,
The bride had consented, the gallant came late:
For a laggard in love, and a dastard in war,
Was to wed the fair Ellen of brave Lochinvar.

So boldly he entered the Netherby hall,
Among bride's-men and kinsmen, and brothers and all:
Then spoke the bride's father, his hand on his sword
(For the poor craven bridegroom said never a word),
" Oh, come ye in peace here, or come ye in war,
Or to dance at our bridal, young Lord Lochinvar ? "

" I long wooed your daughter, my suit you denied ; —
Love swells like the Solway, but ebbs like its tide —
And now I am come, with this lost love of mine,
To lead but one measure, drink one cup of wine.
There are maidens in Scotland more lovely by far,
That would gladly be bride to the young Lochinvar."

The bride kissed the goblet ; the knight took it up,
He quaffed of the wine, and he threw down the cup ;
She looked down to blush, and she looked up to sigh,
With a smile on her lips and a tear in her eye.
He took her soft hand, ere her mother could bar, —
" Now tread we a measure ! " said young Lochinvar.

So stately his form, and so lovely his face,
That never a hall such a galliard did grace ;
While her mother did fret, and her father did fume,
And the bridegroom stood dangling his bonnet and
        plume ;
And the bride-maidens whispered, " 'Twere better by
        far
To have matched our fair cousin with young Lochinvar."

One touch to her hand, and one word in her ear,
When they reached the hall-door, and the charger stood
        near ;

So light to the croupe the fair lady he swung,
So light to the saddle before her he sprung!
" She is won! we are gone, over bank, bush, and scaur;
They'll have fleet steeds that follow," quoth young
      Lochinvar.

There was mounting 'mong Græmes of the Netherby
      clan;
Forsters, Fenwicks, and Musgraves, they rode and they
      ran:
There was racing, and chasing, on Cannobie Lee,
But the lost bride of Netherby ne'er did they see.
So daring in love, and so dauntless in war,
Have ye e'er heard of gallant like young Lochinvar!

— SIR WALTER SCOTT.

———◆———

12.

BLACK–EYED SUSAN.

ALL in the Downs the fleet was moor'd,
   The streamers waving in the wind,
When black-eyed Susan came on board,
   " Oh, where shall I my true-love find?
Tell me, ye jovial sailors, tell me true,
Does my sweet William sail among your crew?"

William, who high upon the yard
   Rock'd by the billows to and fro,
Soon as the well-known voice he heard,
   He sigh'd and cast his eyes below;

The cord flies swiftly through his glowing hands,
And, quick as lightning, on the deck he stands.

So the sweet lark, high poised in air,
  Shuts close his pinions to his breast
If chance his mate's shrill call he hear,
  And drops at once into her nest:—
The noblest captain in the British fleet
Might envy William's lip those kisses sweet.

"O Susan, Susan, lovely dear,
  My vows shall ever true remain;
Let me kiss off that falling tear;
  We only part to meet again.
Change as ye list, ye winds: my heart shall be
The faithful compass that still points to thee.

"Believe not what the landsmen say
  Who tempt with doubts thy constant mind;
They'll tell thee, sailors, when away,
  In every port a mistress find:
Yes, yes, believe them when they tell thee so,
For thou art present wheresoe'er I go."

The boatswain gave the dreadful word,
  The sails their swelling bosom spread;
No longer must she stay aboard;
  They kiss'd, she sigh'd, he hung his head.
Her lessening boat unwilling rows to land;
"Adieu!" she cries; and waves her lily hand.

—JOHN GAY.

13.

SALLY IN OUR ALLEY.

OF all the girls that are so smart
  There's none like pretty Sally;
She is the darling of my heart,
  And she lives in our alley.
There is no lady in the land
  Is half so sweet as Sally;
She is the darling of my heart,
  And she lives in our alley.

Her father he makes cabbage-nets,
  And through the streets does cry 'em;
Her mother she sells laces long
  To such as please to buy 'em;
But sure such folks could ne'er beget
  So sweet a girl as Sally!
She is the darling of my heart,
  And she lives in our alley.

When she is by I leave my work,
  I love her so sincerely;
My master comes like any Turk,
  And bangs me most severely.
But let him bang his bellyful —
  I'll bear it all for Sally;
For she's the darling of my heart,
  And she lives in our alley.

Of all the days that's in the week
  I dearly love but one day,
And that's the day that comes betwixt
  The Saturday and Monday;

L

For then I'm drest all in my best
  To walk abroad with Sally;
She is the darling of my heart,
  And she lives in our alley.

My master carries me to church,
  And often am I blaméd
Because I leave him in the lurch
  As soon as text is naméd:
I leave the church in sermon-time,
  And slink away to Sally, —
She is the darling of my heart,
  And she lives in our alley.

When Christmas comes about again,
  Oh then I shall have money!
I'll hoard it up, and box and all,
  I'll give it to my honey;
Oh, would it were ten thousand pound!
  I'd give it all to Sally;
For she's the darling of my heart,
  And she lives in our alley.

My master and the neighbors all
  Make game of me and Sally,
And but for her I'd better be
  A slave, and row a galley;
But when my seven long years are out,
  Oh then I'll marry Sally!
Oh then we'll wed, and then we'll bed —
  But not in our alley!

— Harry Carey.

14.

AULD ROBIN GRAY.

WHEN the sheep are in the fauld, and the kye at hame,
And a' the warld to rest are gane,
The waes o' my heart fa' in showers frae my e'e,
While my gudeman lies sound by me.

Young Jamie lo'ed me weel, and sought me for his bride;
But saving a croun he had naething else beside :
To make the croun a pund, young Jamie gaed to sea;
And the croun and the pund were baith for me.

He hadna been awa' a week but only twa,
When my father brak his arm, and the cow was stown
      awa';
My mother she fell sick, and my Jamie at the sea —
And auld Robin Gray. came a-courtin' me.

My father couldna work, and my mother couldna spin;
I toiled day and night, but their bread I couldna win;
And Rob maintained them baith, and wi' tears in his e'e
Said, Jennie, for their sakes, oh marry me !

My heart it said nay; I looked for Jamie back;
But the wind it blew high, and the ship it was a wrack;
His ship it was a wrack — why didna Jamie dee?
Or why do I live to cry, Wae's me?

My father urgit sair : my mother didna speak;
But she looked in my face till my heart was like to
      break :
They gi'ed him my hand, but my heart was at the sea;
Sae auld Robin Gray he was gudeman to me.

I hadna been a wife a week but only four,
When mournfu' as I sat on the stane at the door,
I saw my Jamie's wraith, for I couldna think it he —
Till he said, I'm come hame to marry thee.

Oh sair, sair did we greet, and muckle did we say;
We took but ae kiss, and I bad him gang away:
I wish that I were dead, but I'm no like to dee;
And why was I born to say, Wae's me!

I gang like a ghaist, and I carena to spin;
I daurna think on Jamie, for that wad be a sin;
But I'll do my best a gude wife aye to be,
For auld Robin Gray he is kind unto me.

—LADY ANNE BARNARD.

15.

JEANIE MORRISON.

I'VE wandered east, I've wandered west,
    Through mony a weary way;
But never, never can forget
    The love o' life's young day!
The fire that's blawn on Beltane e'en
    May weel be black gin Yule;
But blacker fa' awaits the heart
    Where first fond luve grows cule.

Oh dear, dear Jeanie Morrison,
    The thochts o' bygane years
Still fling their shadows ower my path,
    And blind my een wi' tears!

They blind my een wi' saut, saut tears,
  And sair and sick I pine,
As memory idly summons up
  The blithe blinks o' langsyne.

'Twas then we luvit ilk ither weel,
  'Twas than we twa did part;
Sweet time, sad time! twa bairns at schule,
  Twa bairns, and but ae heart!
'Twas then we sat on ae high bink,
  To leir ilk ither lear:
And tones, and looks, and smiles were shed,
  Remembered ever mair.

I wonder, Jeanie, often yet
  When sitting on that bink,
Cheek touchin' cheek, loof locked in loof,
  What our wee heads could think.
When baith bent doun ower ae braid page,
  Wi' ae buik on our knee,
Thy lips were on thy lesson, but
  My lesson was in thee.

Oh mind ye how we hung our heads,
  How cheeks brent red wi' shame,
Whene'er the school-weans laughin' said,
  We cleeked thegither hame?
And mind ye o' the Saturdays
  (The schule then skail't at noon)
When we ran aft to speel the braes —
  The broomy braes o' June?

My head rins round and round about,
  My heart flows like a sea,
As ane by ane the thochts rush back
  O' schuletime and o' thee.
O mornin' life!   O mornin' luve!
  O lichtsome days and lang,
When hinnied hopes around our hearts,
  Like summer blossoms sprang!

Oh, mind ye, luve, how oft we left
  The deavin' dinsome town,
To wander by the green burnside,
  And hear its water croon.
The summer leaves hung ower our heids,
  The flowers burst round our feet,
And in the gloamin' i' the wud
  The throstle whusslit sweet.

The throstle whusslit i' the wud,
  The burn sang to the trees,
And we with Nature's heart in tune, .
  Concerted harmonies;
And on the knowe abune the burn,
  For hours thegither sat
In the silentest o' joy, till baith
  Wi' very gladness grat!

Aye, aye, dear Jeanie Morrison,
  Tears trinkled down your cheek,
Like dew-beads on a rose, yet nane
  Had ony power to speak!

That was a time, a blessed time,
    When hearts were fresh and young,
When freely gushed all feelings forth
    Unsyllabled — unsung !

I marvel, Jeanie Morrison,
    Gin I hae been to thee,
As closely twined wi' earliest thochts
    As ye hae been to me ?
Oh, tell me gin their music fills
    Thine ear as it does mine ;
Oh, say gin e'er your heart grows grit
    Wi' dreamings o' langsyne ?

I've wandered east, I've wandered west,
    I've borne a weary lot ;
But in my wanderings, far or near,
    Ye never were forgot.
The fount that first burst frae this heart,
    Still travels on its way ;
And channels deeper as it rins
    The luve o' life's long day.

O dear, dear Jeanie Morrison,
    Since we were sindered young,
I've never seen your face, nor heard
    The music of your tongue ;
But I could hug all wretchedness,
    And happy could I die,
Did I but ken your heart still dreamed
    O' bygane days and me.

—WILLIAM MOTHERWELL.

16.

LADY CLARE.

It was the time when lilies blow,
 And clouds are highest up in air,
Lord Ronald brought a lily-white doe
 To give his cousin, Lady Clare.

I trow they did not part in scorn:
 Lovers long-betroth'd were they:
They two will wed the morrow morn:
 God's blessing on the day!

" He does not love me for my birth,
 Nor for my lands so broad and fair;
He loves me for my own true worth,
 And that is well," said Lady Clare.

In there came old Alice the nurse,
 Said, "Who was this that went from thee?"
" It was my cousin," said Lady Clare,
 " To-morrow he weds with me."

" O God be thank'd!" said Alice the nurse,
 " That all comes round so just and fair:
Lord Ronald is heir of all your lands,
 And you are not the Lady Clare."

" Are ye out of your mind, my nurse, my nurse?"
 Said Lady Clare, "that ye speak so wild?"
" As God's above," said Alice the nurse,
 " I speak the truth: you are my child.

"The old Earl's daughter died at my breast;
  I speak the truth, as I live by bread!
I buried her like my own sweet child,
  And put my child in her stead."

" Falsely, falsely have ye done,
  O mother," she said, " if this be true,
To keep the best man under the sun
  So many years from his due."

" Nay now, my child," said Alice the nurse,
  " But keep the secret for your life,
And all you have will be Lord Ronald's,
  When you are man and wife."

" If I'm a beggar born," she said,
  " I will speak out, for I dare not lie.
Pull off, pull off, the broach of gold,
  And fling the diamond necklace by."

" Nay now, my child," said Alice the nurse,
  " But keep the secret all ye can."
She said " Not so: but I will know
  If there be any faith in man."

" Nay now, what faith ?" said Alice the nurse,
  " The man will cleave unto his right."
" And he shall have it," the lady replied,
  "Tho' I should die to-night."

" Yet give one kiss to your mother dear!
  Alas, my child, I sinn'd for thee."
" O mother, mother, mother," she said,
  " So strange it seems to me.

"Yet here's a kiss for my mother dear,
 My mother dear, if this be so,
And lay your hand upon my head,
 And bless me, mother, ere I go."

She clad herself in a russet gown,
 She was no longer Lady Clare:
She went by dale, and she went by down,
 With a single rose in her hair.

The lily-white doe Lord Ronald had brought
 Leapt up from where she lay,
Dropt her head in the maiden's hand,
 And followed her all the way.

Down stept Lord Ronald from his tower:
 "O Lady Clare, you shame your worth!
Why come you drest like a village maid,
 That are the flower of the earth?"

"If I come drest like a village maid,
 I am but as my fortunes are:
I am a beggar born," she said,
 "And not the Lady Clare."

"Play me no tricks," said Lord Ronald,
 "For I am yours in word and in deed.
Play me no tricks," said Lord Ronald,
 "Your riddle is hard to read."

Oh and proudly stood she up!
 Her heart within her did not fail:
She look'd into Lord Ronald's eyes,
 And told him all her nurse's tale.

He laughed a laugh of merry scorn :
　He turn'd and kiss'd her where she stood.
" If you are not the heiress born,
　And I," said he, " the next in blood —

" If you are not the heiress born,
　And I," said he, " the lawful heir,
We two will wed to-morrow morn,
　And you shall still be Lady Clare."

—ALFRED TENNYSON.

17.

LUCY GRAY; OR, SOLITUDE.

OFT I had heard of Lucy Gray :
And, when I crossed the wild,
I chanced to see at break of day
The solitary child.

No mate, no comrade Lucy knew ;
She dwelt on a wide moor,
— The sweetest thing that ever grew
Beside a human door !

You yet may spy the fawn at play,
The hare upon the green ;
But the sweet face of Lucy Gray
Will never more be seen.

" To-night will be a stormy night —
You to the town must go ;
And take a lantern, child, to light
Your mother through the snow."

"That, Father! will I gladly do:
' Tis scarcely afternoon —
The minster-clock has just struck two,
And yonder is the moon!"

At this the father raised his hook,
And snapped a faggot-band;
He plied his work; — and Lucy took
The lantern in her hand.

Not blither is the mountain roe:
With many a wanton stroke
Her feet disperse the powdery snow,
That rises up like smoke.

The storm came on before its time:
She wandered up and down;
And many a hill did Lucy climb,
But never reached the town.

The wretched parents all that night
Went shouting far and wide;
But there was neither sound nor sight
To serve them for a guide.

At day-break on a hill they stood
That overlooked the moor;
And thence they saw the bridge of wood,
A furlong from their door.

They wept — and, turning homeward, cried,
"In heaven we all shall meet!"
— When in the snow the mother spied
The print of Lucy's feet.

Then downwards from the steep hill's edge
They tracked the footmarks small;
And through the broken hawthorn hedge,
And by the long stone-wall:

And then an open field they crossed;
The marks were still the same;
They tracked them on, nor ever lost;.
And to the bridge they came.

They followed from the snowy bank
Those footmarks, one by one,
Into the middle of the plank;
And further there were none!

— Yet some maintain that to this day
She is a living child;
That you may see sweet Lucy Gray
Upon the lonesome wild.

O'er rough and smooth she trips along,
And never looks behind;
And sings a solitary song
That whistles in the wind.

— WILLIAM WORDSWORTH.

NOTES.

NO. 1. ROBIN HOOD'S DEATH AND BURIAL. Robin Hood, a valiant outlaw, living free and bold in the green forest, and waging frank and open war against sheriff and law, was the most popular of English heroes. "It is he," says an old historian, "whom the common people love so dearly to celebrate in games and comedies, and whose history, sung by fiddlers, interests them more than any other."

Grafton, after having related that Robin Hood "practised robberyes," etc., adds that "the King beyng greatly offended therewith caused his proclamation to be made that whosoever would bryng him quicke or dead, the King would give him a great summe of money, as by the recordes in the Exchequer is to be seene." But of this promise no man enjoyed any benefit; for as long as he had his bent bow in his hand it was not safe to meddle with the archer good. Time, however, subdued his strength and spirit. Finding the infirmities of old age increase upon him, and "being troubled with a sicknesse, he came to a certain nonry in Yorkshiere called Bircklies, where desiring to be let blood, he was betrayed and bled to death."

Little John. A stalwart fellow, who upon his first meeting with Robin Hood gave him a sound thrashing, and then, being rechristened by him, became one of his staunchest followers. His original name was John Little.

> " 'This infant was called John Little,' quoth he;
>   ' Which name shall be changed anon.
> The words we'll transpose, so wherever he goes,
>   His name shall be called Little John.' "
>
> *— Ritson, Robin Hood.*

Little John was finally apprehended, and executed on Arbor Hill, Dublin.

l. 9. **Kirkley.** Bircklies, in Yorkshire.

NO. 2. THE WIFE OF USHER'S WELL. This ballad, thought by some to be a fragment of a longer one, entitled *The Clerk's Twa Sons of Owsenford*, was first printed in Scott's *Minstrelsy of the Scottish Border*, 1802.

l. 11. **carline.** Feminine of the word *churl* or *carl*.

l. 17. **Martinmas.** The feast of St. Martin (November 11th).

l. 20. **birk.** Birch.

l. 22. **sheugh.** Shaw, wood, grove.

l. 42. **channerin'.** Charcoal.

No. 3. KING JOHN AND THE ABBOT. From Percy's *Reliques,* "printed from an ancient black-letter copy, to 'The tune of Derry down.'" It seems to have been abridged and modernized about the first of the seventeenth century, from a much older ballad entitled *King John and the Bishop.*

St. Bittel. St. Botolph.

No. 4. THE DOUGLAS TRAGEDY. "This ballad exists in Denmark, and in other European countries. The Scotch have localized it, and point out Blackhouse, on the wild Douglas Burn, a tributary of the Yarrow, as the scene of the tragedy."

No. 5. THE TWA CORBIES.

corbies.	Crows.	**tane.**	The one.
gowden.	Golden.	**theek.**	Thatch.
een.	Eyes.		

An English version contains some additional stanzas, and makes the lady faithful : —

> " She lifted up his bloody head,
>   And kissed his wounds that were so red;
>   She buried him before the prime,
>   She was dead herself ere evensong time."

No. 6. EDWARD OF THE BLOODY BRAND. Printed with the old Scotch spelling, in Percy's *Reliques,* where it stated that it was " transmitted to the editor by Sir David Dalrymple, Bart., late Lord Hailes." It has also been attributed to Lady Wardlaw.

l. 20. dule you drie. Grief you suffer.

No. 7. BARBARA ALLEN'S CRUELTY. This ballad was first published in the *Tea-Table Miscellany,* by Allan Ramsey, in 1724. It is republished in Percy's *Reliques,* with some emendations. That it was in existence long before its publication by Ramsey, is indicated by a reference in Pepys's *Diary,* January 2, 1665, to " the little Scotch song of Barbary Allen."

" These harmless people had several ways of being good company; for while one played the other would sing some soothing ballad, ' Johnny Armstrong's Last Good-Night,' or 'The Cruelty of Barbara Allen.' " — *Goldsmith, Vicar of Wakefield.*

No. 8. BURD HELEN. " Adam Fleming, says tradition, loved Helen Irving, or Helen Bell (for this surname is uncertain, as well as the date of the occurrence), daughter of the Laird of Kirconnel in Dumfriesshire.

The lovers being together one day by the river Kirtle, a rival suitor suddenly appeared on the opposite bank, and pointed his gun.   Helen threw herself before her sweetheart, received the bullet in her breast, and died in his arms.   Then Adam Fleming fought with his guilty rival, and slew him." — *W. Allingham, Book of Ballads.*

Burd.　Maiden.

l. 11. **meikle.**　Much.

l. 34. **een.**　Eyes.

No. 9.　The Twa Sisters.

l. 7. **gowd.**　Gold.

l. 8. **abune.**　Above.

l. 26. **twinned.**　Parted.　**maik.**　Mate.

l. 32. **gar'd.**　Obliged.　**gang.**　To go.

l. 33. **syne.**　Then.

l. 44. **braw.**　Brave, handsome.

No. 10.　The Twa Brothers.

l. 6. **warsell.**　Wrestle.

l. 23. **sark.**　Shirt.

l. 24. **rive it gair by gair.**　Tear it into strips.

l. 26. **syne.**　Then.

l. 31. **sleiding.**　A woven coat.

l. 32. **row.**　Roll.

l. 70. **dule and wae.**　Grief and woe.

No. 11.　Lochinvar.　A song sung by Lady Heron, in Scott's *Marmion.*

No. 12.　Black-Eyed Susan.　This ballad was set to music by Richard Leveridge.　Hazlitt speaks of it as " one of the most delightful songs imaginable."

No. 13.　Sally in Our Alley.　" A little masterpiece in a very difficult style; Catullus himself could hardly have bettered it.　In grace, tenderness, simplicity, and humor, it is worthy of the ancients; and even more so, from the completeness and unity of the picture presented." — *W. G. Palgrave.*

No. 14.　Auld Robin Gray.　The author of this ballad has herself related the peculiar circumstances under which it was written.　A friend of hers used to sing at her father's house in Balcarras an old Scottish melody of which she was passionately fond.　This old melody was marred by the introduction of objectionable words, and Lady Barnard (then Lady

Lindsay) conceived the idea of eliminating this feature by singing the air
to different words, and giving to its plaintive tones some little history of
virtuous distress in humble life.   The song, as it is here printed, was
accordingly written, and became a great favorite.   But its authorship
remained a secret until 1823, when it was divulged by Lady Barnard herself, in a letter to Sir Walter Scott.   The title " Robin Gray " was taken
from the name of a herdsman in Lord Balcarras's service.

No. 15. JEANIE MORRISON.

l. 5. Beltane e'en. In Ireland on June 21, and in Scotland on
May-Day, a fire was kindled on the hills, and the young people danced
around it, feasting on milk and eggs.   The word *Beltane* means *Bel's fire*,
and the custom is supposed to have been a relic of the worship of Baal.

l. 6. Yule. Christmas.

l. 13. saut. Salt.

l. 16. blithe blinks o' langsyne.   Happy moments of the past.

l. 22. leir ilk ither lear.   Learn each other learning.

l. 27. loof. Palm.

l. 36. cleeked. Hooked, clung.

l. 38. skail't. Dismissed, closed.

l. 39. speel the braes. Climb the hills.

l. 50. deavin'. Deafening.

l. 51. burnside. Brookside.

l. 61. Knowe abune the burn. Knoll above the brook.

M

For ofttimes a love-song like a hymn of praise springeth spontaneously from the singer's heart, having been wrought therein through the rapturous contemplation of human beauty and perfectness. Such a song ministereth to the delight of all poetic natures and pointeth them to still loftier ideals of thought and life. And there be love-songs of another sort, mere airy nothings, full of artificial conceits tricked out with strained metaphors and far-fetched figures of speech. These last, like soap-bubbles, are not devoid of beauty, but they are fragile and lifeless, evanescent and cold.

—CECIL DEVEREUX.

I.

OLD LOVE SONG.

BLOW, northern wind, send
Thou me my sweeting; blow
Northern wind, blow, blow, blow. . . .
She's a coral of goodness,
She's a ruby of rich fulness,
She's a crystal of clearness,
And banner of beauty,
She's a lily of largess,
She is parnenke pronesse,
She is salsecle of sweetness
And lady of lealty.

Blow, northern wind, send
Thou me my sweeting; blow
Northern wind, blow, blow.

------◆------

2.

MY SWETE SWETYNG.

Ah! my swete swetyng,
My lytyl pretie swetyng!
My swetyng wyl I loue whereuer I goe:
She is soe proper and pure,
Stedfaste, stabyll, and demure, —
There is nonne suche, ye may be sure,
As my swete swetyng.

In all thys worlde, as thynketh mee,
Is nonne soe plesaunte to my 'ee,
That I am gladde soe ofte to see,
As my swete swetynge.

When I beholde my swetyng swete,
Her face, her haundes, her minion fete,
They seeme to mee ther is nonne soe mete
As my swete swetynge.

Above alle others prayse must I,
And loue my pretie pigsnye;
For nonne I finde so womanlie
As my swete swetynge.

She is soe proper and pure,
Stedfaste, stabyll, and demure, —
There is nonne suche, ye may be sure,
As my swete swetynge.

———◆———

3.

IN PRAISE OF DAPHNE.

My Daphne's hair is twisted gold,
Bright stars a-piece her eyes do hold,
My Daphne's brow enthrones the graces,
My Daphne's beauty stains all faces,
On Daphne's cheek grow rose and cherry,
But Daphne's lip a sweeter berry;
Daphne's snowy hand but touched does melt,
And then no heavenlier warmth is felt;
My Daphne's voice tunes all the spheres,
My Daphne's music charms all ears;
Fond am I thus to sing her praise,
These glories now are turned to bays.

—JOHN LYLY.

———◆———

4.

PHILLIS.

PHILLIS is my only joy,
    Faithless as the winds or seas;
Sometimes coming, sometimes coy,
    Yet she never fails to please.

If with a frown
I am cast down,
Phillis smiling
And beguiling,
Makes me happier than before.

Though, alas! too late I find
Nothing can her fancy fix,
Yet the moment she is kind,
I forgive her all her tricks;
Which though I see,
I can't get free;
She deceiving,
I believing,
What need lovers wish for more?

—SIR CHARLES SEDLEY.

5.

THE LOVER TO HIS LUTE.

My lute, awake! perform the last
Labor that thou and I shall waste;
And end that I have now begun:
And when this song is sung and past,
My lute! be still, for I have done.

As to be heard where ear is none;
As lead to grave in marble stone,
My song may pierce her heart as soon;
Should we then sing, or sigh, or moan?
No, no, my lute! for I have done.

The rock doth not so cruelly,
Repulse the waves continually,
As she my suit and affection:
So that I am past remedy;
Whereby my lute and I have done.

Proud of the spoil that thou hast got
Of simple hearts thorough Love's shot,
By whom, unkind, thou hast them won;
Think not he hath his bow forgot,
Although my lute and I have done.

Vengeance shall fall on thy disdain,
That makest but game of earnest pain;
Trow not alone under the sun
Unquit to cause thy lovers plain,
Although my lute and I have done.

May chance thee lie withered and old
In winter nights, that are so cold,
Plaining in vain unto the moon;
Thy wishes then dare not be told:
Care then who list, for I have done.

And then may chance thee to repent
The time that thou hast lost and spent
To cause thy lovers sigh and swoon;
Then shalt thou know beauty but lent,
And wish and want, as I have done.

Now cease, my lute! This is the last
Labor that thou and I shall waste;

And ended is that we begun :
Now is thy song both sung and past ;
My lute, be still, for I have done.

— SIR THOMAS WYATT.

6.

THE LOVER TO HIS LYRE.

AWAKE, awake my Lyre!
And tell thy silent master's humble tale
 In sounds that may prevail, —
 Sounds that gentle thoughts inspire :
  Though so exalted she
  And I so lowly be,
Tell her such different notes make all thy harmony.

 Hark! how the strings awake ;
And though the moving hand approach not near,
 Themselves with awful fear
 A kind of numerous trembling make.
  Now all thy forces try ;
  Now all thy charms apply :
Revenge upon her ear the conquests of her eye!

 Weak Lyre! thy virtue sure
Is useless here, since thou art only found
 To cure, but not to wound —
 And she to wound, but not to cure.
  Too weak too wilt thou prove,
  My passion to remove :
Physic to other ills, thou'rt nourishment to love.

Sleep, sleep again, my Lyre!
For thou canst never tell my humble tale
In sounds that will prevail,
Nor gentle thoughts in her inspire.
All thy vain mirth lay by,
Bid thy strings silent lie:
Sleep, sleep again, my Lyre, and let thy master die!

—ABRAHAM COWLEY.

7.

THE LOVER'S APPEAL.

AND wilt thou leave me thus?
Say nay! say nay! for shame,
To save thee from the blame
Of all my grief and grame.
And wilt thou leave me thus?
Say nay! say nay!

And wilt thou leave me thus,
That hath loved thee so long
In wealth and woe among:
And is thy heart so strong
As for to leave me thus?
Say nay! say nay!

And wilt thou leave me thus,
That hath given thee my heart
Never for to depart
Neither for pain nor smart:
And wilt thou leave me thus?
Say nay! say nay!

And wilt thou leave me thus,
And have no more pity
Of him that loveth thee?
Alas! thy cruelty!
And wilt thou leave me thus?
Say nay! say nay!
                    —SIR THOMAS WYATT.

8.

A LOST LOVE.

THE tide is high, and stormy beams
Of sunlight scud across the down:
Above, the cloudy squadrons frown;
On their broad front a rainbow gleams.

Cease, boisterous wind.   The west is gray
With glory-coated mists, that swell
From distant seas, and gathering tell
Of coming storm and darkened day.

Leave the dank clouds to droop, and guide
Toward their fair port yon sleeping sails:
Close-furled they wait the wakening gales;
Shower-sprinkled shines the pennon wide.

Sail seaward, stately ships, and view
Some blessèd isle where love is bred.
Bring me again my love that's dead
And all I have I'll give to you.
                    —JOHN ADDINGTON SYMONDS.

9.

TO THE VIRGINS TO MAKE MUCH OF TIME.

GATHER ye rose-buds while ye may,
  Old Time is still a-flying :
And this same flower that smiles to-day,
  To-morrow will be dying.

The glorious Lamp of Heaven, the Sun,
  The higher he's a-getting
The sooner will his race be run,
  And nearer he's to setting.

That age is best which is the first,
  When youth and blood are warmer ;
But being spent, the worse, and worst
  Times, still succeed the former.

Then be not coy, but use your time ;
  And while ye may, go marry :
For having lost but once your prime,
  You may for ever tarry.
                    — ROBERT HERRICK.

10.

THE ROSE'S MESSAGE.

Go, lovely rose !
Tell her, that wastes her time and me,
  That now she knows
When I resemble her to thee,
How sweet and fair she seems to be.

Tell her that's young,
And shuns to have her graces spy'd,
That had'st thou sprung
In deserts where no men abide,
Thou must have uncommended dy'd.

Small is the worth
Of beauty from the light retir'd:
Bid her come forth,
Suffer herself to be desir'd,
And not blush so to be admir'd.

Then die! that she
The common fate of all things rare
May read in thee:
How small a part of time they share,
That are so wondrous sweet and fair!

—EDMUND WALLER.

II.

GO, HAPPY ROSE!

Go, happy rose! and, interwove
With other flowers, bind my love!
Tell her, too, she must not be
Longer flowing, longer free,
That so oft hath fettered me.

Say, if she's fretful, I have bands
Of pearl and gold to bind her hands;
Tell her, if she struggles still,
I have myrtle rods at will,
For to tame, though not to kill.

Take then my blessing thus, and go,
And tell her this, — but do not so !
 Lest a handsome anger fly,
 Like a lightning from her eye,
 And burn thee up, as well as I.

     — ROBERT HERRICK.

—————◆—————

12.

PHILLIDA FLOUTS ME.

OH, what a plague is love !
 I cannot bear it ;
She will unconstant prove,
 I greatly fear it :
It so torments my mind
 That my heart faileth ;
She wavers with the wind
 As a ship saileth.
Please her the best I may,
She loves still to gainsay :
Alack, and well-a-day !
 Phillida flouts me.

At the fair, t'other day,
 As she passed by me,
She looked another way,
 And would not spy me.
I wooed her for to dine,
 But could not get her ;
Dick had her to The Vine —
 He might entreat her ;

With Daniel she did dance,
On me she would not glance:
Oh, thrice unhappy chance!
    Phillida flouts me.

Fair maid, be not so coy —
    Do not disdain me;
I am my mother's joy, —
    Sweet, entertain me!
I shall have, when she dies,
    All things that's fitting, —
Her poultry and her bees,
    And her goose sitting;
A pair of mattress beds,
A barrelful of shreds;
And yet, for all these gauds,
        Phillida flouts me!

I often heard her say
    That she loved posies:
In the last month of May
    I gave her roses;
Cowslips and gillyflowers,
    And the sweet lily,
I got to deck the bowers
    Of my dear Philly:
She did them all disdain,
And threw them back again:
Therefore 'tis flat and plain,
        Phillida flouts me.

Thou shalt eat curds and cream
    All the year lasting,
And drink the crystal stream,
    Pleasant in tasting;

Swig whey until thou burst,
  Eat bramble-berries,
Pye-lid and pastry crust,
  Pears, plums, and cherries;
Thy garments shall be thin,
Made of a wether's skin:
Yet, all's not worth a pin, —
  Phillida flouts me!

Which way soe'er I go,
  She still torments me;
And whatsoe'er I do,
  Nothing contents me.
I fade and pine away,
  With griefs and sorrow;
I fall quite to decay,
  Like any shadow:
I shall be dead, I fear,
Within a thousand year;
And all because my dear
  Phillida flouts me.

Fair maiden, have a care!
  And in time take me;
I can have those as fair,
  If you forsake me:
There's Doll, the dairy-maid,
  Smiled on me lately;
And wanton Winifred
  Favors me greatly:
She throws milk on my clothes,
Th'other plays with my nose:
What pretty toys are those!
  Phillida flouts me!

She has a cloth of mine,
   Wrought with blue coventry,
Which she keeps as a sign
   Of my fidelity ;
But if she frowns on me,
   She ne'er shall wear it :
I'll give it to my maid Joan,
   And she shall tear it.
Since 'twill no better be,
I'll bear it patiently ;
Yet all the world may see
    Phillida flouts me.

—ANONYMOUS.

13.

AN APPEAL.

FORGET not yet the tried intent
Of such a truth as I have meant;
My great travail so gladly spent
        Forget not yet !

Forget not yet when first began
The weary life ye know, since whan
The suit, the service none tell can ;
        Forget not yet !

Forget not yet the great assays,
The cruel wrong, the scornful ways ;
The painful patience in delays,
        Forget not yet !

Forget not! oh! forget not this,
How long ago hath been, and is
The mind that never meant amiss —
        Forget not yet!

Forget not then thine own approved,
The which so long hath thee so loved,
Whose steadfast faith yet never moved —
        Forget not this!

                —SIR THOMAS WYATT.

14.

THE PASSIONATE SHEPHERD TO HIS LOVE.

COME live with me, and be my love,
And we will all the pleasures prove,
That valleys, groves, [or] hills and fields,
Woods or steepy mountains yields.

And we will sit upon the rocks,
Seeing the shepherds feed their flocks
By shallow rivers, to whose falls
Melodious birds sing madrigals.

And I will make thee beds of roses,
And a thousand fragrant posies,
A cap of flowers, and a kirtle,
Embroidered all with leaves of myrtle;

A gown made of the finest wool,
Which from our pretty lambs we pull;

Fair-linèd slippers for the cold,
With buckles of the purest gold;

A belt of straw and ivy-buds,
With coral clasps and amber studs:
And if these pleasures may thee move,
Come live with me, and be my love.

Thy silver dishes for thy meat,
As precious as the gods do eat,
Shall, on an ivory table, be
Prepared each day for thee and me.

The shepherd swains shall dance and sing
For thy delight each May-morning.
If these delights thy mind may move,
Come live with me, and be my love.

— CHRISTOPHER MARLOWE.

———◆———

15.

THE SHEPHERDESS'S REPLY.

IF all the world and Love were young,
And truth in every shepherd's tongue,
These pretty pleasures might me move
To live with thee, and be thy love.

Time drives the flocks from field to fold,
When rivers rage, and rocks grow cold;
Then Philomel becometh dumb,
The rest complains of cares to come.

N

The flowers do fade, and wanton fields
To wayward winter reckoning yields;
A honey tongue, a heart of gall,
Is fancy's spring, but sorrow's fall.

Thy gowns, thy shoes, thy beds of roses,
Thy cap, thy kirtle, and thy posies,
Soon break, soon wither, soon forgotten;
In folly ripe, in reason rotten.

Thy belt of straw and ivy-buds,
Thy coral clasps and amber studs,
All these in me no means can move,
To come to thee and be thy love.

What should we talk of dainties, then,
Of better meat than's fit for men?
These are but vain : that's only good
Which God hath bless'd and sent for food.

But could youth last, and love still breed,
Had joys no date, nor age no need ;
Then those delights my mind might move,
To live with thee and be thy love.

—SIR WALTER RALEIGH.

16.

LITTLE BUT LONG.

Love me little, love me long,
Is the burden of my song.
Love that is too hot and strong
    Burneth soon to waste.

Still I would not have thee cold,
Not too backward or too bold;
Love that lasteth till 'tis old
    Fadeth not in haste.

If thou lovest me too much,
It will not prove as true as touch;
Love me little, more than such,
    For I fear the end.
I am with little well content,
And a little from thee sent
Is enough, with true intent,
    To be steadfast, friend.

Say thou lov'st me while thou live,
I to thee my love will give,
Never dreaming to deceive
    While that life endures:
Nay, and after death, in sooth,
I to thee will keep my truth,
As now, when in my May of youth,
    This my love assures.

Constant love is moderate ever,
And it will through life persever;
Give me that — with true endeavor
    I will it restore.
A suit of durance let it be,
For all weathers; that for me,
For the land or for the sea,
    Lasting evermore.

Winter's cold or summer's heat,
Autumn's tempests on it beat,
It can never know defeat,
    Never can rebel.
Such the love that I would gain,
Such the love, I tell thee plain,
Thou must give, or woo in vain ;
    So to thee farewell.

------◆------

17.

PASTORAL.

My banks they are furnished with bees
    Whose murmur invites one to sleep ;
My grottos are shaded with trees,
    And my hills are white over with sheep.
I seldom have met with a loss,
    Such health do my fountains bestow —
My fountains all bordered with moss,
    Where the harebells and violets grow.

Not a pine in my grove is there seen
    But with tendrils of woodbine is bound ;
Not a beech's more beautiful green
    But a sweetbrier entwines it around.
Not my fields in the prime of the year
    More charms than my cattle unfold ;
Not a brook that is limpid and clear
    But it glitters with fishes of gold.

One would think she might like to retire
  To the bow'r I have labored to rear;
Not a shrub that I heard her admire
  But I hastened and planted it there.
Oh, how sudden the jessamine strove
  With the lilac, to render it gay!
Already it calls for my love,
  To prune the wild branches away.

From the plains, from the woodlands and groves,
  What strains of wild melody flow!
How the nightingales warble their loves
  From thickets of roses that blow!
And when her bright form shall appear,
  Each bird shall harmoniously join
In a concert, so soft and so clear
  As she may not be fond to resign.

I have found out a gift for my fair —
  I have found where the wood-pigeons breed;
But let me that plunder forbear —
  She will say 'twas a barbarous deed.
For he ne'er could be true, she averr'd,
  Who would rob a poor bird of her young;
And I loved her the more when I heard
  Such tenderness fall from her tongue.

I have heard her with sweetness unfold
  How that Pity was due to a dove;
That it ever attended the bold,
  And she called it the sister of Love.

But her words such a pleasure convey,
　So much I her accents adore,
Let her speak, and whatever she say,
　Methinks I should love her the more.

Can a bosom so gentle remain
　Unmoved when her Corydon sighs?
Will a nymph that is fond of the plain,
　These plains and this valley despise?
Dear regions of silence and shade!
　Soft scenes of contentment and ease!
Where I could have pleasingly strayed,
　If aught in her absence could please.

But where does my Phyllida stray?
　And where are her grots and her bowers?
Are the groves and the valleys as gay,
　And the shepherds as gentle as ours?
The groves may perhaps be as fair,
　And the face of the valleys as fine;
The swains may in manners compare —
　But their love is not equal to mine.

— WILLIAM SHENSTONE.

18.

SILENT MUSIC.

ROSE-CHEEKED Laura, come!
Sing thou smoothly with thy beauty's
Silent music, either other
　Sweetly gracing.

Lovely forms do flow
From concent divinely framed;
Heaven is music, and thy beauty's
Birth is heavenly.

These dull notes we sing
Discords need for helps to grace them;
Only beauty purely loving
Knows no discord;

But still moves delight,
Like clear springs renewed by flowing,
Ever perfect, ever in them-
Selves eternal.

— THOMAS CAMPION.

19.

SAMELA.

LIKE to Diana in her summer weed,
Girt with a crimson robe of brightest dye,
Goes fair Samela!
Whiter than be the flocks that straggling feed,
When washed by Arethusa faint they lie,
Is fair Samela!
As fair Aurora in her morning gray,
Decked with the ruddy glister of her love,
Is fair Samela!
Like lovely Thetis on a calméd day,
Whenas her brightness Neptune's fancies move,
Shines fair Samela!
Her tresses gold, her eyes like glassy streams;
Her teeth are pearl, the breasts are ivory
Of fair Samela!

Her cheeks, like rose and lily, yield forth gleams;
Her brows' bright arches framed of ebony:
      Thus fair Samela
Passeth fair Venus in her bravest hue,
And Juno in the show of majesty,
      For she's Samela!
Pallas in wit, — all three, if you will view,
For beauty, wit, and matchless dignity,
      Yield to Samela.

— ROBERT GREENE.

20.

TO HELEN.

HELEN, thy beauty is to me
    Like those Nicéan barks of yore,
That gently o'er a perfumed sea,
    The weary way-worn wanderer bore
    To his own native shore.

On desperate seas long wont to roam,
    Thy hyacinth hair, thy classic face,
Thy Naiad airs have brought me home
    To the glory that was Greece,
    And the grandeur that was Rome.

Lo! in yon brilliant window-niche
    How statue-like I see thee stand,
    The agate lamp within thy hand!
Ah, Psyche, from the regions which
    Are Holy Land!

— EDGAR ALLAN POE.

21.

MY JEAN.

OF a' the airts the wind can blaw,
  I dearly like the west,
For there the bonnie lassie lives,
  The lassie I lo'e best:
There wild woods grow, and rivers row,
  And mony a hill between;
But, day and night, my fancy's flight
  Is ever wi' my Jean.

I see her in the dewy flowers,
  I see her sweet and fair:
I hear her in the tunefu' birds,
  I hear her charm the air:
There's not a bonnie flower that springs
  By fountain, shaw, or green;
There's not a bonnie bird that sings,
  But minds me o' my Jean.

—ROBERT BURNS.

22.

MARY MORISON.

TUNE — "Bide ye yet."

O MARY, at thy window be,
  It is the wished, the trysted hour!
Those smiles and glances let me see,
  That make the miser's treasure poor;

How blithely wad I bide the stoure,
　A weary slave frae sun to sun ;
Could I the rich reward secure,
　The lovely Mary Morison.

Yestreen, when to the trembling string
　The dance gaed thro' the lighted ha',
To thee my fancy took its wing,
　I sat, but neither heard nor saw ;
Tho' this was fair, and that was braw,
　And yon the toast of a' the town,
I sigh'd, and said amang them a',
　"Ye are na Mary Morison."

O Mary, canst thou wreck his peace,
　Wha for thy sake wad gladly die ?
Or canst thou break that heart of his,
　Whase only faut is loving thee ?
If love for love thou wilt na gie,
　At least be pity to me shown !
A thought ungentle canna be
　The thought o' Mary Morison.

—ROBERT BURNS.

23.

HIGHLAND MARY.

YE banks and braes and streams around
　The castle o' Montgomery,
Green be your woods, and fair your flowers,
　Your waters never drumlie !

There simmer first unfauld her robes,
  And there the langest tarry;
For there I took the last fareweel
  O' my sweet Highland Mary.

How sweetly bloomed the gay green birk,
  How rich the hawthorn's blossom,
As underneath their fragrant shade
  I clasped her to my bosom!
The golden hours on angel wings
  Flew o'er me and my dearie;
For dear to me as light and life
  Was my sweet Highland Mary.

Wi' mony a vow and locked embrace
  Our parting was fu' tender;
And pledging aft to meet again,
  We tore oursels asunder;
But, oh! fell Death's untimely frost,
  That nipt my flower sae early!
Now green's the sod, and cauld's the clay,
  That wraps my Highland Mary!

Oh pale, pale now, those rosy lips,
  I aft hae kissed sae fondly!
And closed for aye the sparkling glance
  That dwelt on me sae kindly;
And mouldering now in silent dust
  That heart that lo'ed me dearly!
But still within my bosom's core
  Shall live my Highland Mary.

— ROBERT BURNS.

24.

TO MARY IN HEAVEN.

TUNE — " Miss Forbes' Farewell to Banff."

THOU ling'ring star, with less'ning ray,
  That lov'st to greet the early morn,
Again thou usher'st in the day
  My Mary from my soul was torn.
O Mary! dear departed shade!
  Where is thy place of blissful rest?
Seest thou thy lover lowly laid?
  Hear'st thou the groans that rend his breast?

That sacred hour can I forget,
  Can I forget the hallow'd grove,
Where by the winding Ayr we met,
  To live one day of parting love!
Eternity will not efface
  Those records dear of transports past;
Thy image at our last embrace;
  Ah! little thought we 'twas our last!

Ayr gurgling kissed his pebbled shore,
  O'erhung with wild woods, thick'ning green;
The fragrant birch, and hawthorn hoar,
  Twined am'rous round the raptured scene.
The flowers sprang wanton to be prest,
  The birds sang love on ev'ry spray, —
Till too, too soon, the glowing west
  Proclaim'd the speed of winged day.

Still o'er these scenes my mem'ry wakes,
  And fondly broods with miser care;
Time but th'impression deeper makes,
  As streams their channels deeper wear.

My Mary, dear departed shade !
  Where is thy place of blissful rest?
Seest thou thy lover lowly laid?
  Hear'st thou the groans that rend his breast?

                  —ROBERT BURNS.

25.

THE AUTHOR'S RESOLUTION IN A SONNET.

SHALL I, wasting in despaire
Dye, because a woman's fair?
Or make pale my cheeks with care
Cause another's rosie are?
    Be she fairer than the Day
    Or the flowry Meads in May,
    If she thinke not well of me,
    What care I *how* faire she be?

Shall my seely heart be pin'd
Cause I see a woman kind?
Or a well-disposed Nature
Joyned with a lovely feature?
    Be she Meeker, Kinder than
    Turtle-dove or *Pellican:*
    If she be not so to me,
    What care I how kind she be?

Shall a woman's Vertues move
Me to perish for her Love?
Or her wel deservings knowne
Make me quite forget mine own?

Be she with that Goodness blest
Which may merit name of best:
If she be not such to me,
What care I how Good she be?

Cause her *Fortune* seems too high
Shall I play the fool and die?
She that beares a Noble mind,
If not outward helpes she find,
　　Thinks what with them he wold do,
　　That without them dares her woe.
　　And unlesse that *Minde* I see
　　What care I how great she be?

Great, or Good, or Kind, or Faire
I will ne're the more despaire:
If she love me (this beleeve)
I will Die ere she shall grieve.
　　If she slight me when I woe,
　　I can scorne and let her goe,
　　For if she be not for me
　　What care I for whom she be?

　　　　　　　　　—GEORGE WITHER.

26.

THE SOLDIER GOING TO THE FIELD.

PRESERVE thy sighs, unthrifty girl,
To purify the air;
Thy tears to thread, instead of pearl,
On bracelets of thy hair.

The trumpet makes the echo hoarse,
And wakes the louder drum ;
Expense of grief gains no remorse,
When sorrow should be dumb :

For I must go, where lazy peace
Will hide her drowsy head ;
And, for the sport of kings, increase
The number of the dead.

But first I'll chide thy cruel theft ;
Can I in war delight,
Who, being of my heart bereft,
Can have no heart to fight ?

Thou know'st the sacred laws of old
Ordained a thief should pay,
To quit him of his theft, sevenfold
What he had stol'n away.

Thy payment shall but double be ;
Oh then with speed resign
My own seducèd heart to me,
Accompanied with thine.

—Sir William Davenant.

27.

SONG TO CHLORIS.

Ah ! Chloris, that I now could sit
　As unconcerned as when
Your infant beauty could beget
　No pleasure, nor no pain !

When I the dawn used to admire
    And praised the coming day,
I little thought the growing fire
    Must take my rest away.

Your charms in harmless childhood lay,
    Like metals in the mine,
Age from no face took more away
    Than youth concealed in thine.

But as your charms insensibly
    To their perfection prest,
Fond love as unperceived did fly,
    And in my bosom rest.

My passion with your beauty grew,
    And Cupid at my heart,
Still as his mother favored you,
    Threw a new flaming dart.

Each gloried in their wanton part;
    To make a lover, he
Employed the utmost of his art,
    To make a beauty she.

Though now I slowly bend to love,
    Uncertain of my fate,
If your fair self my chains approve
    I shall my freedom hate.

Lovers, like dying men, may well
    At first disordered be,
Since none alive can truly tell
    What fortune they must see.

—SIR CHARLES SEDLEY.

28.

SONG.

WELCOME, welcome do I sing
 Far more welcome than the spring:
He that parteth from you never
 Shall enjoy a spring for ever.

Love, that to the voice is near
 Breaking from your ivory pale,
Need not walk abroad to hear
 The delightful nightingale.

 Welcome, welcome then I sing
  Far more welcome than the spring:
 He that parteth from you never
  Shall enjoy a spring for ever.

Love, that looks still on your eyes,
 Tho' the winter have begun
To benumb our arteries,
 Shall not want the summer's sun.

 Welcome, welcome, &c.

Love, that still may see your cheeks,
 Where all rareness still reposes,
Is a fool if ere he seeks
 Other lilies, other roses.

 Welcome, welcome, &c.

Love, to whom your soft lip yields,
 And perceives your breath in kissing,
All the odors of the fields
 Never, never shall be missing.

 Welcome, welcome, &c.

o

Love, that question would anew
　　What fair Eden was of old,
Let him rightly study you,
　　And a brief of that behold.

　　Welcome, welcome, &c.

—WILLIAM BROWNE.

29.

TO ALTHEA — FROM PRISON.

WHEN Love with unconfinéd wings
　　Hovers within my gates,
And my divine Althea brings
　　To whisper at the grates;
When I lie tangled in her hair
　　And fetter'd to her eye,
The birds that wanton in the air
　　Know no such liberty.

When flowing cups run swiftly round
　　With no allaying Thames,
Our careless heads with roses crown'd,
　　Our hearts with loyal flames;
When thirsty grief in wine we steep,
　　When healths and draughts go free—
Fishes that tipple in the deep
　　Know no such liberty.

When, linnet-like confinéd, I
　　With shriller throat shall sing
The sweetness, mercy, majesty
　　And glories of my King;

When I shall voice aloud how good
  He is, how great should be,
Enlargéd winds, that curl the flood,
  Know no such liberty.

Stone walls do not a prison make,
  Nor iron bars a cage ;
Minds innocent and quiet take
  That for an hermitage :
If I have freedom in my love
  And in my soul am free,
Angels alone, that soar above,
  Enjoy such liberty.

— COLONEL RICHARD LOVELACE.

30.

HER GOLDEN HAIR.

AMARANTHA, sweet and fair,
O braid no more that shining hair !
Let it fly, as unconfined
As its calm ravisher, the wind
Who hath left his darling east
To wanton o'er that spicy nest.
Ev'ry tress must be confest,
But neatly tangled at the best —
Like a clew of golden thread
Most excellently ravelléd ;
Do not, then, wind up that light
In ribbons, and o'ercloud in night,
Like the sun's in early ray ;
But shake your head, and scatter day !

— COLONEL RICHARD LOVELACE.

31.

TO LUCASTA (ON GOING TO THE WARS).

Tell me not, sweet, I am unkind, —
  That from the nunnery
Of thy chaste breast and quiet mind
  To war and arms I fly.

True, a new mistress now I chase,
  The first foe in the field;
And with a stronger faith embrace
  A sword, a horse, a shield.

Yet this inconstancy is such
  As you, too, shall adore;
I could not love thee, dear, so much,
  Loved I not Honor more.

—Colonel Richard Lovelace.

32.

APPRENTICED.

(OLD STYLE.)

"Come out and hear the waters shoot, the owlet hoot,
    the owlet hoot;
  Yon crescent moon, a golden boat, hangs dim behind
    the tree, O!
The dropping thorn makes white the grass, O sweetest
    lass, and sweetest lass;
  Come out and smell the ricks of hay adown the croft
    with me, O!"

"My granny nods before her wheel, and drops her
  reel, and drops her reel;
My father with his crony talks as gay as gay can be, O !
But all the milk is yet to skim, ere light wax dim, ere
  light wax dim;
How can I step adown the croft, my 'prentice lad,
  with thee, O ? "

"And must ye bide, yet waiting's long, and love is
  strong, and love is strong;
And O! had I but served the time that takes so long
  to flee, O !
And thou, my lass, by morning's light, wast all in white,
  wast all in white;
And parson stood within the rails, a-marrying me and
  thee, O ! "

—JEAN INGELOW.

———◆———

33.

THE LONG WHITE SEAM.

As I came round the harbor buoy,
  The lights began to gleam,
No wave the land-locked harbor stirred,
  The crags were white as cream;
And I marked my love by candlelight
  Sewing her long white seam.
    It's aye sewing ashore, my dear,
      Watch and steer at sea,
    It's reef and furl, and haul the line,
      Set sail and think of thee.

I climbed to reach her cottage door;
  Oh sweetly my love sings!
Like a shaft of light her voice breaks forth,
  My soul to meet it springs,
As the shining water leaped of old
  When stirred by angel wings.
    Aye longing to list anew,
      Awake and in my dream,
    But never a song she sang like this,
      Sewing her long white seam.

Fair fall the lights, the harbor lights,
  That brought me in to thee,
And peace drop down on that low roof,
  For the sight that I did see,
And the voice, my dear, that rang so clear,
  All for the love of me.
    For O, for O, with brows bent low,
      By the flickering candle's gleam,
    Her wedding gown it was she wrought,
      Sewing the long white seam.

—JEAN INGELOW.

———◆———

34.

A BRIDAL SONG.

ROSES, their sharp spines being gone,
Not royal in their smells alone,
  But in their hue;
Maiden-pinks, of odor faint;
Daisies smell-less, yet most quaint,
  And sweet thyme true;

Primrose, first-born child of Ver,
Merry spring-time's harbinger,
  With her bells dim ;
Oxlips in their cradles growing,
Marigolds on death-beds blowing,
  Lark-heels trim ;

All, dear Nature's children sweet,
Lie 'fore bride and bridegroom's feet,
  Blessing their sense !
Not an angel of the air,
Bird melodious, or bird fair,
  Be absent hence !

The crow, the slanderous cuckoo, nor
The boding raven, nor chough hoar,
  Nor chattering pie,
May on our bride-house perch or sing,
Or with them any discord bring,
  But from it fly !

— BEAUMONT AND FLETCHER.

35.

CONSTANCY.

OUT upon it, I have loved
  Three whole days together ;
And am like to love three more,
  If it þrove fair weather.

> Time shall moult away his wings,
>   Ere he shall discover
> In the whole wide world again
>   Such a constant lover.
>
> But the spite on't is, no praise
>   Is due at all to me :
> Love with me had made no stays,
>   Had it any been but she.
>
> Had it any been but she,
>   And that very face,
> There had been at least ere this
>   A dozen dozen in her place.

— SIR JOHN SUCKLING.

36.

COME O'ER THE SEA.

> COME o'er the sea,
> Maiden, with me,
> Mine through sunshine, storm, and snows ;
> Seasons may roll,
> But the true soul
> Burns the same, where'er it goes.
> Let fate frown on, so we love and part not ;
> 'Tis life where thou art, 'tis death where thou art not.
> Then come o'er the sea,
> Maiden, with me,
> Come wherever the wild wind blows ;
> Seasons may roll,
> But the true soul
> Burns the same, where'er it goes.

Was not the sea
Made for the free,
Land for courts and chains alone?
Here we are slaves,
But on the waves
Love and liberty's all our own.
No eye to watch, and no tongue to wound us,
All earth forgot, and all heaven around us —
Then come o'er the sea,
Maiden, with me,
Mine through sunshine, storm, and snows;
Seasons may roll,
But the true soul
Burns the same, where'er it goes.

—THOMAS MOORE.

37.

THE BANKS OF DOON.

YE banks and braes o' bonnie Doon,
How can ye bloom sae fair!
How can ye chant, ye little birds,
And I sae fu' o' care!

Thou'll break my heart, thou bonnie bird,
That sings upon the bough;
Thou minds me o' the happy days
When my fause Luve was true.

Thou'll break my heart, thou bonnie bird,
That sings beside thy mate;
For sae I sat, and sae I sang,
And wist na o' my fate.

Aft hae I roved by bonnie Doon
To see the woodbine twine,
And ilka bird sang o' its love;
And sae did I o' mine.

Wi' lightsome heart I pu'd a rose,
Frae aff its thorny tree;
And my fause luver staw the rose,
But left the thorn wi' me.

— ROBERT BURNS.

38.

SONG.

LAY a garland on my hearse
Of the dismal yew;
Maidens, willow branches bear:
Say, I died true.

My love was false, but I was firm
From my hour of birth.
Upon my buried body lie
Lightly, gentle earth!

— BEAUMONT AND FLETCHER.

39.

PENTHEA'S DYING SONG.

OH no more, no more, too late
  Sighs are spent; the burning tapers
Of a life as chaste as fate,
  Pure as are unwritten papers,

Are burnt out; no heat, no light
Now remains; 'tis ever night.
    Love is dead; let lovers' eyes,
    Locked in endless dreams,
    Th'extremes of all extremes,
    Ope no more, for now Love dies.
Now Love dies — implying
Love's martyrs must be ever, ever dying.

—JOHN FORD.

———◆———

40.

STANZAS FOR MUSIC.

THERE be none of Beauty's daughters
    With a magic like thee;
And like music on the waters
    Is thy sweet voice to me:
When, as if its sound were causing
The charmed ocean's pausing,
The waves lie still and gleaming,
And the lull'd winds seem dreaming:

And the midnight moon is weaving
    Her bright chain o'er the deep;
Whose breast is gently heaving,
    As an infant's asleep:
So the spirit bows before thee,
To listen and adore thee;
With a full but soft emotion,
Like the swell of Summer's ocean.

—LORD BYRON.

NOTES.

No. 1. LOVE SONG. These lines are adapted from what Warton says is the earliest love-song in our language. The original is among the Harleian manuscripts in the British Museum, and was written probably before the year 1200.

No. 2. MY SWETE SWETYNG. Written, it is supposed, in the time of Henry VIII. The author is unknown.

l. 13. **minion.** Dainty, neat.

l. 17. **pigsnye.** A word of endearment for a girl or a woman. From Danish *pige*, a girl.

"She was a primerole, a piggesnie." — *Chaucer, Canterbury Tales*, 3268.

No. 3. IN PRAISE OF DAPHNE. Daphne, the daughter of a river-god, fleeing from Apollo, was changed into a laurel, or bay, tree. The bay is the tree of Apollo.

No. 6. THE LOVER TO HIS LYRE. The resemblance between this song and that which precedes it, although not approaching imitation, needs no comment. Dr. Johnson says of Cowley's love-songs that they are " such as might have been written for penance by a hermit, or for hire by a philosophical rhymer who had only heard of another sex."

No. 7. THE LOVER'S APPEAL.

l. 4. **grame.** Sorrow. See Chaucer, *Canterbury Tales*, 16,871 : —

> " Lo swiche a lucre is this lusty game,
> A man's mirth it wol turn all to grame."

No. 9. THE VIRGINS. See *Wisdom of Solomon*, ii., 8 : —

> " Let us crown ourselves with rosebuds, before they be withered."

No. 10. THE ROSE'S MESSAGE. " Waller's fame has sadly, but not undeservedly, declined since the time when it used to be taken for granted that he had virtually invented English poetry, or, one might almost say, the English language; since an editor[1] of his poems (1690) could write that his was ' a name that carries everything in it that is either great or graceful in poetry. He was indeed the parent of English verse, and the first that showed us our tongue had beauty and numbers in it. The tongue came into his hands like a rough diamond; he polished it first, and to that degree that all artists since him have admired the workmanship without pretending to mend it.' " — *Dean Trench.*

---

[1] Thought to be Francis Atterbury, Bishop of Rochester.

l. 7. **graces spy'd.** " These syllables drag painfully on the tongue and I remember to have heard the greatest living authority on melodious numbers suggest that Waller must have written *graces eyed.* The first edition of 1645, however, has, by an obvious misprint, *grace spy'd,* and I believe that what Waller wrote was *grace espy'd.*"

ll. 9, 10. Compare with Gray's *Elegy :* —
> " Full many a flower is born to blush unseen,
> And waste its sweetness on the desert air."

No. 14. THE PASSIONATE SHEPHERD TO HIS LOVE. " It would be ludicrous," says Mr. Palgrave, " to criticize this little poem on the ground of the unshepherdlike or unreal character of some images suggested."

No. 15. THE SHEPHERDESS'S REPLY. There are reasons for doubting that this poem was written by Sir Walter Raleigh. It was first published in *England's Helicon,* in 1600. " In all known copies of this edition," says Dean Trench, " ' Ignoto ' has been pasted over W. R., the original signature which the poem bore. This may have arisen from a discovery on the part of the editor that the poem was not Raleigh's; but also may be explained by his unwillingness to have his authorship of it declared; so that there is here nothing decisive one way or the other."

Izaak Walton, writing of these two poems, in 1653, speaks of " that smooth song which was made by Kit Marlowe, now at least fifty years ago. And the milkmaid's mother sang an answer to it which was made by Sir Walter Raleigh in his younger days."

No. 16. LITTLE BUT LONG. Written about the year 1570. Author unknown.

l. 1. This is a favorite expression among the poets. Marlowe has it, in the *Jew of Malta,* iv. : —
> " Love me little, love me long ; let music rumble,
> Whilst I in thy incony lap do tumble."

It is the subject of a poem by Herrick, and a novel by Charles Reade. It appears also in Heywood's *Proverbs* (1546), and in Bacon's *Formularies.*

No. 18. SILENT MUSIC. This beautiful little piece was published in Campion's *Observations on the Art of English Poetry,* 1602, and was written as illustration of the position taken by the author that rhyme is an unnecessary appendage to English verse. Trench says : " Had he offered to his readers many lyrics like this, he might have done much more than by all his arguments he has done to bring them to his opinion."

No. 21. MY JEAN.

l. 1. **airts.** Quarters of the heavens.

l. 5. **row.** Roll.

l. 14. **shaw.** Copse, grove.

No. 22. Mary Morison. This is one of Burns's earlier poems.

l. 5. **stoure.** Dust, labor.

l. 13. **braw.** Brave.

No. 23. Highland Mary. This poem was considered by Burns to be one of his happiest efforts. Highland Mary is supposed by some to have been Mary Campbell, the poet's first love. It is more likely, however, that Mary Morison is meant — to whom also the songs *Will ye go to the Indies, my Mary?* and *To Mary in Heaven,* were addressed.

> **braes.** Hill-slopes.   **drumlie.** Troubled.
> **birk.** Birch.

No. 25. The Author's Resolution in a Sonnet. "I have transcribed this song," says T. H. Ward, "*verbatim et literatim* (for it is too precious not to be given exactly as it first saw the light) from the original edition of *Fidelia,* in which it first appeared. Mr. W. C. Hazlitt, in his *Handbook to English Literature,* assumes the existence of an edition in 1617, before the well-known second edition in the latter part of the same year; but he says : 'This first edition is supposed to have been privately printed. No copy of it is at present known.' There is, however, a copy of this treasure in the Bodleian Library. As I write, the title-page of it is before me : '*Fidelia,* London, Printed by Nicholas Okes, 1615.'"

No. 26. The Soldier Going to the Field. "Davenant is scarcely known at all except by his strong-thoughted, but heavy, poem of *Gondibert;* and very little known, I should suppose, by that. But this poem shows that in another vein, that of graceful half play, half earnest, few have surpassed him." — *Trench.*

No. 27. Song to Chloris. From *The Mulberry Garden,* a play published in 1668. Sir Charles Sedley, according to Macaulay, was "one of the most brilliant and profligate wits of the Restoration."

No. 29. To Althea — from Prison. Althea was Lucy Sacheverell, whom the poet also calls Lucasta. This poem was written in the prison to which he had been consigned by the Long Parliament for presenting a petition from Kent. The two following poems were probably addressed to the same lady. It is said that "Lucasta," on hearing a false report of Colonel Lovelace's death after he had gone to the wars, married another man. Lovelace died in great poverty, in 1658.

No. 39. Penthea's Dying Song. From the tragedy of *The Broken Heart,* printed in 1633, and reckoned one of the finest of Ford's dramatic works.

Sonnets.

Scorn not the Sonnet: Critic you have frowned
  Mindless of its just honors; with this key
  Shakespeare unlocked his heart; the melody
Of this small lute gave ease to Petrarch's wound:
A thousand times this pipe did Tasso sound;
  With it Camoëns soothed an exile's grief;
  The sonnet glittered like a gay myrtle leaf
Amid the cypresses with which Dante crowned
  His visionary brow; a glow-worm lamp
It cheered mild Spenser, called from Faery-land
  To struggle through dark ways; and when a damp
Fell round the path of Milton, in his hand
  The thing became a trumpet; whence he blew
  Soul-animating strains — alas, too few!

—WILLIAM WORDSWORTH.

I.

DESCRIPTION AND PRAISE OF HIS LOVE GERALDINE.

FROM Tuscan' came my lady's worthy race;
  Fair Florence was some time their ancient seat;
The western isle, whose pleasant shore doth face
  Wild Camber's cliffs, did give her lively heat:
Fostered she was with milk of Irish breast;
  Her sire an earl; her dame of princes' blood:

From tender years, in Britain she doth rest
  With king's child, where she tasteth costly food.
Hunsdon did first present her to my een :
  Bright is her hue, and Geraldine she hight :
Hampton me taught to wish her first for mine :
  And Windsor, alas, doth chase me from her sight.
Her beauty of kind, her virtues from above ;
Happy is he that can obtain her love.

— EARL OF SURREY.

2.

HERSELF ALL TREASURE.

YE tradefull Merchants, that, with weary toyle
  Do seeke most pretious things to make your gain ;
And both the Indias of their treasure spoile ;
  What needeth you to seeke so farre in vaine ?
  For loe, my Love doth in herselfe containe
All this world's riches that may farre be found :
  If Saphyres, loe, her eies be Saphyres plaine ;
If Rubies, loe, her lips be Rubies sound ;
If Pearles, her teeth be Pearles, both pure and round ;
  If Ivorie, her forhead Ivorie weene ;
If Gold, her locks are finest Gold on ground :
  If Silver, her faire hands are Silver sheene :
But that which fairest is, but few behold —
Her mind adorned with vertues manifold.

— EDMUND SPENSER.

3.

A VISION UPON THE FAERIE QUEENE.

METHOUGHT I saw the grave where Laura lay,
  Within that temple where the vestal flame
Was wont to burn; and passing by that way
  To see that buried dust of living fame,
Whose tomb fair Love and fairer Virtue kept,
  All suddenly I saw the Faerie Queene:
At whose approach the soul of Petrarch wept;
  And from thenceforth those Graces were not seen,
For they this Queen attended; in whose stead
  Oblivion laid him down on Laura's hearse.
Hereat the hardest stones were seen to bleed,
  And groans of buried ghosts the heavens did pierce,
Where Homer's spright did tremble all for grief,
And cursed the accèss of that celestial thief.

— SIR WALTER RALEIGH.

4.

ON FIRST LOOKING INTO CHAPMAN'S HOMER.

MUCH have I travelled in the realms of gold,
  And many goodly states and kingdoms seen;
  Round many western islands have I been
Which bards in fealty to Apollo hold.
Oft of one wide expanse had I been told
  That deep-browed Homer ruled as his demesne:
  Yet did I never breathe its pure serene
Till I heard Chapman speak out loud and bold:

P

Then felt I like some watcher of the skies
  When a new planet swims into his ken;
Or like stout Cortez when with eagle eyes
  He stared at the Pacific — and all his men
Looked at each other with a wild surmise —
  Silent, upon a peak in Darien.

               — JOHN KEATS.

5.

ON HIS BLINDNESS.

WHEN I consider how my light is spent,
  Ere half my days, in this dark world and wide,
  And that one talent, which is death to hide,
  Lodged with me useless, though my soul more bent
To serve therewith my Maker, and present
  My true account, lest he, returning, chide;
  " Doth God exact day-labor, light denied ? "
  I fondly ask: but Patience, to prevent
That murmur, soon replies, "God doth not need
  Either man's work, or his own gifts; who best
  Bear his mild yoke, they serve him best: his state
Is kingly; thousands at his bidding speed,
  And post o'er land and ocean without rest;
  They also serve who only stand and wait."

               — JOHN MILTON.

6.

TO MILTON.

MILTON ! thou shouldst be living at this hour;
  England hath need of thee: she is a fen

Of stagnant waters : altar, sword, and pen,
Fireside, the heroic wealth of hall and bower,
Have forfeited their ancient English dower
  Of inward happiness. We are selfish men :
  Oh ! raise us up, return to us again ;
And give us manners, virtue, freedom, power.
  Thy soul was like a star, and dwelt apart :
Thou hadst a voice whose sound was like the sea ;
Pure as the naked heavens, majestic, free ;
So didst thou travel on life's common way,
  In cheerful godliness ; and yet thy heart
The lowliest duties on itself did lay.

—WILLIAM WORDSWORTH.

7.

THE PARTING.

SINCE there's no help, come let us kiss and part —
  Nay, I have done, you get no more of me ;
And I am glad, yea, glad with all my heart,
  That thus so cleanly I myself can free ;
Shake hands for ever, cancel all our vows,
  And when we meet at any time again,
Be it not seen in either of our brows
  That we one jot of former love retain.
Now at the last gasp of love's latest breath,
  When, his pulse failing, passion speechless lies,
When faith is kneeling by his bed of death,
  And innocence is closing up his eyes, —
Now if thou would'st, when all have given him over,
From death to life thou might'st him yet recover !

— MICHAEL DRAYTON.

8.

EASTER MORNING.

MOST glorious Lord of life, that on this day
    Didst make thy triumph over death and sin,
And, having harrowed hell, didst bring away
    Captivity thence captive, us to win ;
This joyous day, dear Lord, with joy begin,
    And grant that we, for whom Thou diddest die,
Being with thy dear blood clean washed from sin,
    May live for ever in felicity :
    And that thy love we weighing worthily,
May likewise love Thee for the same again :
    And for thy sake, that all like dear didst buy,
With love may one another entertain.
So let us love, dear Lord, like as we ought ;
Love is the lesson which the Lord us taught.

— EDMUND SPENSER.

9.

QUATUOR NOVISSIMA.

THAT time of year thou mayst in me behold
    When yellow leaves, or none, or few, do hang
Upon those boughs which shake against the cold,
    Bare ruin'd choirs, where late the sweet birds sang.
In me thou see'st the twilight of such day
    As after sunset fadeth in the west,

Which by and by black night doth take away,
  Death's second self, that seals up all in rest.
In me thou see'st the glowing of such fire
  That on the ashes of his youth doth lie,
As the death-bed whereon it must expire
  Consumed with that which it was nourish'd by.
This thou perceivest, which makes thy love more strong,
To love that well which thou must leave ere long.
                              —WILLIAM SHAKESPEARE.

10.

A LOVER'S LETTERS.

My letters! all dead paper, mute and white!
  And yet they seem alive and quivering
  Against my tremulous hands which loose the string
And let them drop down on my knee to-night.
This said, — he wished to have me in his sight
  Once, as a friend: this fixed a day in spring
  To come and touch my hand — a simple thing,
Yet I wept for it! this — the paper's light —
  Said, *Dear, I love thee;* and I sank and quailed
As if God's future thundered on my past.
  This said, *I am thine* — and so its ink has paled
With lying at my heart that beat too fast:
  And this — O Love, thy words have ill availed,
If, what this said, I dared repeat at last!
                              —ELIZABETH BARRETT BROWNING.

11.

LIFE'S LESSONS.

Lord, with what care hast Thou begirt us round!
  Parents first season us: then schoolmasters
Deliver us to laws; they send us bound,
  To rules of reason, holy messengers,
Pulpits and Sundays, sorrow dogging sin,
  Afflictions sorted, anguish of all sizes,
Fine nets and stratagems to catch us in,
  Bibles laid open, millions of surprises,
Blessings beforehand, ties of gratefulness,
  The sound of glory ringing in our ears;
Without, our shame; within, our consciences;
  Angels and grace, eternal hopes and fears.
Yet all these fences and their whole array
One cunning bosom-sin blows quite away.

— George Herbert.

12.

SAD AND SWEET.

Sad is our youth, for it is ever going,
  Crumbling away beneath our very feet;
Sad is our life, for onward it is flowing
  In current unperceived, because so fleet;
Sad are our hopes, for they were sweet in sowing —
  But tares, self-sown, have overtopped the wheat;
Sad are our joys, for they were sweet in blowing —
  And still, oh still, their dying breath is sweet;
And sweet is youth, although it hath bereft us
  Of that which made our childhood sweeter still;

And sweet is middle life, for it hath left us
    A newer good to cure an older ill ;
And sweet are all things when we learn to prize them
Not for their sake, but His who grants them or denies
          them.

—AUBREY DE VERE.

13.

TO THE MOON.

WITH how sad steps, O Moon, thou climb'st the skies!
    How silently, and with how wan a face!
    What, may it be that even in heavenly place
That busy archer his sharp arrows tries!
Sure, if that long-with-love-acquainted eyes
    Can judge of love, thou feel'st a lover's case,
    I read it in thy looks ; thy languisht grace,
To me, that feel the like, thy state descries.
    Then, even of fellowship, O Moon, tell me,
Is constant love deem'd there but want of wit?
    Are beauties there as proud as here they be ?
Do they above love to be lov'd, and yet
    Those lovers scorn whom that love doth possess ?
    Do they call virtue there ungratefulness?

—SIR PHILIP SIDNEY.

14.

THE COMMON GRAVE.

LAST night beneath the foreign stars I stood,
    And saw the thoughts of those at home go by
To the great grave upon the hill of blood.

Upon the darkness they went visibly,
Each in the vesture of its own distress.
    Among them there came One, frail as a sigh,
And like a creature of the wilderness
    Dug with her bleeding hands.   She neither cried
Nor wept ; nor did she see the many stark
    And dead that lay unburied at her side.
All night she toiled ; and at that time of dawn,
When Day and Night do change their More and Less,
And Day is More, I saw the melting Dark
Stir to the last, and knew she labored on.

— SYDNEY DOBELL.

15.

TO HIS LUTE.

MY lute, be as thou wert when thou didst grow
    With thy green mother in some shady grove,
    When immelodious winds but made thee move,
And birds their ramage did on thee bestow.
    Since that dear Voice which did thy sounds approve,
Which wont in such harmonious strains to flow,
    Is reft from Earth to tune those spheres above,
What art thou but a harbinger of woe ?
    Thy pleasing notes be pleasing notes no more,
But orphans' wailings to the fainting ear ;
Each stroke a sigh, each sound draws forth a tear ;
    For which be silent as in woods before :
Or if that any hand to touch thee deign,
Like widow'd turtle still her loss complain.

—WILLIAM DRUMMOND.

16.

RESIGNATION AND DESPAIR.

As due by many titles, I resign
  Myself to Thee, O God.   First I was made
  By Thee and for Thee; and, when I was decayed,
Thy blood bought that, the which before was thine:
I am thy son, made with Thyself to shine;
  Thy servant, whose pains Thou hast still repaid,
  Thy sheep, thine image; and, till I betrayed
Myself, a temple of thy Spirit divine.
  Why doth the devil then usurp on me?
Why doth he steal, nay, ravish that's thy right?
Except Thou rise, and for thine own work fight,
  Oh! I shall soon despair, when I shall see
That Thou lov'st mankind well, yet wilt not choose me
And Satan hates me, yet is loth to lose me.

—JOHN DONNE.

17.

LAST SONNET.

BRIGHT star! would I were steadfast as thou art —
  Not in lone splendor hung aloft the night,
And watching, with eternal lids apart,
  Like Nature's patient sleepless Eremite,
The moving waters at their priestlike task
  Of pure ablution round earth's human shores,

Or gazing on the new soft fallen mask
  Of snow upon the mountains and the moors.—
No — yet still steadfast, still unchangeable,
  Pillowed upon my fair love's ripening breast,
To feel for ever its soft fall and swell,
  Awake for ever in a sweet unrest;
Still, still to hear her tender-taken breath,
And so live ever — or else swoon to death.

—JOHN KEATS.

———◆———

18.

RETIREMENT.

GIVE me a cottage on some Cambrian wild
  Where, far from cities, I may spend my days,
And by the beauties of the scene beguil'd,
  May pity man's pursuits, and shun his ways,
While on the rock I mark the browsing goat,
  List to the mountain-torrent's distant noise,
Or the hoarse bittern's solitary note,
  I shall not want the world's delusive joys;
But with my little scrip, my book, my lyre,
  Shall think my lot complete, nor covet more;
And when, with time, shall wane the vital fire,
  I'll raise my pillow on the desert shore,
And lay me down to rest where the wild wave
Shall make sweet music o'er my lonely grave.

— HENRY KIRKE WHITE.

19.

EVENING.

ALREADY evening! In the duskiest nook
  Of yon dusk corner, under the Death's-head,
  Between the alembics, thrust this legended
And iron-bound, and melancholy book;
For I will read no longer. The loud brook
  Shelves his sharp light up shallow banks thin-spread;
  The slumbrous west grows slowly red, and red:
Up from the ripen'd corn her silver hook
  The moon is lifting: and deliciously
Along the warm blue hills the day declines.
  The first star brightens while she waits for me,
  And round her swelling heart the zone grows tight:
Musing, half-sad, in her soft hair she twines
  The white rose, whispering "He will come to-night! '
          —OWEN MEREDITH (LORD LYTTON).

20.

TWILIGHT.

IT is the hour when from the boughs
    The nightingale's high note is heard;
It is the hour when lovers' vows
    Seem sweet in every whispered word;
And gentle winds, and waters near,
Make music to the lonely ear.

Each flower the dews have lightly wet,
And in the sky the stars are met,
And on the wave is deeper blue,
And on the leaf a browner hue,
And in the heaven that clear obscure,
So softly dark, and darkly pure,
Which follows the decline of day,
As twilight melts beneath the moon away.

—LORD BYRON.

———◆———

21.

ILLUSIONS.

A GOOD that never satisfies the mind,
A beauty fading like the April flow'rs,
A sweet with floods of gall, that run combin'd,
A pleasure passing ere in thought made ours,
An honour that more fickle is than wind,
A glory at opinion's frown that low'rs,
A treasury which bankrupt time devours,
A knowledge than grave ignorance more blind,
A vain delight our equals to command,
A style of greatness, in effect a dream,
A swelling thought of holding sea and land,
A servile lot, deck'd with a pompous name,
    Are the strange ends we toil for here below,
    Till wisest death make us our errors know.

—WILLIAM DRUMMOND.

22.

SWEET AND BITTER.

Sweet is the rose, but grows upon a brere;
   Sweet is the juniper, but sharp his bough;
Sweet is the eglantine, but pricketh near;
   Sweet is the firbloom, but his branches rough;
   Sweet is the cyprus, but his rind is tough;
Sweet is the nut, but bitter is his pill;
   Sweet is the broom flower, but yet sour enough;
And sweet is moly, but his root is ill;
So, every sweet with sour is tempered still,
   That maketh it be coveted the more:
For easy things that may be got at will
   Most sorts of men do set but little store.
Why then should I account of little pain,
That endless pleasure shall unto me gain?

               — Edmund Spenser.

23.

THE NILE.

It flows through old hushed Egypt and its sands,
   Like some grave mighty thought threading a dream;
   And times and things, as in that vision, seem
Keeping along it their eternal stands, —
Caves, pillars, pyramids, the shepherd bands
   That roamed through the young world, the glory
      extreme

Of high Sesostris, and that southern beam,
The laughing queen that caught the world's great
        hands.
    Then comes a mightier silence, stern and strong,
As of a world left empty of its throng,
    And the void weighs on us; and then we wake,
And hear the fruitful stream lapsing along
    'Twixt villages, and think how we shall take
    Our own calm journey on for human sake.

— LEIGH HUNT.

———◆———

24.

IN SAN LORENZO.

Is thine hour come to wake, O slumbering Night?
    Hath not the Dawn a message in thine ear?
    Though thou be stone and sleep, yet shalt thou hear
When the word falls from heaven — Let there be Light.
Thou knowest we would not do thee the despite
    To wake thee while the old sorrow and shame were
        near.
    We spake not loud for thy sake, and for fear
Lest thou should'st lose the rest that was thy right,
The blessing given thee that was thine alone,
The happiness to sleep and to be stone.
    Yea, we kept silence of thee for thy sake,
Albeit we knew thee alive, and left with thee
The great good gift to feel not nor to see;
    But will not yet thine Angel bid thee wake?

— A. C. SWINBURNE.

25.

HER EYES.

Long-while I sought to what I might compare
  Those powerful eyes, which lighten my dark spright:
Yet found I nought on earth, to which I dare
  Resemble th'image of their goodly light.
  Not to the Sun; for they do shine by night;
Nor to the Moon; for they are changéd never;
  Nor to the Stars; for they have purer sight;
Nor to the Fire; for they consume not never;
Nor to the Lightning; for they still persever;
  Nor to the Diamond; for they are more tender;
Nor unto Crystal; for naught may them sever;
  Nor unto Glasse; such baseness might offend her.
Then to the Maker's self they likest be,
Whose light doth lighten all that here we see.

—Edmund Spenser.

26.

CUPID AND CAMPASPE.

Cupid and my Campaspe play'd
At cards for kisses; Cupid paid:
He stakes his quiver, bow, and arrows,
His mother's doves, and team of sparrows;
Loses them too; then down he throws
The coral of his lip, the rose

Growing on's cheek (but none knows how);
With these, the crystal of his brow,
And then the dimple on his chin;
All these did my Campaspe win:
At last he set her both his eyes —
She won, and Cupid blind did rise.
     O Love! has she done this to thee?
     What shall, alas! become of me?
             — JOHN LYLY.

27.

THE GRASSHOPPER AND THE CRICKET.

GREEN little vaulter on the sunny grass,
Catching your heart up at the feel of June,
Sole voice that's heard amidst the lazy noon,
When ev'n the bees lag at the summoning brass;
And you, warm little housekeeper, who class
With those who think the candles come too soon,
Loving the fire, and with your tricksome tune
Nick the glad silent moments as they pass;
O sweet and tiny cousins, that belong,
One to the fields, the other to the hearth,
Both have your sunshine; both, though small, are strong
At your clear hearts, and both seem given to earth
To sing in thoughtful ears this natural song,
In doors and out, summer and winter, mirth.
             — LEIGH HUNT.

28.

FANCY IN NUBIBUS.

Oh, it is pleasant, with a heart at ease,
Just after sunset, or by moonlight skies,
To make the shifting clouds be what you please,
Or let the easily-persuaded eyes
Own each quaint likeness issuing from the mould
Of a friend's fancy; or, with head bent low,
And cheek aslant, see rivers flow of gold,
'Twixt crimson banks; and then a traveller go
From mount to mount, through Cloudland, gorgeous
    land!
Or, listening to the tide with closèd sight,
Be that blind Bard, who on the Chian strand,
By those deep sounds possessed with inward light,
Beheld the Iliad and the Odyssee
Rise to the swelling of the voiceful sea.

—Samuel Taylor Coleridge.

------◆------

NOTES.

No. 3. A Vision upon the Faerie Queene. This is the first of the
commendatory verses prefixed to the first edition of *The Faerie Queene.*
— "Two persons, I have no doubt, were included in the magnificent flat-
tery of this sonnet — Queen Elizabeth as well as Spenser; for it was she
whom the poet expressly imaged in his Queen of Fairyland; and Sir W.
Raleigh was not the man to let the occasion pass for extolling that great
woman, their joint mistress. His abolition of Laura, Petrarch, and Homer
all in a lump, in honour of his friend Spenser is in the highest style of his
wilful and somewhat domineering genius; but everything in the poem is
as grandly as it is summarily done." — *Leigh Hunt.*

Q

No. 15. To his Lute. This sonnet was later expanded by Shelley in his beautiful poem entitled *To a Lady, with a Guitar* (see page 336).

ramage. Wood-song.

harbinger. Messenger, herald.

turtle. Turtle dove.

No. 22. Sweet and Bitter.

brere. Briar.   eglantine. Hawthorn.

moly. A herb with a black root and white blossoms, mentioned in the *Odyssey*.

No. 23. The Nile. One of the finest of Leigh Hunt's poems. Sisostris. One of the greatest of Egypt's ancient rulers. A name given to the third king of the nineteenth dynasty, 2300 B.C. The laughing queen. Cleopatra.

No. 24. In San Lorenzo. Line 1. *"O slumbering Night."* The famous statue of sleeping Night, on the tomb of Giuliano de' Medici, by Michael Angelo, in the Medici Chapel of San Lorenzo, Florence. The poet supposes the dawn of Italian liberty to be at hand as indeed it was, when this fine sonnet was written.

No. 26. Cupid and Campaspe. From the drama entitled *Alexander and Campaspe*, published in 1584. "It is full," says Hazlitt, "of sweetness and point, of Attic salt and the honey of Hymettus."

Lyrics of Life.

The poet's mission is not to disguise men from themselves, but to reveal to them their own nature, and make them better acquainted with the world around them. True. poetry is the remembrance of love, the embodiment in words of the happiest and holiest moments of life, of the noblest thoughts of man, of the greatest deeds of the past. — PROFESSOR JOWETT.

I.

MAN'S MORTALITY.

LIKE as the damask rose you see,
Or like the blossom on the tree,
Or like the dainty flower in May,
Or like the morning of the day,
Or like the sun, or like the shade,
Or like the gourd which Jonas had —
E'en such is man; whose thread is spun,
Drawn out, and cut, and so is done.
The rose withers; the blossom blasteth;
The flower fades; the morning hasteth;
The sun sets, the shadow flies;
The gourd consumes; and man he dies!

Like to the grass that's newly sprung,
Or like a tale that's new begun,
Or like the bird that's here to-day,
Or like the pearlèd dew of May,
Or like an hour, or like a span,
Or like the singing of a swan —
E'en such is man; who lives by breath,
Is here, now there, in life and death.
The grass withers, the tale is ended;
The bird is flown, the dew's ascended;
The hour is short, the span is long;
The swan's near death; man's life is done!

— SIMON WASTELL.

2.

THE LIFE OF MAN.

LIKE to the falling of a star,
Or as the flights of eagles are,
Or like the fresh spring's gaudy hue,
Or silver drops of morning dew,
Or like a wind that chafes the flood,
Or bubbles which on water stood:
Even such is man, whose borrowed light
Is straight called in and paid to night:
The wind blows out; the bubble dies;
The spring intomb'd in autumn lies;
The dew's dry'd up; the star is shot;
The flight is past; and man forgot!

— FRANCIS BEAUMONT.

3.

LIFE AND THE FLOWERS.

I MADE a posy while the day ran by:
" Here will I smell my remnant out, and tie
    My life within this band."

But Time did beckon to the flowers, and they
By noon most cunningly did steal away,
    And withered in my hand.

My hand was next to them, and then my heart.
I took, without more thinking, in good part
    Time's gentle admonition;

Who did so sweetly death's sad taste convey,
Making my mind to smell my fatal day,
    Yet sugaring the suspicion.

Farewell, dear flow'rs! sweetly your time ye spent;
Fit, while ye lived, for smell or ornament;
    And after death, for cures.

I follow straight, without complaints or grief;
Since, if my scent be good, I care not if
    It be as short as yours.

               —GEORGE HERBERT.

4.

THE RETREAT.

Happy those early days, when I
Shin'd in my angel-infancy!
Before I understood this place
Appointed for my second race,
Or taught my soul to fancy ought
But a white, celestial thought;
When yet I had not walk'd above
A mile or two, from my first love,
And looking back — at that short space —
Could see a glimpse of His bright face;
When on some gilded cloud or flower
My gazing soul would dwell an hour,
And in those weaker glories spy
Some shadows of eternity;
Before I taught my tongue to wound
My conscience with a sinful sound,
Or had the black art to dispense,
A sev'ral sin to ev'ry sense,
But felt through all this fleshly dress
Bright shoots of everlastingness.
  Oh how I long to travel back,
And tread again that ancient track!
That I might once more reach that plain,
Where first I left my glorious train;
From whence th' enlightened spirit sees
That shady city of palm trees.
But ah! my soul with too much stay
Is drunk, and staggers in the way!

Some men a forward motion love,
But I by backward steps will move;
And when this dust falls to the urn,
Into that state I came, return.
— HENRY VAUGHAN.

5.

THE PIPER.

PIPING down the valleys wild,
Piping songs of pleasant glee,
On a cloud I saw a child,
And he laughing said to me: —

"Pipe a song about a lamb:"
So I piped with merry cheer.
"Piper, pipe that song again:"
So I piped; he wept to hear.

"Drop thy pipe, thy happy pipe,
Sing thy songs of happy cheer:"
So I sung the same again,
While he wept with joy to hear.

"Piper, sit thee down and write
In a book that all may read"—
So he vanished from my sight;
And I plucked a hollow reed,

And I made a rural pen,
And I stained the water clear,
And I wrote my happy songs,
Every child may joy to hear.
—WILLIAM BLAKE.

6.

THE ROMANCE OF THE SWAN'S NEST.

> "So the dreams depart,
>   So the fading phantoms flee,
>   And the sharp reality
>   Now must act its part."
>
> —WESTWOOD'S *Beads from a Rosary.*

I.

LITTLE Ellie sits alone
  'Mid the beeches of a meadow,
    By a stream-side on the grass,
And the trees are showering down
  Doubles of their leaves in shadow,
    On her shining hair and face.

II.

She has thrown her bonnet by,
  And her feet she has been dipping
    In the shallow water's flow;
Now she holds them nakedly
  In her hands, all sleek and dripping,
    While she rocketh to and fro.

III.

Little Ellie sits alone,
  And the smile she softly uses
    Fills the silence like a speech,
While she thinks what shall be done,
  And the sweetest pleasure chooses
    For her future within reach.

IV.

Little Ellie in her smile
　　Chooses, " I will have a lover,
　　　　Riding on a steed of steeds :
He shall love me without guile,
　　And to *him* I will discover
　　　　The swan's nest among the reeds.

· V.

" And the steed shall be red-roan,
　　And the lover shall be noble,
　　　　With an eye that takes the breath.
And the lute he plays upon
　　Shall strike ladies into trouble,
　　　　As his sword strikes men to death.

VI.

" And the steed it shall be shod
　　All in silver, housed in azure ;
　　　　And the mane shall swim the wind ;
And the hoofs along the sod
　　Shall flash onward, and keep measure,
　　　　Till the shepherds look behind.

VII.

" But my lover will not prize
　　All the glory that he rides in,
　　　　When he gazes in my face.
He will say, ' O Love, thine eyes
　　Build the shrine my soul abides in,
　　　　And I kneel here for thy grace ! '

VIII.

" Then, ay, then he shall kneel low,
 With the red-roan steed anear him,
  Which shall seem to understand,
Till I answer, 'Rise and go !
 For the world must love and fear him
  Whom I gift with heart and hand.

IX.

" Then he will arise so pale,
 I shall feel my own lips tremble
  With a *yes* I must not say :
Nathless maiden-brave, ' Farewell,'
 I will utter, and dissemble —
  ' Light to-morrow with to-day ! '

X.

" Then he'll ride among the hills
 To the wide world past the river,
  There to put away all wrong,
To make straight distorted wills,
 And to empty the broad quiver
  Which the wicked bear along.

XI.

" Three times shall a young foot-page
 Swim the stream, and climb the mountain,
  And kneel down beside my feet :
' Lo ! my master sends this gage,
 Lady, for thy pity's counting.
  What wilt thou exchange for it ? '

XII.

" And the first time I will send
　A white rosebud for a guerdon :
　　And the second time, a glove ;
But the third time I may bend
　From my pride, and answer,— ' Pardon,
　　If he comes to take my love.'

XIII.

"Then the young foot-page will run ;
　Then my lover will ride faster,
　　Till he kneeleth at my knee :
' I am a duke's eldest son,
　Thousand serfs do call me master,
　　But, O Love, I love but *thee !* '

XIV.

" He will kiss me on the mouth
　Then, and lead me as a lover
　　Through the crowds that praise his deeds ;
And, when soul-tied by one troth,
　Unto *him* I will discover
　　That swan's nest among the reeds."

XV.

Little Ellie, with her smile
　Not yet ended, rose up gayly,
　　Tied the bonnet, donned the shoe,
And went homeward, round a mile,
　Just to see, as she did daily,
　　What more eggs were with the two.

XVI.

Pushing through the elm-tree copse,
  Winding up the stream, light-hearted,
    Where the osier pathway leads,
Past the boughs she stoops, and stops.
  Lo, the wild swan had deserted,
    And a rat had gnawed the reeds!

XVII.

Ellie went home sad and slow.
  If she found the lover ever,
    With his red-roan steed of steeds,
Sooth I know not; but I know
  She could never show him — never,
    That swan's nest among the reeds.
                    —Elizabeth Barrett Browning.

7.

A BOY'S SONG.

Where the pools are bright and deep,
Where the grey trout lies asleep,
Up the river and o'er the lea,
That's the way for Billy and me.

Where the blackbird sings the latest,
Where the hawthorn blooms the sweetest,
Where the nestlings chirp and flee,
That's the way for Billy and me.

Where the mowers mow the cleanest,
Where the hay lies thick and greenest;
There to trace the homeward bee,
That's the way for Billy and me.

Where the hazel bank is steepest,
Where the shadow falls the deepest,
Where the clustering nuts fall free,
That's the way for Billy and me.

Why the boys should drive away
Little maidens from their play,
Or love to banter and fight so well,
That's the thing I never could tell.

But this I know, I love to play,
Through the meadow, among the hay:
Up the water and o'er the lea,
That's the way for Billy and me.

—JAMES HOGG.

8.

YOUTH AND AGE.

WHEN all the world is young, lad,
  And all the trees are green;
And every goose a swan, lad,
  And every lass a queen;
Then hey for boot and horse, lad,
  And round the world away;
Young blood must have its course, lad,
  And every dog his day.

When all the world is old, lad,
   And all the trees are brown;
And all the sport is stale, lad,
   And all the wheels run down;
Creep home, and take your place there,
   The spent and maimed among:
God grant you find one face there,
   You loved when all was young.

—CHARLES KINGSLEY.

9.

THE SPRING JOURNEY.

OH, green was the corn as I rode on my way,
And bright were the dews on the blossoms of May,
And dark was the sycamore's shade to behold,
And the oak's tender leaf was of emerald and gold.

The thrush from his holly, the lark from his cloud,
Their chorus of rapture sang jovial and loud:
From the soft vernal sky to the soft grassy ground,
There was beauty above me, beneath, and around.

The mild southern breeze brought a shower from the hill;
And yet, though it left me all dripping and chill,
I felt a new pleasure as onward I sped,
To gaze where the rainbow gleamed broad overhead.

Oh, such be life's journey, and such be our skill,
To lose in its blessings the sense of its ills;
Through sunshine and shower may our progress be
   even,
And our tears add a charm to the prospect of heaven!

—REGINALD HEBER.

10.

OVER THE HILL.

" TRAVELLER, what lies over the hill?
  Traveller, tell to me :
I am only a child — from the window-sill
  Over I cannot see."

" Child, there's a valley over there,
  Pretty and wooded and shy ;
And a little brook that says, ' Take care,
  Or I'll drown you by-and-by.' "

" And what comes next ? "   " A little town,
  And a towering hill again ;
More hills and valleys, up and down,
  And a river now and then."

" And what comes next ? "   "A lonely moor
  Without a beaten way ;
And grey clouds sailing slow before
  A wind that will not stay."

" And then ? "   " Dark rocks and yellow sand,
  And a moaning sea beside."
" And then ? "   " More sea, more sea, more land,
  And rivers deep and wide."

" And then ? "   " Oh, rock and mountain and vale,
  Rivers and fields and men,
Over and over — a weary tale —
  And round to your home again."

"And is that all?   Have you told me the best?"
  "No, neither the best nor the end.
On summer eves, away in the west,
  You will see a stair ascend,

"Built of all colors of lovely stones,
  A stair up into the sky —
Where no one is weary, and no one moans,
  Or wants to be laid by."

"I will go."   "But the steps are very steep;
  If you would climb up there,
You must lie at the foot, as still as sleep,
  A very step of the stair."

— GEORGE MACDONALD.

II.

YOUTH AND AGE.

VERSE, a breeze 'mid blossoms straying,
Where Hope clung feeding, like a bee —
Both were mine!   Life went a-Maying
  With Nature, Hope, and Poesy,
    When I was young!
When I was young? — Ah, woful when!
Ah, for the change 'twixt Now and Then!
This breathing house not built with hands,
This body that does me grievous wrong,
O'er aery cliffs and glittering sands
How lightly then it flash'd along:
Like those trim skiffs, unknown of yore,
On winding lakes and rivers wide,

That ask no aid of sail or oar,
That fear no spite of wind or tide!
Nought cared this body for wind or weather
When Youth and I lived in't together.

Flowers are lovely; Love is flower-like;
Friendship is à sheltering tree;
Oh, the joys, that came down shower-like,
Of Friendship, Love, and Liberty,
    Ere I was old!

Ere I was old? Ah woful Ere,
Which tells me, Youth's no longer here!
O Youth! for years so many and sweet
'Tis known that thou and I were one;
I'll think it but a fond conceit —
It cannot be, that thou art gone!
Thy vesper-bell hath not yet toll'd: —
And thou wert aye a masker bold!
What strange disguise hast now put on
To make believe that thou art gone?
I see these locks in silvery slips,
This drooping gait, this alter'd size:
But Springtide blossoms on thy lips,
And tears like sunshine from thine eyes!
Life is but Thought: so think I will
That Youth and I are housemates still.

Dew-drops are the gems of morning,
But the tears of mournful eve!
Where no hope is, life's a warning
That only serves to make us grieve
    When we are old:

R

— That only serves to make us grieve
With oft and tedious taking-leave,
Like some poor nigh-related guest
That may not rudely be dismisst,
Yet hath out-stay'd his welcome while,
And tells the jest without the smile.

—S. T. COLERIDGE.

12.

THE STREAM OF LIFE.

O STREAM descending to the sea,
   Thy mossy banks between,
The flowerets blow, the grasses grow,
   The leafy trees are green.

In garden plots the children play,
   The fields the laborers till,
And houses stand on either hand,
   And thou descendest still.

O life descending into death,
   Our waking eyes behold,
Parent and friend thy lapse attend,
   Companions young and old.

Strong purposes our minds possess,
   Our hearts affections fill,
We toil and earn, we seek and learn,
   And thou descendest still.

O end to which our currents tend,
  Inevitable sea,
To which we flow, what do we know,
  What shall we guess of thee?

A roar we hear upon thy shore,
  As we our course fulfil;
Scarce we divine a sun will shine
  And be above us still.

— ARTHUR HUGH CLOUGH.

13.

A PETITION TO TIME.

TOUCH us gently, Time!
  Glide us adown thy stream
Gently, — as we sometimes glide
  Through a quiet dream!
Humble voyagers are we,
Husband, wife, and children three —
(One is lost, — an angel, fled
To the azure overhead!)

Touch us gently, Time!
  We've not proud nor soaring wings:
Our ambition, *our* content
  Lies in simple things.
Humble voyagers are we,
O'er Life's dim unsounded sea,
Seeking only some calm clime: —
Touch us *gently*, gentle Time!

— BRYAN WALLER PROCTER.

14.

A PROPER MAN.

Of your trouble, Ben, to ease me,
I will tell what man would please me.
I would have him if I could
Noble; or of greater blood;
Titles, I confess, do take me,
And a woman God did make me;
French to boot, at least in fashion,
And his manners of that nation.

Young I'd have him too, and fair,
Yet a man; with crispèd hair,
Cast in thousand snares and rings,
For love's fingers and his wings:
Chestnut color, or more slack,
Gold upon a ground of black.
Venus and Minerva's eyes,
For he must look wanton-wise.

Eyebrows bent like Cupid's bow,
Front, an ample field of snow;
Even nose, and cheek withal,
Smooth as is the billiard-ball;
Chin as woolly as the peach;
And his lip should kissing teach,
Till he cherished too much beard,
And made Love or me afeard.

He should have a hand as soft
As the down, and show it oft;
Skin as smooth as any rush,
And so thin to see a blush
Rising through it, ere it came;
All his blood should be a flame,

Quickly fired, as in beginners
In Love's school, and yet no sinners.
　　'Twere too long to speak of all;
What we harmony do call
In a body should be there.
Well he should his clothes, too, wear,
Yet no tailor help to make him;
Drest, you still for man should take him,
And not think h' had eat a stake,
Or were set up in a brake.
　　Valiant he should be as fire,
Showing danger more than ire.
Bounteous as the clouds to earth,
And as honest as his birth;
All his actions to be such,
As to do no thing too much:
Nor o'er praise, nor yet condemn,
Nor out-value, nor contemn;
Nor do wrongs, nor wrongs receive,
Nor tie knots, nor knots unweave;
And from baseness to be free,
As he durst love Truth and me.
　　Such a man, with every part,
I could give my very heart;
But of one if short he came,
I can rest me where I am.

—Ben Jonson.

15.

A PROPER WOMAN.

HE that loves a rosy cheek
  Or a coral lip admires,
Or from star-like eyes doth seek
  Fuel to maintain his fires ;
As old time makes these decay,
So his flames must waste away.

But a smooth and steadfast mind,
  Gentle thoughts and calm desires,
Hearts with equal love combined,
  Kindle never dying fires ; —
Where these are not, I despise
Lovely cheeks, or lips, or eyes.

—THOMAS CAREW.

16.

THE COMMON LOT.

ONCE, in the flight of ages past,
There lived a man : — and WHO WAS HE ? —
Mortal ! howe'er thy lot be cast,
That man resembled thee.

Unknown the region of his birth,
The land in which he died unknown :
His name has perished from the earth ;
This truth survives alone : —

That joy and grief, and hope and fear,
Alternate triumphed in his breast;
His bliss and woe, — a smile, a tear! —
Oblivion hides the rest.

The bounding pulse, the languid limb,
The changing spirits' rise and fall,
We know that these were felt by him,
For these are felt by all.

He suffered, — but his pangs are o'er;
Enjoyed, — but his delights are fled;
Had friends, — his friends are now no more;
And foes, — his foes are dead.

He loved, — but whom he loved, the grave
Hath lost in its unconscious womb:
Oh, she was fair! — but nought could save
Her beauty from the tomb.

He saw whatever thou hast seen;
Encountered all that troubles thee:
He was — whatever thou hast been;
He is — what thou shalt be.

The rolling seasons, day and night,
Sun, moon, and stars, the earth and main,
Erewhile his portion, life and light,
To him exist in vain.

The clouds and sunbeams o'er his eye
That once their shades and glory threw,
Have left in yonder silent sky
No vestige where they flew.

The annals of the human race,
Their ruins since the world began,
Of HIM afford no other trace
Than this, — THERE LIVED A MAN !

—JAMES MONTGOMERY.

17.

THE PERFECT LIFE.

IT is not growing like a tree
In bulk, doth make Man better be ;
Or standing long an oak, three hundred year,
To fall a log at last, dry, bald, and sere :
A lily of a day
Is fairer far in May,
Although it fall and die that night —
It was the plant and flower of Light.
In small proportions we just beauties see ;
And in short measures life may perfect be.

— BEN JONSON.

18.

THE CONTENTED MIND.

I WEIGH not fortune's frown or smile ;
I joy not much in earthly joys ;
I seek not state, I seek not style ;
I am not fond of fancy's toys ;
I rest so pleased with what I have,
I wish no more, no more I crave.

I quake not at the thunder's crack;
  I tremble not at noise of war;
I swound not at the news of wrack;
  I shrink not at a blazing star;
I fear not loss, I hope not gain,
I envy none, I none disdain.

I see ambition never pleased;
  I see some Tantals starved in store;
I see gold's dropsy seldom eased;
  I see e'en Midas gape for more:
I neither want, nor yet abound —
Enough's a feast, content is crowned.

I feign not friendship, where I hate;
  I fawn not on the great in show;
I prize, I praise a mean estate —
  Neither too lofty nor to low:
This, this is all my choice, my cheer —
A mind content, a conscience clear.

— JOSHUA SYLVESTER.

19.

A WISH.

THIS only grant me, that my means may lie
Too low for envy, for contempt too high.
  Some honor I would have
Not from great deeds, but good alone.
The unknown are better than ill known;
  Rumor can ope the grave.
Acquaintance I would have, but when 't depends
Not on the number, but the choice of friends.

Books should, not business, entertain the light,
And sleep, as undisturb'd as death, the night.
    My house a cottage, more
Than palace, and should fitting be,
For all my use, not luxury.
    My garden painted o'er
With nature's hand, not art's; and pleasures yield,
Horace might envy in his Sabine field.

Thus would I double my life's fading space,
For he that runs it well, twice runs his race.
    And in this true delight,
These unbought sports, this happy state,
I would not fear nor wish my fate,
    But boldly say each night,
To-morrow let my sun his beams display,
Or in clouds hide them; I have liv'd to-day.

—ABRAHAM COWLEY.

20.

A WISH.

MINE be a cot beside the hill;
A bee-hive's hum shall soothe my ear;
A willowy brook that turns a mill,
With many a fall shall linger near.

The swallow, oft, beneath my thatch
Shall twitter from her clay-built nest;
Oft shall the pilgrim lift the latch,
And share my meal, a welcome guest.

Around my ivied porch shall spring
Each fragrant flower that drinks the dew;
And Lucy, at her wheel, shall sing
In russet-gown and apron blue.

The village church among the trees,
Where first our marriage vows were given,
With merry peals shall swell the breeze
And point with taper spire to Heaven.

—SAMUEL ROGERS.

21.

THE CHARACTER OF A HAPPY LIFE.

How happy is he born and taught
  That serveth not another's will;
Whose armor is his honest thought,
  And simple truth his utmost skill;

Whose passions not his masters are;
  Whose soul is still prepared for death,
Untied unto the world by care
  Of public fame or private breath;

Who envies none that chance doth raise,
  Nor vice; who never understood
How deepest wounds are given by praise;
  Nor rules of state, but rules of good;

Who hath his life from rumors freed;
  Whose conscience is his strong retreat;
Whose state can neither flatterers feed,
  Nor ruin make oppressors great;

Who God doth late and early pray
  More of his grace than gifts to lend;
And entertains the harmless day
  With a religious book or friend.

This man is freed from servile bands
  Of hope to rise or fear to fall:
Lord of himself, though not of lands,
  And, having nothing, yet hath all.

—Sir Henry Wotton.

✦

22.

THE QUIET LIFE.

Happy the man whose wish and care
A few paternal acres bound,
Content to breathe his native air
    In his own ground.

Whose herds with milk, whose fields with bread,
Whose flocks supply him with attire;
Whose trees in summer yield him shade,
    In winter, fire.

Blest, who can unconcern'dly find
Hours, days, and years, slide soft away
In health of body; peace of mind;
    Quiet by day;

Sound sleep by night; study and ease
Together mix'd; sweet recreation,
And innocence, which most does please
    With meditation.

Thus let me live, unseen, unknown;
Thus unlamented let me die;
Steal from the world, and not a stone
Tell where I lie.

— ALEXANDER POPE.

23.

THE EASY LIFE.

Is this a life, to break thy sleep,
To rise as soon as day doth peep?
To tire thy patient ox or ass
By noon, and let thy good days pass,
Not knowing this, that Jove decrees
Some mirth, t'adulce man's miseries?
— No: 'tis a life to have thine oil
Without extortion from thy soil;
Thy faithful fields to yield thee grain,
Although with some, yet little pain;
To have thy mind, and nuptial bed,
With fears and cares uncumberèd;
A pleasing wife, that by thy side
Lies softly panting like a bride;
— This is to live, and to endear
Those minutes Time has sent us here.
Then, while fates suffer, live thou free,
As is that air that circles thee;
And crown thy temples too; and let
Thy servant, not thy own self, sweat,
To strut thy barns with sheaves of wheat.
— Time steals away like to a stream,
And we glide hence away with them;

No sound recalls the hours once fled,
Or roses, being witherèd;
Nor us, my friend, when we are lost,
Like to a dew, or melted frost.
— Then live we mirthful while we should,
And turn the iron age to gold;
Let's feast and frolic, sing and play,
And thus less last, than live our day.
Whose life with care is overcast,
That man's not said to live, but last;
Nor is't a life, seven years to tell,
But for to live that half seven well;
And that we'll do, as men who know,
Some few sands spent, we hence must go,
Both to be blended in the urn,
From whence there's never a return.

—ROBERT HERRICK.

————◆————

24.

CONTENT.

ART thou poor, yet hast thou golden slumbers?
        O sweet Content!
Art thou rich, yet is thy mind perplexed?
        O Punishment!
Dost laugh to see how fools are vexed
To add to golden numbers golden numbers?
        O sweet Content, O sweet, O sweet Content!

Work apace, apace, apace, apace,
Honest labor bears a lovely face.
Then hey noney, noney; hey noney, noney.

Canst drink the waters of the crisped spring?
      O sweet Content!
Swim'st thou in wealth, yet sink'st in thine own tears?
      O Punishment!
Then he that patiently Want's burden bears,
No burden bears, but is a king, a king.
    O sweet Content, O sweet, O sweet Content!

Work apace, apace, etc.

                    —THOMAS DEKKER.

25.

MELANCOLIA.

HENCE, all you vain delights,
As short as are the nights
Wherein you spend your folly:
There's nought in this life sweet,
If man were wise to see't,
But only melancholy,
O sweetest melancholy!
Welcome, folded arms, and fixéd eyes,
A sigh that piercing mortifies,
A look that's fasten'd to the ground,
A tongue chain'd up without a sound!
Fountain heads and pathless groves,
Places which pale passion loves!
Moonlight walks, when all the fowls
Are warmly housed, save bats and owls!
A midnight bell, a parting groan!
These are the sounds we feed upon;
Then stretch our bones in a still gloomy valley;
Nothing's so dainty sweet as lovely melancholy.

                    —FRANCIS BEAUMONT.

26.

ON MELANCHOLY.

I.

WHEN I go musing all alone,
Thinking of divers things foreknown;
When I build castles in the air,
Void of sorrow, void of care,
Pleasing myself with phantasms sweet,
Methinks the time runs very fleet.
    All my joys to this are folly;
    Naught so sweet as melancholy!

2.

When I go walking all alone,
Recounting what I have ill-done,
My thoughts on me then tyrannise,
Fear and sorrow me surprise,
Whether I tarry still, or go,
Methinks the time moves very slow.
    All my griefs to this are jolly;
    Naught so sad as melancholy.

3.

When to myself I act and smile,
With pleasing thoughts the time beguile,
By a brookside or wood so green,
Unheard, unsought for, or unseen,
A thousand pleasures do me bless,
And crown my soul with happiness.
    All my joys besides are folly;
    None so sweet as melancholy.

4.

When I lie, sit, or walk alone,
I sigh, I grieve, making great moan ;
In a dark grove or irksome den,
With discontents and furies then,
A thousand miseries at once
Mine heavy heart and soul ensconce.
    All my griefs to this are jolly ;
    None so sour as melancholy.

5.

Methinks I hear, methinks I see
Sweet music, wondrous melody,
Towns, palaces, and cities fine ;
Here now, then there, the world is mine;
Rare beauties, gallants, ladies shine,
Whate'er is lovely, is divine.
    All other joys to this are folly ;
    None so sweet as melancholy.

6.

Methinks I hear, methinks I see
Ghosts, goblins, fiends : my fantasy
Presents a thousand ugly shapes ;
Headless bears, black men, and apes ;
Doleful outcries, fearful sights
My sad and dismal soul affrights.
    All my griefs to this are jolly ;
    None so damn'd as melancholy.

— ROBERT BURTON.

27.

BREAK, BREAK, BREAK!

Break, break, break,
　On thy cold gray stones, O Sea!
And I would that my tongue could utter
　The thoughts that arise in me.

Oh well for the fisherman's boy,
　That he shouts with his sister at play!
Oh well for the sailor lad,
　That he sings in his boat on the bay!

And the stately ships go on
　To their haven under the hill;
But oh for the touch of a vanished hand,
　And the sound of a voice that is still!

Break, break, break,
　At the foot of thy crags, O Sea!
But the tender grace of a day that is dead
　Will never come back to me.

— ALFRED TENNYSON.

28.

THE SOUL'S ERRAND.

Go, Soul, the body's guest,
　Upon a thankless errand;
Fear not to touch the best;
　The truth shall be thy warrant.
Go, since I must die,
And give the world the lie.

Say to the Court it glows
  And shines like rotten wood;
Say to the Church it shows
  What's good, and doth no good.
If Church and Court reply,
Then give them both the lie.

Tell Potentates they live
  Acting but others' actions;
Not loved unless they give,
  Not strong but by their factions.
If Potentates reply,
Give Potentates the lie.

Tell men of high condition,
  That manage the estate,
Their purpose is ambition,
  Their practice only hate.
And if they once reply,
Then give them all the lie.

Tell them that brave it most,
  They beg for more by spending,
Who in their greatest cost
  Like nothing but commending:
And if they make reply,
Then tell them all they lie.

Tell Zeal it wants devotion;
  Tell Love it is but lust;
Tell Time it is but motion;
  Tell Flesh it is but dust.
And wish them not reply,
For thou must give the lie.

Tell Age it daily wasteth;
  Tell Honor how it alters;
Tell Beauty how she blasteth;
  Tell Favor how it falters.
And as they shall reply,
Give every one the lie.

Tell Wit how much it wrangles
  In tickle points of niceness;
Tell Wisdom she entangles
  Herself in over-wiseness.
And when they do reply,
Straight give them both the lie.

Tell Physic of her boldness;
  Tell Skill it is pretension;
Tell Charity of coldness;
  Tell Law it is contention.
And as they do reply,
So give them still the lie.

Tell Fortune of her blindness;
  Tell Nature of decay;
Tell Friendship of unkindness;
  Tell Justice of delay.
And if they will reply,
Then give them all the lie.

Tell Arts they have no soundness,
  But vary by esteeming;
Tell Schools they want profoundness,
  And stand too much on seeming.
If Arts and Schools reply,
Give Arts and Schools the lie.

Tell Faith it's fled the city;
  Tell how the country erreth;
Tell Manhood shakes off pity;
  Tell Virtue least preferreth.
And if they do reply,
Spare not to give the lie.

So when thou hast, as I
  Commanded thee, done babbling,
Although to give the lie
  Deserves no less than stabbing,
Yet stab at thee who will,
No stab the soul can kill.

—SIR WALTER RALEIGH (?).

29.

THE LIGHT OF OTHER DAYS.

OFT in the stilly night
  Ere slumber's chain has bound me,
Fond Memory brings the light
  Of other days around me;
    The smiles, the tears
    Of boyhood's years,
  The words of love then spoken;
    The eyes that shone,
    Now dimmed and gone,
  The cheerful hearts now broken!
Thus in the stilly night
  Ere slumber's chain has bound me,
Sad Memory brings the light
  Of other days around me.

When I remember all
  The friends so linked together
I've seen around me fall
  Like leaves in wintry weather,
    I feel like one
    Who treads alone
  Some banquet-hall deserted,
    Whose lights are fled,
    Whose garlands dead,
  And all but he departed!
Thus in the stilly night
  Ere slumber's chain has bound me,
Sad Memory brings the light
  Of other days around me.

— THOMAS MOORE.

30.

JOHN ANDERSON.

JOHN ANDERSON my jo, John,
When we were first acquent
Your locks were like the raven,
Your bonnie brow was brent;
But now your brow is bald, John,
Your locks are like the snow;
But blessings on your frosty pow,
John Anderson my jo.

John Anderson my jo, John,
We clamb the hill thegither,
And mony a canty day, John,
We've had wi' ane anither:

Now we maun totter down, John,
But hand in hand we'll go,
And sleep thegither at the foot,
John Anderson my jo.
—ROBERT BURNS.

31.

AULD LANG SYNE.

SHOULD auld acquaintance be forgot,
  And never brought to mind?
Should auld acquaintance be forgot,
  And days o' lang syne?

Chorus.

For auld lang syne, my dear,
  For auld lang syne,
We'll tak a cup o' kindness yet,
  For auld lang syne.

And surely ye'll be your pint-stowp,
  And surely I'll be mine;
And we'll tak a cup o' kindness yet
  For auld lang syne.
    For auld, &c.

We twa hae run about the braes,
  And pu'd the gowans fine;
But we've wander'd mony a weary foot
  Sin' auld lang syne.
    For auld, &c.

We twa hae paidl'd i' the burn,
From morning sun till dine ;
But seas between us braid hae roar'd
Sin' auld lang syne.
For auld, &c.

And here's a hand, my trusty fiere,
And gie's a hand o' thine ;
And we'll tak a right guid willie-waught,
For auld lang syne.
For auld, &c.

— ROBERT BURNS.

32.

THE LAND O' THE LEAL.

I'M wearin' awa', John,
Like snaw-wreaths in thaw, John,
I'm wearin' awa'
To the land o' the leal.
There's nae sorrow there, John,
There's neither cauld nor care, John,
The day is aye fair
In the land o' the leal.

Our bonnie bairn's there, John,
She was baith gude and fair, John,
And oh ! we grudg'd her sair
To the land o' the leal.
But sorrow's sel' wears past, John,
And joy's a-comin' fast, John,
And joy that's aye to last
In the land o' the leal.

Sae dear that joy was bought, John,
Sae free the battle fought, John,
That sinfu' man e'er brought
  To the land o' the leal.
Oh! dry your glistening e'e, John,
My soul langs to be free, John,
And angels beckon me
  To the land o' the leal.

Oh! haud ye leal and true, John,
Your day it's wearin' thro', John,
And I'll welcome you
  To the land o' the leal.
Now fare ye weel, my ain John,
This warld's cares are vain, John;
We'll meet, and we'll be fain,
  In the land o' the leal.

— LADY NAIRNE.

33.

GROWING OLD.

WHAT is it to grow old?
Is it to lose the glory of the form,
The lustre of the eye?
Is it for beauty to forego her wreath?
Yes, but not this alone.

Is it to feel our strength —
Not our bloom only, but our strength — decay?
Is it to feel each limb
Grow stiffer, every function less exact,
Each nerve more weakly strung?

Yes, this, and more! but not,
Ah, 'tis not what in youth we dream'd 'twould be!
'Tis not to have our life
Mellow'd and soften'd as with sunset glow,
A golden day's decline!

'Tis not to see the world
As from a height, with rapt prophetic eyes,
And heart profoundly stirr'd;
And weep, and feel the fulness of the past,
The years that are no more!

It is to spend long days
And not once feel that we were ever young.
It is to add, immured
In the hot prison of the present, month
To month with weary pain.

It is to suffer this,
And feel but half, and feebly, what we feel.
Deep in our hidden heart
Festers the dull remembrance of a change,
But no emotion — none.

It is — last stage of all —
When we are frozen up within, and quite
The phantom of ourselves,
To hear the world applaud the hollow ghost
Which blamed the living man.

— MATTHEW ARNOLD.

34.

TO MY GRANDMOTHER.

THIS Relative of mine,
Was she seventy-and-nine
    When she died?
By the canvas may be seen
How she looked at seventeen,
    As a Bride.

Beneath a summer tree,
Her maiden reverie
    Has a charm;
Her ringlets are in taste;
What an arm! . . . what a waist
    For an arm!

With her bridal-wreath, bouquet,
Lace farthingale, and gay
    Falbala, —
If Romney's art be true,
What a lucky dog were you,
    Grandpapa!

Her lips are sweet as love;
They are parting!   Do they move?
    Are they dumb?
Her eyes are blue, and beam
Beseechingly, and seem
    To say, "Come!"

What funny fancy slips
From atween these cherry lips?
    •   Whisper me,

Fair Sorceress in paint,
What canon says I mayn't
    Marry thee?

That good-for-nothing Time
Has a confidence sublime!
    When I first
Saw this Lady, in my youth,
Her winters had, forsooth,
    Done their worst.

Her locks, as white as snow,
Once shamed the swarthy crow:
    By-and-by
That fowl's avenging sprite
Set his cruel foot for spite
    Near her eye.

Her rounded form was lean,
And her silk was bombazine:
    Well I wot
With her needles would she sit,
And for hours would she knit, —
    Would she not?

Ah, perishable clay;
Her charms had dropt away
    One by one:
But if she heaved a sigh
With a burthen, it was, "Thy
    Will be done."

In travail, as in tears,
With the fardel of her years
    Overprest,

In mercy she was borne
Where the weary and the worn
   Are at rest.

Oh, if you now are there,
And sweet as once you were,
   Grandmamma,
This nether world agrees
You'll all the better please
   Grandpapa.
      —FREDERICK LOCKER-LAMPSON.

35.

UP–HILL.

DOES the road wind up-hill all the way?
  Yes, to the very end.
Will the day's journey take the whole long day?
  From morn till night, my friend.

But is there for the night a resting-place?
  A roof for when the slow dark hours begin.
May not the darkness hide it from my face?
  You cannot miss that inn.

Shall I meet other wayfarers at night?
  Those who have gone before.
Then must I knock, or call when just in sight?
  They will not keep you standing at that door.

Shall I find comfort, travel-sore and weak?
  Of labor you shall find the sum.
Will there be beds for me and all who seek?
  Yea, beds for all who come.
      —CHRISTINA ROSSETTI.

36.

A PARTING IN DREAMLAND.

AMONG the poppies by the well
    Of Lethe, where I weary lay,
Upon my soul a slumber fell,
    Making the light of summer gray;
Nepenthé too I ate of him,
Whose eyes were eyes of Seraphim.

But ere I slept, while still it seemed
    That sleep was a delicious thing,
The splendor of a vision streamed
    Above the poppy-heads that fling
Their drowsy juice and drowsy scent
Through blood and brain with ravishment.

For there he stood whose eyes are eyes
    Of Seraphim : and lo ! his lips
Seemed quivering with the winds of sighs ;
    And all his forehead in eclipse
Burned not, but showered well-heads of tears
Amid the deserts of dead years.

Yea, and his heart fed living fire ;
    And both his cheeks like ashes wan
Were cinders of a spent desire
    For lack of food to feed upon :
Therewith the Spirit smiled and spake
Words sweet as breath from buds that break :

" I go ; take now, dear soul, thy rest ;
    Slumber beneath the poppy-flowers !
The mole within her winter nest
    Be not so folded from sad hours

As thou, who of the thought of me
Eatest Nepenthé wearily.

"I go; but when thy dream is o'er,
    When thou awakest cold perchance,
And haply from sleep's golden door
    Gazest upon the drear expanse
Of barren years and vacant life
And long monotony of strife,

"Think then of me: though hence I go;
    Though I am withered, worn, and old,
With waiting, praying, weeping through
    Long days that shiver in the cold
Of thy scant love — yet will I come,
And, when thou callest, bear thee home."

He spake; and fire with sudden pain
    Flashed in his face.   Then slumber fell
Upon my lids like summer rain;
    And through faint dreams the terrible
Flame of that head, of those wild eyes,
Died; and my sleep was Paradise.

—J. A. SYMONDS.

37.

THE VOYAGE OF LIFE.

Let not the water floods overflow me, neither let the deeps swallow me up.
Psalm lxii. 15.

THE world's a sea; my flesh a ship that's manned
With lab'ring thoughts, and steered by reason's hand,
My heart's the seaman's card whereby she sails;
My loose affections are the greater sails;

The top-sail is my fancy, and the gusts
That fill these wanton sheets, are worldly lusts.
Prayer is the cable, at whose end appears
The anchor hope, ne'er slipped but in our fears:
My will's th' unconstant pilot, that commands
The stagg'ring keel; my sins are like the sands:
Repentance is the bucket, and mine eye
The pump unused (but in extremes) and dry:
My conscience is the plummet that does press
The deeps, but seldom cries, O *fathomless:*
Smooth calm's security: the gulf, despair;
My freight's corruption, and this life's my fare:
My soul's the passenger, confusedly driven
From fear to fright; her landing port is heaven.
My seas are stormy, and my ship doth leak;
My sailors rude; my steersman faint and weak:
My canvas torn, it flaps from side to side:
My cable's crack'd, my anchor's slightly tied,
My pilot's crazed; my ship-wrack sands are cloaked:
My bucket's broken, and my pump is choked;
My calm's deceitful; and my gulf too near;
My wares are slubbered, and my fare's too dear:
My plummet's light, it cannot sink nor sound;
Oh shall my rock-bethreaten'd soul be drown'd?
Lord, still the seas, and shield my ship from harm;
Instruct my sailors, guide my steersman's arm:
Touch thou my compass, and renew my sails,
Send stiffer courage or send milder gales;
Make strong my cable, bind my anchor faster;
Direct my pilot, and be thou his master;
Object the sands to my more serious view,
Make sound my bucket, bore my pump anew:
New-cast my plummet, make it apt to try

Where the rocks lurk, and where the quick-sands lie ;
Guard thou the gulf with love, my calms with care ;
Cleanse thou my freight ; accept my slender fare ;
Refresh the sea-sick passenger ; cut short
His voyage ; land him in his wished port :
Thou, then, whom winds and stormy seas obey,
That through the deep gavest grumbling Israel way,
Say to my soul, be safe ; and then mine eye
Shall scorn grim death, although grim death stand by.
O thou whose strength-reviving arm did cherish
Thy sinking Peter, at the point to perish,
Reach forth thy hand, or bid me tread the wave,
I'll come, I'll come : the voice that calls will save.

— FRANCIS QUARLES.

The confluence of lust makes a great tempest, which in this sea disturbeth the sea-faring soul, that reason cannot govern it. — ST. AMBROSE. *Apol. post. pro David*, cap. 3.

We labour in the boisterous sea : thou standest upon the shore and seest our dangers ; give us grace to hold a middle course between Scylla and Charybdis, that, both dangers escaped, we may arrive at the port secure. — ST. AUGUSTINE. *Soliloq.* cap. 35.

EPIG. II.

My soul, the seas are rough, and thou a stranger
In these false coasts ; O keep aloof ; there's danger :
Cast forth thy plummet ; see a rock appears ;
Thy ship wants sea-room ; make it with thy tears.

T

38.

CROSSING THE BAR.

Sunset and evening star,
  And one clear call for me !
And may there be no moaning at the bar
  When I put out to sea,
But such a tide as moving seems asleep,
  Too full for sound and foam,
When that which drew from out the boundless deep
  Turns again home.

Twilight and evening bell,
  And after that the dark!
And may there be no sadness of farewell
  When I embark ;
For though from out our bourne of Time and Place
  The flood may bear me far,
I hope to see my Pilot face to face
  When I have crossed the bar.

                  — Alfred Tennyson.

39.

LIFE AND DEATH.

Life ! I know not what thou art,
But know that thou and I must part;
And when, or where, or how we met
I own to me's a secret yet.

Life ! we've been long together
Through pleasant and through cloudy weather;
'Tis hard to part when friends are dear —
Perhaps 'twill cost a sigh, a tear ; —

Then steal away, give little warning,
Choose thine own time;
Say not Good-night,— but in some brighter clime
Bid me Good-morning.

> —ANNA LETITIA BARBAULD.

40.

SWEET PERIL.

ALAS! how easily things go wrong —
A sigh too much, or a kiss too long,
And there follows a mist and a weeping rain,
And life is never the same again.

Alas! how hardly things go right —
'Tis hard to watch in a summer night,
For the sigh will come, and the kiss will stay,
And the summer night is a winter day.

> —GEORGE MACDONALD.

41.

DEATH.

THEY die — the dead return not.   Misery
  Sits near an open grave, and calls them over,
A youth with hoary hair and haggard eye.
  They are the names of kindred, friend, and lover,
Which he so feebly calls.   They all are gone,
Fond wretch, all dead! Those vacant names alone,
    This most familiar scene, my pain,
      These tombs, — alone remain.

Misery, my sweetest friend, oh! weep no more!
 Thou wilt not be consoled?   I wonder not:
For I have seen thee from thy dwelling's door
 Watch the calm sunset with them, and this spot
Was even as bright and calm but transitory, —
And now thy hopes are gone, thy hair is hoary.
 This most familiar scene, my pain,
 These tombs, — alone remain.

— PERCY BYSSHE SHELLEY.

42.

SORROW-SONG.

O SORROW, sorrow, say where dost thou dwell?
 In the lowest room of hell.
Art thou born of human race?
 No, no, I have a furier face.
Art thou in city, town, or court?
 I to every place resort.
Oh, why into the world is sorrow sent?
 Men afflicted best repent.
What dost thou feed on?
  Broken sleep.
What tak'st thou pleasure in?
  To weep,
  To sigh, to sob, to pine, to groan,
  To wring my hands, to sit alone.
Oh, when, oh, when shall sorrow quiet have?
 Never, never, never, never.
 Never till she finds a grave.

— SAMUEL ROWLEY.

43.

DEATH'S TRIUMPH.

THE glories of our blood and state
   Are shadows, not substantial things;
There is no armor against fate:
   Death lays his icy hand on kings.
         Sceptre and crown
         Must tumble down,
And in the dust be equal made
With the poor crooked scythe and spade.

Some men with swords may reap the field,
   And plant with laurels where they kill;
But their strong nerves at last must yield,
   They tame but one another still;
         Early or late,
         They stoop to fate,
And must give up their murmuring breath,
When they, pale captives! creep to death.

The garlands wither on your brow;
   Then boast no more your mighty deeds;
Upon death's purple altar, now,
   See where the victor victim bleeds!
         All heads must come
         To the cold tomb,
Only the actions of the just
Smell sweet and blossom in the dust.
                         —JAMES SHIRLEY.

44.

TO LIFE'S PILGRIM.

FLY from the press, and dwell with soothfastness;
  Suffice unto thy good, though it be small,
For hoard hath hate, and climbing tickleness;
  Preise hath envie, and weal is blent o'er all.
  Savour no more than thee behoven shall,
Rede well thyself that other folk can'st rede,
And Truth thee shalt deliver — 'tis no drede.

That thee is sent receive in buxomness:
  The wrestling of this world, asketh a fall.
Here is no home, here is but wilderness.
  Forth, pilgrim, forth — on, best out of thy stall;
  Look up on high, and thank the God of all!
Weivith thy lust, and let thy ghost thee lead,
And Truth thee shalt deliver — 'tis no drede.

— GEOFFREY CHAUCER.

45.

LAST LINES.

EVEN such is time, that takes in trust
Our youth, our joys, our all we have,
And pays us but with earth and dust;
Who, in the dark and silent grave,
When we have wandered all our ways,
Shuts up the story of our days;
But from this earth, this grave, this dust,
My God shall raise me up I trust.

— SIR WALTER RALEIGH.

NOTES.

NO. 1. MAN'S MORTALITY.   First published in the second edition of Wastell's *Microbiblion*, 1629.   There are doubts concerning its authorship.
l. 6. gourd which Jonas had.   See Jonah, iv.

NO. 4. THE RETREAT.   "This poem, apart from its proper beauty, has a deeper interest, as containing in the germ Wordsworth's still higher strain, namely, his *Ode on Intimations of Immortality from Recollections of Early Childhood.*   I proceeded in my first edition to say, ' I do not mean that Wordsworth had ever seen this poem when he wrote his own.   The coincidences are so remarkable that it is certainly difficult to esteem them accidental; but Wordsworth was so little a reader of anything out of the way, and at the time when his Ode was composed, the *Silex Scintillans* was altogether out of the way, a book of such excessive rarity, that an explanation of the points of contact between the poems must be sought for elsewhere.'   That this was too rashly spoken I have since had proof.   A correspondent, with date July 13, 1869, has written to me, ' I have a copy of the first edition of the *Silex*, incomplete and very much damp-stained, which I bought in a lot with several other books at the poet Wordsworth's sale.'   The entire forgetfulness into which poetry, which, though not of the very highest order of all, is yet of a very high one, may fall, is strikingly exemplified in the fact that as nearly as possible two centuries intervened between the first and second editions of Vaughan's poems.   The first edition of the first part of the *Silex Scintillans* appeared in 1650, the second edition of the book in 1847.   That which is sometimes referred to as a second edition, bearing date 1655, is indeed only the first, with a new title-page and preface, and some eighty-four pages of additional matter.   Oblivion overtook him from the first.   Phillips in his *Theatrum Poetarum*, 1675, just mentions him and no more; and knows him only by his *Olor Iscanus*, a juvenile production, of comparatively little worth; which yet, seeing that it yields such lines as the following — they form part of a poem addressed to the unfortunate Elizabeth of Bohemia, daughter of our first James — cannot be affirmed to be of none :

> ' Thou seem'st a rosebud born in snow ;
> A flower of purpose sprung to bow
> To heedless tempests and the rage
> Of an incensèd stormy age :

> ' And yet as balm-trees gently spend
> Their tears for those that do them rend,
> Thou didst not murmur nor revile,
> But drank'st thy wormwood with a smile.'

As a theologian Vaughan may be inferior, but as a poet he is certainly superior, to Herbert, who never wrote anything so purely poetical as *The Retreat.* Still Vaughan would probably never have written as he has, if Herbert, whom he gratefully owns as his master, had not shown him the way." — *Trench.*

No. 5. THE PIPER. This poem forms the introduction to Blake's *Songs of Innocence,* 1789.

No. 8. YOUTH AND AGE. A song from the story of *The Water-Babies,* 1863.

No. 11. YOUTH AND AGE. Leigh Hunt says: " This is one of the most perfect poems for style, feeling, and everything, that ever was written."

No. 12. THE STREAM OF LIFE. From *Poems on Life and Duty.*

No. 20. THE CHARACTER OF A HAPPY LIFE. First published in the *Reliquiæ Wottonianæ,* in 1651, twelve years after Wotton's death.

No. 21. A WISH. First published in *Poetical Blossomes,* 1633.

No. 22. THE QUIET LIFE. It is said that these lines were written by Pope in 1700, when only twelve years old.

No. 24. CONTENT. From the drama entitled *Patient Grissell.*

No. 25. MELANCOLIA. This might be supposed to have suggested Milton's *Il Penseroso,* were it not that it did not appear until two years after the publication of that poem (1637).

No. 26. ON MELANCHOLY. From *The Anatomy of Melancholy,* 1621, — the book of which Dr. Johnson said it was the only one that ever took him out of bed two hours sooner than he wished to rise.

No. 28. THE SOUL'S ERRAND. Published in Davison's *Poetical Rhapsody,* 1608. It is ascribed to Sir Walter Raleigh by no better evidence than tradition. As it appeared some ten years before his death, there can be no truth in the statement which is sometimes made that it was written on the night before his execution.

No. 30. JOHN ANDERSON.
    jo. Darling.   **brent.** Brown.
    pow. Poll, head.   **canty.** Happy.
    maun. Must.

No. 31. AULD LANG SYNE.
    pint-stowp. Flagon.
    braes. Hill-slopes.
    gowan. Daisy.
    burn. Brook.
    sun till dine. Sunrise to sunset.
    fiere. Companion.
    willie-waught. Hearty pull.

No. 32. THE LAND o' THE LEAL.
    leal. True.   **aye.** Ever.
    bairn. Child.   **sair.** Sorely.
    e'e. Eye.   **haud ye.** Keep yourself.
    fain. Glad.

No. 34. TO MY GRANDMOTHER. The poem was suggested by a picture by Mr. Romney.

No. 37. THE VOYAGE OF LIFE. From *Emblems, Divine and Moral,* 1635. "He uses language almost as greatly as Shakespeare," says Thoreau; "and although there is not much straight grain in him, there is plenty of tough crooked timber."
    l. 27. **slubbered.** Smeared over.
    l. 28. **plummet.** Lead.

No. 42. SORROW-SONG. The writer of this poem was one of the players in the service of Henry, Prince of Wales. His best known work is a play called *The Spanish Writer,* from which this little song has been taken.

No. 43. DEATH'S TRIUMPH. From the drama entitled *The Contentions of Ajax and Ulysses,* 1659.

No. 44. LAST LINES. These verses are said to have been written by Sir Walter Raleigh in his Bible on the night before his execution, October 29, 1618.

Religious Songs and Melodies.

With Christians, a poetical view of things is a duty,—we are bid to color all things with hues of faith, to see a Divine meaning in every event, and a superhuman tendency. Even our friends around are invested with unearthly brightness—no longer imperfect men, but beings taken into Divine favor, stamped with His seal, and in training for future happiness. Religion presents us with those ideal forms of excellence in which a poetical mind delights, and with which all grace and harmony are associated.—JOHN HENRY NEWMAN.

I.

PEACE.

My soul, there is a country,
  Afar beyond the stars,
Where stands a wingèd sentry,
  All skilful in the wars.
There, above noise and danger,
  Sweet Peace sits crowned with smiles,
And One born in a manger
  Commands the beauteous files.
He is thy gracious friend,
  And (O my soul, awake!)
Did in pure love descend,
  To die here for thy sake.

If thou canst get but thither,
　　There grows the flower of peace,
The rose that cannot wither,
　　Thy fortress, and thy ease.
Leave then thy foolish ranges;
　　For none can thee secure,
But One who never changes,
　　Thy God, thy Life, thy Cure.

—HENRY VAUGHAN.

2.

THE HEAVENLY JERUSALEM.

JERUSALEM, my happy home,
When shall I come to thee?
When shall my sorrows have an end,
Thy joys when shall I see?

O happy harbor of the saints!
O sweet and pleasant soil!
In thee no sorrow may be found,
No grief, no care, no toil.

In thee no sickness may be seen,
Nor hurt, nor ache, nor sore:
There is no death, nor ugly dole,
But Life for evermore.

There lust and lucre cannot dwell,
There envy bears no sway:
There is no hunger, heat, nor cold,
But pleasure every way.

Thy walls are made of precious stones,
Thy bulwarks diamonds square;

Thy gates are of right orient pearl,
Exceeding rich and rare.

Thy turrets and thy pinnacles
With carbuncles do shine;
Thy very streets are paved with gold,
Surpassing clear and fine.

Thy houses are of ivory,
Thy windows crystal clear;
Thy tiles are made of beaten gold;—
O God, that I were there!

Ah, my sweet home, Jerusalem,
Would God I were in thee!
Would God my woes were at an end,
Thy joys that I might see!

Thy saints are crowned with glory great;
They see God face to face;
They triumph still, they still rejoice,
Most happy is their case.

We that are here in banishment
Continually do moan,
We sigh, and sob, we weep and wail,
Perpetually we groan.

Our sweet is mixed with bitter gall,
Our pleasure is but pain,
Our joys scarce last the looking on,
Our sorrows still remain.

But there they live in such delight,
Such pleasure and such play,

As that to them a thousand years
Doth seem as yesterday.

Thy gardens and thy gallant walks
Continually are green;
There grow such sweet and pleasant flowers
As nowhere else are seen.

Quite through the streets, with silver sound,
The flood of Life doth flow;
Upon whose banks on every side
The wood of Life doth grow.

There trees for evermore bear fruit,
And evermore do spring;
There evermore the angels sit,
And evermore do sing.

Jerusalem, my happy home,
Would God I were in thee!
Would God my woes were at an end,
Thy joys that I might see!

—ANON.

3.

SUNDAY.

O DAY most calm, most bright!
The fruit of this, the next world's bud;
The endorsement of supreme delight,
Writ by a Friend, and with his blood;
The couch of Time; Care's calm and bay:
The week were dark but for thy light;
Thy torch doth show the way.

The other days and thou
Make up one man, whose face thou art,
   Knocking at heaven with thy brow:
The working-days are the back part;
   The burden of the week lies there,
   Making the whole to stoop and bow,
   Till thy release appear.

   Man had straightforward gone
To endless death; but thou dost pull
   And turn us round, to look on One,
Whom, if we were not very dull,
   We could not choose but look on still;
   Since there is no place so alone
   The which He doth not fill.

   Sundays the pillars are
On which heaven's palace archèd lies
   The other days fill up the spare
And hollow room with vanities;
   They are the fruitful beds and borders
   In God's rich garden; that is bare
   Which parts their ranks and orders.

— GEORGE HERBERT.

———◆———

4.

THE VIRTUOUS SOUL.

SWEET day, so cool, so calm, so bright,
The bridal of the earth and sky,
Sweet dews shall weep thy fall to-night,
   For thou must die.

Sweet rose, whose hue, angry and brave,
Bids the rash gazer wipe his eye,
Thy root is ever in its grave,
    And thou must die.

Sweet spring, full of sweet days and roses,
A box where sweets compacted lie,
My music shows you have your closes,
    And all must die.

Only a sweet and virtuous soul,
Like seasoned timber, never gives;
But when the whole world turns to coal,
    Then chiefly lives.
        —GEORGE HERBERT.

5.

THE FLOWER.

How fresh, O Lord, how sweet and clean
Are thy returns! e'en as the flowers in spring;
    To which, besides their own demean,
The late-past frosts tributes of pleasure bring.
      Grief melts away,
      Like snow in May,
As if there were no such cold thing.

Who could have thought my shrivelled heart
Could have recovered greenness? It was gone
    Quite under ground; as flowers depart
To see their mother-root, when they have blown;
      Where they together
      All the hard weather,
Dead to the world, keep house unknown.

These are thy wonders, Lord of power,
Killing and quickening, bringing down to hell
    And up to heaven in an hour;
Making a chiming of a passing bell.
            We say amiss,
            This or that is:
Thy word is all, if we could spell.

    Oh, that I once past changing were,
Fast in thy Paradise, where no flower can wither!
    Many a spring I shoot up fair,
Offering at heaven, growing and groaning thither:
            Nor doth my flower
            Want a spring-shower,
My sins and I joining together.

    But while I grow in a straight line,
Still upwards bent, as if heaven were mine own,
    Thy anger comes, and I decline:
What frost to that? what pole is not the zone
            Where all things burn,
            When thou dost turn,
And the least frown of thine is shown?

    And now in age I bud again,
After so many deaths I live and write;
    I once more smell the dew and rain,
And relish versing: O my only Light,
            It cannot be
            That I am he
On whom thy tempests fell at night.

    These are thy wonders, Lord of love,
To make us see we are but flowers that glide;

Which when we once can find and prove,
Thou hast a garden for us, where to bide.
Who would be more,
Swelling through store,
Forfeit their Paradise by their pride.

—George Herbert.

6.

THE PULLEY.

When God at first made man,
Having a glass of blessing standing by;
Let us (said he) pour on him all we can:
Let the world's riches which dispersed lie
Contract into a span.

So strength first made a way;
Then beauty flow'd, then wisdom, honor, pleasure;
When almost all was out, God made a stay,
Perceiving that alone, of all his treasure,
Rest in the bottom lay.

For if I should (said he)
Bestow this jewel also on my creature,
He would adore my gifts instead of me,
And rest in Nature, not the God of Nature;
So both should losers be.

Yet let him keep the rest,
But keep them with repining restlessness:
Let him be rich and weary, that at least,
If goodness lead him not, yet weariness
May toss him to my breast.

U

Man cannot serve thee: let him go
And serve the swine — there, there is his delight:
He doth not like this virtue, no;
Give him his dirt to wallow in all night:
   These preachers make
    His head to shoot and ache.

*   *   *   *   *   *   *   *

Indeed, at first man was a treasure,
A box of jewels, shop of rarities,
 A ring whose posy was "My pleasure";
He was a garden in a Paradise;
   Glory and grace
    Did crown his heart and face.

But sin hath fool'd him; now he is
A lump of flesh, without a foot or wing
 To raise him to a glimpse of bliss;
A sick-toss'd vessel, dashing on each thing,
   Nay, his own self;
    My God, I mean myself.

       — GEORGE HERBERT.

7.

TRANSLATION OF THE TWENTY-THIRD PSALM.

THE Lord my pasture shall prepare,
And feed me with a shepherd's care;
His presence shall my wants supply,
And guard me with a watchful eye;
My noonday walks he shall attend,
And all my midnight hours defend.

When in the thirsty glebe I faint,
Or on the thirsty mountain pant,
To fertile vales and dewy meads
My weary, wand'ring steps he leads;
Where peaceful rivers, soft and slow,
Amid the verdant landscape flow.

Though in the paths of death I tread,
With gloomy horrors overspread,
 My steadfast heart shall feel no ill,
For thou, O Lord, art with me still!
Thy friendly crook shall give me aid,
And guide me through the dreadful shade.

Though in a bare and rugged way,
Through devious, lonely wilds I stray,
Thy bounty shall my wants beguile;
The barren wilderness shall smile,
With sudden greens and herbage crowned,
And streams shall murmur all around.

—JOSEPH ADDISON.

8.

THE DYING CHRISTIAN TO HIS SOUL.

VITAL spark of heavenly flame!
Quit, oh, quit this mortal frame!
Trembling, hoping, lingering, flying,
Oh, the pain, the bliss of dying!
Cease, fond nature, cease thy strife,
And let me languish into life.

Hark! they whisper; angels say,
"Sister spirit, come away!"
What is this absorbs me quite?
Steals my senses, shuts my sight,
Drowns my spirits, draws my breath?
Tell me, my soul, can this be death?

The world recedes; it disappears!
Heaven opens on my eyes! My ears
With sounds seraphic ring:
Lend, lend your wings! I mount! I fly!
O Grave! where is thy victory?
O Death! where is thy sting?

—ALEXANDER POPE.

9.

RESIGNATION.

O LORD my God, do thou thy holy will —
    I will lie still —
I will not stir, lest I forsake thine arm,
    And break the charm
Which lulls me, clinging to my Father's breast,
    In perfect rest.

Wild Fancy, peace! thou must not me beguile
    With thy false smile:
I know thy flatteries and thy cheating ways;
    Be silent, Praise,
Blind guide with siren voice, and blinding all
    That hear thy call.

Come, Self-devotion, high and pure,
Thoughts that in thankfulness endure,
Though dearest hopes are faithless found,
And dearest hearts are bursting round.
Come, Resignation, spirit meek,
And let me kiss thy placid cheek,
And read in thy pale eye serene
Their blessing, who by faith can wean
Their hearts from sense, and learn to love
God only, and the joys above.
They say, who know the life divine,
And upward gaze with eagle eyne,
That by each golden crown on high,
Rich with celestial jewelry,
Which for our Lord's redeem'd is set,
There hangs a radiant coronet,
All gemm'd with pure and living light,
Too dazzling for a sinner's sight,
Prepar'd for virgin souls, and them
Who seek the martyr's diadem.

Nor deem, who to that bliss aspire,
Must win their way through blood and fire.
The writhings of a wounded heart
Are fiercer than a foeman's dart.
Oft in Life's stillest shade reclining,
In Desolation unrepining,
Without a hope on earth to find
A mirror in an answering mind,
Meek souls there are, who little dream
Their daily strife an Angel's theme,
Or that the rod they take so calm
Shall prove in Heaven a martyr's palm.

And there are souls that seem to dwell
Above this earth — so rich a spell
Floats round their steps, where'er they move,
From hopes fulfilled, and mutual love.
Such, if on high their thoughts are set,
Nor in the stream the source forget,
If prompt to quit the bliss they know,
Following the Lamb where'er He go,
By purest pleasures unbeguiled
To idolise or wife or child;
Such wedded souls our God shall own
For faultless virgins round his throne.

Thus everywhere we find our suffering God,
          And where he trod
May set our steps : the Cross on Calvary
          Uplifted high
Beams on the martyr host, a beacon light
          In open fight.

To the still wrestlings of the lonely heart
          He doth impart
The virtue of his midnight agony,
          When none was nigh,
Save God and one good angel, to assuage
          The tempest's rage.

Mortal ! if life smile on thee, and thou find
          All to thy mind,
Think, who did once from Heaven to Hell descend,
          Thee to befriend :
So shalt thou dare forego, at his dear call,
          Thy best, thine all.

"O Father! not my will, but thine be done" —
　　So spake the Son.
Be this our charm, mellowing Earth's ruder noise
　　Of griefs and joys;
That we may cling forever to thy breast
　　In perfect rest!

—JOHN KEBLE.

———◆———

10.

FROM "THE WATERFALL."

Go where the waters fall,
Sheer from the mountain's height —

Mark how a thousand streams in one,—
One in a thousand on they fare,
　Now flashing to the sun,
　Now still as beast in lair.

Now round the rock, now mounting o'er,
In lawless dance they win their way,
　Still seeming more and more
　To swell as we survey,

They rush and roar, they whirl and leap,
Not wilder drives the wintry storm.
　Yet a strong law they keep,
　Strange powers their course inform.

Even so the mighty skyborn stream
Its living waters from above,
　All marred and broken seem,
　No union and no love.

Yet in dim caves they softly blend
In dreams of mortals unespied :
  One is their awful end,
  One their unfailing Guide.

            —JOHN KEBLE.

II.

THE LILIES OF THE FIELD.

SWEET nurslings of the vernal skies,
  Bathed in soft airs, and fed with dew,
What more than magic in you lies,
  To fill the heart's fond view?
In childhood's sports, companions gay,
In sorrow, on Life's downward way,
How soothing ! in our last decay
  Memorials prompt and true.

Relics ye are of Eden's bowers,
  As pure, as fragrant, and as fair,
As when ye crowned the sunshine hours
  Of happy wanderers there.
Fall'n all beside — the world of life,
How it is stained with fear and strife !
In Reason's world what storms are rife,
  What passions range and glare !

            — JOHN KEBLE.

12.

CHRIST'S COMING TO JERUSALEM IN TRIUMPH.

LORD, come away,
Why dost thou stay?
Thy road is ready: and thy paths, made straight,
With longing expectation wait
The consecration of thy beauteous feet.
Ride on triumphantly; behold we lay
Our lusts and proud wills in thy way.
Hosanna! welcome to our hearts.   Lord, here
Thou hast a temple too, and full as dear
As that of Sion; and as full of sin;
Nothing but thieves and robbers dwell therein.
Enter, and chase them forth, and cleanse the floor;
Crucify them, that they may never more
Profane that holy place,
Where thou hast chose to set thy face.
And then if our stiff tongues shall be
Mute in the praises of thy Deity,
The stones out of the temple wall
Shall cry aloud, and call
Hosanna! and thy glorious footsteps greet.

—JEREMY TAYLOR.

13.

THE LITANY.

IN the hour of my distress,
When temptations me oppress,
And when I my sins confess,
• Sweet Spirit, comfort me!

When I lie within my bed,
Sick in heart, and sick in head,
And with doubts discomforted,
    Sweet Spirit, comfort me!

When the house doth sigh and weep,
And the world is drown'd in sleep,
Yet mine eyes the watch do keep,
    Sweet Spirit, comfort me!

When the artless doctor sees
No one hope, but of his fees,
And his skill runs on the lees,
    Sweet Spirit, comfort me!

When his potion and his pill,
Has, or none, or little skill,
Meet for nothing but to kill,
    Sweet Spirit, comfort me!

When the passing-bell doth toll,
And the furies in a shoal
Come to fright a parting soul,
    Sweet Spirit, comfort me!

When the tapers now burn blue,
And the comforters are few,
And that number more than true,
    Sweet Spirit, comfort me!

When the priest his last hath pray'd,
And I nod to what is said,
'Cause my speech is now decay'd,
    Sweet Spirit, comfort me!

When, God knows, I'm tost about,
Either with despair or doubt;
Yet, before the glass be out,
    Sweet Spirit, comfort me!

When the tempter me pursu'th
With the sins of all my youth,
And half damns me with untruth,
    Sweet Spirit, comfort me!

When the flames and hellish cries
Fright mine ears, and fright mine eyes,
And all terrors me surprise,
    Sweet Spirit, comfort me!

When the Judgment is reveal'd,
And that open'd which was seal'd;
When to Thee I have appeal'd,
    Sweet Spirit, comfort me!

            —ROBERT HERRICK.

14.

A THANKSGIVING.

LORD, in this dust thy sovereign voice
First quickened love divine;
I am all thine — thy care and choice,
My very praise is thine.

I praise thee, while thy providence
In childhood frail I trace,
For blessings given, ere dawning sense
Could seek or scan thy grace;

Blessings in boyhood's marvelling hour,
Bright dreams and fancyings strange;
Blessings, when reason's awful power
Gave thought a bolder range;

Blessings of friends, which to my door
Unasked, unhoped, have come;
And choicer still, a countless store
Of eager smiles at home.

Yet, Lord, in memory's fondest place
I shrine those seasons sad,
When looking up, I saw thy face
In kind austereness clad.

I would not miss one sigh or tear,
Heart-pang or throbbing brow;
Sweet was the chastisement severe,
And sweet its memory now.

Yes! let the fragrant scars abide,
Love-tokens in thy stead,
Faint shadows of the spear-pierced side,
And thorn-encompassed head.

And such thy tender force be still,
When self would swerve or stray,
Shaping to truth the froward will
Along thy narrow way.

Deny me wealth; far, far remove
The lure of power or name;
Hope thrives in straits, in weakness love,
And faith in this world's shame.

—JOHN HENRY NEWMAN.

15.

CHRIST OUR EXAMPLE.

Lamb of God, I look to thee;
Thou shalt my example be;
Thou art gentle, meek, and mild;
Thou wast once a little child.

Fain I would be as thou art;
Give me thy obedient heart!
Thou art pitiful and kind;
Let me have thy loving mind!

Meek and lowly may I be;
Thou art all humility!
Let me to my betters bow;
Subject to thy parents thou.

Let me above all fulfil
God my heavenly Father's will;
Never his good Spirit grieve;
Only to his glory live!

Thou didst live to God alone;
Thou didst never seek thine own;
Thou thyself didst never please;
God was all thy happiness.

Loving Jesu, gentle Lamb,
In thy gracious hands I am;
Make me, Saviour, what thou art!
Live thyself within my heart!

I shall then shew forth thy praise;
Serve thee all my happy days;
Then the world shall always see
Christ, the Holy Child, in me.

—CHARLES WESLEY.

16.

EASTER HYMN.

CHRIST the Lord is risen to-day,
Sons of men and angels say:
Raise your joys and triumphs high,
Sing, ye heavens, and earth reply.

Love's redeeming work is done,
Fought the fight, the battle won:
Lo! our Sun's eclipse is o'er;
Lo! he sets in blood no more.

Vain the stone, the watch, the seal;
Christ hath burst the gates of hell!
Death in vain forbids his rise;
Christ hath opened Paradise!

Lives again our glorious King:
Where, O Death, is now thy sting?
Once he died, our souls to save:
Where thy victory, O Grave?

Soar we now where Christ has led,
Following our exalted Head;

Made like him, like him we rise;
Ours the cross, the grave, the skies.

What though once we perished all,
Partners in our parents, fall?
Second life we all receive,
In our heavenly Adam live.

Risen with him, we upward move;
Still we seek the things above;
Still pursue, and kiss the Son
Seated on his Father's throne.

Scarce on earth a thought bestow,
Dead to all we leave below;
Heav'n our aim, and loved abode,
Hid our life with Christ in God:

Hid, till Christ our Life appear
Glorious in his members here;
Join'd to him, we then shall shine,
All immortal, all divine.

Hail the Lord of Earth and Heaven!
Praise to thee by both be given!
Thee we greet triumphant now!
Hail, the Resurrection thou!

King of glory, Soul of bliss!
Everlasting life is this,
Thee to know, thy power to prove,
Thus to sing, and thus to love!

—CHARLES WESLEY.

17.

AN HYMN FOR SERIOUSNESS.

Thou God of glorious majesty,
To thee against myself, to thee
　A worm of earth I cry,
An half-awakened child of man,
An heir of endless bliss or pain,
　A sinner born to die.

Lo! on a narrow neck of land,
'Twixt two unbounded seas I stand
　Secure, insensible :
A point of life, a moment's space
Removes me to that heavenly place,
　Or shuts me up in hell.

O God, mine inmost soul convert,
And deeply on my thoughtful heart
　Eternal things impress,
Give me to feel their solemn weight,
And tremble on the brink of fate,
　And wake to righteousness.

Before me place in dread array
The pomp of that tremendous day,
　When thou with clouds shalt come
To judge the nations at thy bar :
And tell me, Lord, shall I be there
　To meet a joyful doom ?

Be this my one great business here,
With serious industry, and fear,
　My future bliss to insure,

Thine utmost counsel to fulfil,
And suffer all thy righteous will,
  And to the end endure.

Then, Saviour, then my soul receive,
Transported from the vale, to live
  And reign with thee above,
Where faith is sweetly lost in sight,
And hope in full supreme delight,
  And everlasting love.
—JOHN WESLEY.

x

Miscellaneous Lyrics.

—◦◦⁑◦◦—

Poetry makes immortal all that is best and most beautiful in the world; it arrests the vanishing apparitions which haunt the inter-lunations of life, and veiling them or in language or in form, sends them forth among mankind, bearing sweet news of kindred joy to those with whom their sisters abide — abide, because there is no portal of expression from the caverns of the spirit which they inhabit into the universe of things.   Poetry redeems from decay the visita-tions of the divinity in man. — Percy Bysshe Shelley.

I.

SONGS FROM "THE PRINCESS."

I.

Sweet and low, sweet and low,
  Wind of the western sea —
Low, low, breathe and blow,
  Wind of the western sea!
Over the rolling waters go,
Come from the dying moon, and blow,
  Blow him again to me:
While my little one, while my pretty one, sleeps.

Sleep and rest, sleep and rest,
   Father will come to thee soon ;
Rest, rest, on mother's breast,
   Father will come to thee soon ;
Father will come to his babe in the nest,
Silver sails all out of the west
   Under the silver moon :
Sleep, my little one, sleep, my pretty one, sleep.

II.

The splendor falls on castle walls
   And snowy summits old in story :
The long light shakes across the lakes,
   And the wild cataract leaps in glory.
Blow, bugle, blow, set the wild echoes flying,
Blow, bugle ; answer, echoes, dying, dying, dying.

O hark ! O hear, how thin and clear,
   And thinner, clearer, farther going !
O sweet and far from cliff and scar
   The horns of Elfland faintly blowing !
Blow, let us hear the purple glens replying ;
Blow, bugle ; answer, echoes, dying, dying, dying.

O love ! they die in yon rich sky,
   They faint on hill or field or river :
Our echoes roll from soul to soul,
   And grow for ever and for ever.
Blow, bugle, blow, set the wild echoes flying,
And answer, echoes, answer, dying, dying, dying.

III.

Ask me no more: the moon may draw the sea;
  The cloud may stoop from heaven and take the shape,
  With fold to fold, of mountain or of cape;
But O too fond, when have I answer'd thee?
           Ask me no more.

Ask me no more: what answer should I give?
  I love not hollow cheek or faded eye:
  Yet, O my friend, I will not have thee die!
Ask me no more, lest I should bid thee live;
           Ask me no more.

Ask me no more: thy fate and mine are seal'd:
  I strove against the stream and all in vain:
  Let the great river take me to the main:
No more, dear love, for at a touch I yield;
           Ask me no more.

IV.

Home they brought her warrior dead:
  She nor swoon'd, nor utter'd cry.
All her maidens, watching, said,
  "She must weep, or she will die."

Then they praised him, soft and low,
  Call'd him worthy to be loved,
Truest friend and noblest foe;
  Yet she neither spoke nor moved.

Stole a maiden from her place,
  Lightly to the warrior stept,
Took the face-cloth from the face;
  Yet she neither moved nor wept.

Rose a nurse of ninety years,
  Set his child upon her knee —
Like summer tempest came her tears —
  " Sweet my child, I live for thee."

— ALFRED TENNYSON.

2.

MUSIC.

CHARM me asleep, and melt me so
  With thy delicious numbers,
That being ravish'd, hence I go
  Away in easy slumbers.
    Ease my sick head,
    And make my bed,
  Thou Power that canst sever
    From me this ill ; —
    And quickly still,
    Though thou not kill
      My fever.

Thou sweetly canst convert the same
  From a consuming fire,
Into a gentle-licking flame,
  And make it thus expire.
    Then make me weep
    My pains asleep,
  And give me such reposes,
    That I, poor I,
    May think, thereby,
    I live and die
      'Mongst roses.

Fall on me like a silent dew,
   Or like those maiden showers,
Which, by the peep of day, do strew
   A baptism o'er the flowers.
     Melt, melt my pains
     With thy soft strains;
   That having ease me given,
     With full delight,
     I leave this light,
     And take my flight
      For Heaven.
        —ROBERT HERRICK.

3.

PRAISE OF MUSIC.

WHEN whispering strains do softly steal
   With creeping passion through the heart,
And when at ev'ry touch we feel
   Our pulses beat and bear a part;
     When threads can make
     A heart-string quake,
     Philosophy
     Can scarce deny
The soul consists of harmony.

Oh lull me, lull me, charming air,
   My sense is rock'd with wonder sweet!
Like snow on wool thy fallings are —
   Soft like a spirit's are thy feet.
     Grief who need fear
     That hath an ear?

Down let him lie,
And slumb'ring die,
And change his soul for harmony.

—WILLIAM STRODE.

4.

THE SPIRIT OF DELIGHT.

RARELY, rarely comest thou,
　Spirit of Delight!
Wherefore hast thou left me now
　Many a day and night?
Many a weary night and day
'Tis since thou art fled away.

How shall ever one like me
　Win thee back again?
With the joyous and the free,
　Thou wilt scoff at pain.
Spirit false! thou hast forgot
All but those who need thee not.

As a lizard with the shade
　Of a trembling leaf,
Thou with sorrow art dismayed;
　Even the sighs of grief
Reproach thee that thou art not near,
And reproach thou wilt not hear.

Let me set my mournful ditty
　To a merry measure; —
Thou wilt never come for pity,
　Thou wilt come for pleasure;

Pity then will cut away
Those cruel wings, and thou wilt stay.

I love all that thou lovest,
    Spirit of Delight!
The fresh earth in new leaves dressed,
    And the starry night,
Autumn evening, and the morn
When the golden mists are born.

I love snow, and all the forms
    Of the radiant frost;
I love waves and winds and storms, —
    Everything almost
Which is Nature's, and may be
Untainted by man's misery.

I love tranquil solitude,
    And such society
As is quiet, wise, and good.
    Between thee and me
What difference?   But thou dost possess
The things I seek, not love them less.

I love Love, though he has wings,
    And like light can flee;
But above all other things,
    Spirit, I love thee —
Thou art love and life! Oh, come!
Make once more my heart thy home!
                    — PERCY BYSSHE SHELLEY.

5.

TO ECHO.

Sweet Echo, sweetest nymph, that liv'st unseen
    Within thy aery shell,
  By slow Meander's margent green,
And in the violet-embroider'd vale,
    Where the love-lorn nightingale
Nightly to thee her sad song mourneth well;
Canst thou not tell me of a gentle pair
    That likest thy Narcissus are?
    Oh if thou have
  Hid them in some flowery cave,
    Tell me but where,
  Sweet queen of parley, daughter of the sphere!
So may'st thou be translated to the skies,
And give resounding grace to all Heaven's harmonies.

          — John Milton.

6.

THE FAIRY QUEEN.

  Come follow, follow me,
  You fairy elves that be:
  Which circle on the greene,
  Come follow Mab your queene.
Hand in hand let's dance around,
For this place is fairye ground.

  When mortals are at rest,
  And snoring in their nest;
  Unheard, and unespy'd,
  Through key-holes we do glide;

Over tables, stools, and shelves,
We trip it with our fairy elves.

Upon a mushroome's head
Our table-cloth we spread;
A grain of rye, or wheat,
Is manchet, which we eat;
Pearly drops of dew we drink,
In acorn cups fill'd to the brink.

The brains of nightingales,
With unctuous fat of snailes,
Between two cockles stew'd,
Is meat that's easily chew'd;
Tailes of wormes, and marrow of mice,
Do make a dish that's wondrous nice.

The grasshopper, gnat, and fly,
Serve for our minstrelsie;
Grace said, we dance a while,
And so the time beguile:
And if the moon doth hide her head,
The gloe-worm lights us home to bed.

On tops of dewie grasse
So nimbly do we passe,
The young and tender stalk
Ne'er bends when we do walk:
Yet in the morning may be seen
Where we the night before have been.

— ANONYMOUS.

7.

AS I LAYE A-THYNKYNGE.

(Last Lines of Thomas Ingoldsby.)

As I laye a-thynkynge, a-thynkynge, a-thynkynge,
Merrie sang the Birde as she sat upon the spraye;
   There came a noble Knyghte,
   With his hauberke shynynge brighte,
   And his gallant heart was lyghte,
      Free and gaye;
As I laye a-thynkynge, he rode upon his waye.

As I laye a-thynkynge, a-thynkynge, a-thynkynge,
Sadly sang the Birde as she sat upon the tree!
   There seemed a crimson plain,
   Where a gallant Knyghte lay slayne,
   And a steed with broken rein
      Ran free.
As I laye a-thynkynge, most pitiful to see.

As I laye a-thynkynge, a-thynkynge, a-thynkynge,
Merrie sang the Birde as she sat upon the boughe;
   A lovely Mayde came bye,
   And a gentil Youth came nighe
   And he breathed many a syghe
      And a vowe;
As I laye a-thynkynge, her heart was gladsome now.

As I laye a-thynkynge, a-thynkynge, a-thynkynge,
Sadly sang the Birde as she sat upon the thorne;
   No more a Youth was there,
   But a Maiden rent her haire,

And cried in sad despaire,
  "That I was borne!"
As I lay a-thynkynge, she perishèd forlorne.

As I laye a-thynkynge, a-thynkynge, a-thynkynge,
Sweetly sang the Birde as she sat upon the briar;
 There came a lovely Childe,
 And his face was meek and milde,
 Yet joyously he smiled
  On his Sire;
As I laye a-thynkynge, a Cherub mote admire.

But I laye a-thynkynge, a-thynkynge, a-thynkynge,
And sadly sang the Birde as it perched upon a bier;
 That joyous smile was gone,
 And the face was white and wan,
 As the downe upon the Swan
  Doth appear,
As I laye a-thynkynge — O! bitter flowed the tear!

As I laye a-thynkynge, the golden sun was sinking,
Oh merrie sang that Birde as it glittered on her breast,
 With a thousand gorgeous dyes,
 While soaring to the skies,
 'Mid the stars she seemed to rise,
  As to her nest;
As I laye a-thynkynge, her meaning was exprest:—
 "Follow, follow me away,
 It boots not to delay,"—
 'Twas so she seemed to saye,
  "HERE IS REST!"
       —R. H. BARHAM.

8.

THE PALM-TREE AND THE PINE.

BENEATH an Indian palm a girl
Of other blood reposes;
Her cheek is clear and pale as pearl,
Amid that wild of roses.

Beside a northern pine a boy
Is leaning fancy-bound,
Nor listens where with noisy joy
Awaits the impatient hound.

Cool grows the sick and feverish calm,
Relaxt the frosty twine;
The pine-tree dreameth of the palm,
The palm-tree of the pine.

As soon shall nature interlace
Those dimly-visioned boughs,
As these young lovers face to face
Renew their early vows.
— LORD HOUGHTON.

9.

THE SANDS OF DEE.

"O MARY, go and call the cattle home,
And call the cattle home,
And call the cattle home,
Across the sands of Dee."
The western wind was wild and dank with foam,
And all alone went she.

The creeping tide crept up along the sand,
    And o'er and o'er the sand,
    And round and round the sand,
  As far as eye could see.
The blinding mist came down, and hid the land:
  And never home came she.

"Oh! is it weed, or fish, or floating hair —
    A tress of golden hair,
    A drownèd maiden's hair,
  Above the nets at sea?
Was never salmon yet that shone so fair
  Among the stakes on Dee."

They rowed her in across the rolling foam,
    The cruel crawling foam,
    The cruel hungry foam,
  To her grave beside the sea:
But still the boatmen hear her call the cattle home
  Across the sands of Dee.

— CHARLES KINGSLEY.

10.

KUBLA KHAN.

In Xanadu did Kubla Khan
A stately pleasure-dome decree:
Where Alph, the sacred river, ran
Through caverns measureless to man
Down to a sunless sea.
So twice five miles of fertile ground
With walls and towers were girdled round:

And here were gardens bright with sinuous rills
Where blossomed many an incense-bearing tree;
And here were forests ancient as the hills,
Enfolding sunny spots of greenery.

But oh! that deep romantic chasm which slanted
Down the green hill athwart a cedarn cover!
A savage place! as holy and enchanted
As e'er beneath a waning moon was haunted
By woman wailing for her demon-lover!
And from this chasm, with ceaseless turmoil seething,
As if this earth in fast thick pants were breathing,
A mighty fountain momently was forced:
Amid whose swift half-intermitted burst
Huge fragments vaulted like rebounding hail,
Or chaffy grain beneath the thresher's flail:
And 'mid those dancing rocks at once and ever
It flung up momently the sacred river,
Five miles meandering with a mazy motion
Through wood and dale the sacred river ran,
Then reached the caverns measureless to man,
And sank in tumult to a lifeless ocean :
And 'mid this tumult Kubla heard from far
Ancestral voices prophesying war!

 The shadow of the dome of pleasure
 Floated midway on the waves;
 Where was heard the mingled measure
 From the fountain and the caves.
It was a miracle of rare device,
A sunny pleasure-dome with caves of ice!

 A damsel with a dulcimer
 In a vision once I saw:

It was an Abyssinian maid,
And on her dulcimer she played,
Singing of Mount Abora.
Could I revive within me
Her symphony and song,
To such a deep delight 'twould win me,
That with music loud and long,
I would build that dome in air,
That sunny dome! those caves of ice!
And all who heard should see them there,
And all should cry, Beware! Beware!
His flashing eyes, his floating hair,
Weave a circle round him thrice,
And close your eyes with holy dread,
For he on honey-dew hath fed,
And drunk the milk of Paradise.

—SAMUEL TAYLOR COLERIDGE

II.

TO A LADY, WITH A GUITAR.

ARIEL to Miranda:—Take
This slave of music, for the sake
Of him, who is the slave of thee;
And teach it all the harmony
In which thou canst, and only thou,
Make the delighted spirit glow,
Till joy denies itself again,
And, too intense, is turned to pain.
For, by permission and command
Of thine own Prince Ferdinand,

Poor Ariel sends this silent token
Of more than ever can be spoken;
Your guardian spirit Ariel, who
From life to life must still pursue
Your happiness, for thus alone
Can Ariel ever find his own.
From Prospero's enchanted cell,
As the mighty verses tell,
To the throne of Naples he
Lit you o'er the trackless sea,
Flitting on, your prow before,
Like a living meteor.

When you die, the silent Moon
In her interlunar swoon
Is not sadder in her cell
Than deserted Ariel.
When you live again on earth, —
Like an unseen star of birth,
Ariel guides you o'er the sea
Of life from your nativity.
Many changes have been run
Since Ferdinand and you begun
Your course of love, and Ariel still
Has tracked your steps and served your will.
Now, in humbler, happier lot,
This is all remembered not;
And now, alas! the poor Sprite is
Imprisoned for some fault of his
In a body like a grave:
From you he only dares to crave,
For his service and his sorrow,
A smile to-day, a song to-morrow.

Y

The artist who this idol wrought,
To echo all harmonious thought,
Felled a tree while on the steep
The woods were in their winter sleep,
Rocked in that repose divine
On the wind-swept Apennine,
And dreaming, some of Autumn past,
And some of Spring approaching fast,
And some of April buds and showers,
And some of songs in July bowers,
And all of love.   And so this tree —
Oh, that such our death may be ! —
Died in sleep, and felt no pain,
To live in happier form again :
From which, beneath heaven's fairest star
The artist wrought this loved Guitar,
And taught it justly to reply,
To all who question skilfully,
In language gentle as thine own ;
Whispering in enamored tone
Sweet oracles of woods and dells,
And summer winds in sylvan cells.
For it had learnt all harmonies
Of the plains and of the skies,
Of the forests and the mountains,
And the many-voicèd fountains ;
The clearest echoes of the hills,
The softest notes of falling rills,
The melodies of birds and bees,
The murmuring of summer seas,
And pattering rain, and breathing dew,
And airs of evening ; and it knew
That seldom-heard mysterious sound

Which, driven on its diurnal round,
As it floats through boundless day,
Our world enkindles on its way:
— All this it knows, but will not tell
To those who cannot question well
The spirit that inhabits it;
It talks according to the wit
Of its companions; and no more
Is heard than has been felt before
By those who tempt it to betray
These secrets of an elder day.
But, sweetly as its answers will
Flatter hands of perfect skill,
It keeps its highest, holiest tone
For one beloved Friend alone.

—PERCY BYSSHE SHELLEY.

12.

DAVID PLAYING BEFORE SAUL.

THEN I tuned my harp, — took off the lilies we twine
round its chords
Lest they snap 'neath the stress of the noontide —
those sunbeams like swords!
And I first played the tune all our sheep know, as, one
after one,
So docile they come to the pen-door till folding be
done.
They are white and untorn by the bushes, for lo, they
have fed
Where the long grasses stifle the water within the
stream's bed;

And now one after one seeks its lodging, as star follows
     star
Into eve and the blue far above us, — so blue and so
     far !

— Then the tune, for which quails on the cornland will
     each leave his mate
To fly after the player; then, what makes the crickets
     elate
Till for boldness they fight one another: and then,
     what has weight
To set the quick jerboa a-musing outside his sand
     house —
There are none such as he for a wonder, half bird and
     half mouse !
God made all the creatures and gave them our love and
     our fear,
To give sign, we and they are his children, one family
     here.

Then I played the help-tune of our reapers, their wine-
     song, when hand
Grasps at hand, eye lights eye in good friendship, and
     great hearts expand
And grow one in the sense of this world's life. — Then,
     the last song
When the dead man is praised on his jouney — " Bear,
     bear him along
With his few thoughts shut up like dead flowerets ! Are
     balm seeds not here
To console us ?   The land has none left such as he on
     the bier.
Oh, would we might keep thee, my brother ! " — And
     then, the glad chaunt

Of the marriage, — first go the young maidens, next, she
    whom we vaunt
As the beauty, the pride of our dwelling. — And then,
    the great march
Wherein man runs to man to assist him and buttress an
    arch
Nought can break; who shall harm them, our friends?
    Then, the chorus intoned
As the Levites go up to the altar in glory enthroned.
But I stopped here: for here in the darkness Saul
    groaned.

                      —ROBERT BROWNING.

13.

STANZAS FROM "WINE OF CYPRUS."

Go, — let others praise the Chian!
  This is soft as Muses' string,
This is tawny as Rhea's lion,
  This is rapid as his spring,
Bright as Paphia's eyes e'er met us,
  Light as ever trod her feet;
And the brown bees of Hymettus
  Make their honey not so sweet.

Very copious are my praises,
  Though I sip it like a fly!
Ah — but, sipping, — times and places
  Change before me suddenly:
As Ulysses' old libation
  Drew the ghosts from every part,
So your Cyprus wine, dear Grecian,
  Stirs the Hades of my heart.

And I think of those long mornings
    Which my thoughts go far to seek,
When, betwixt the folio's turnings,
    Solemn flowed the rhythmic Greek:
Past the pane the mountain spreading,
    Swept the sheep-bells' tinkling noise,
While a girlish voice was reading,
    Somewhat low for *αις* and *οις*.

Then, what golden hours were for us!
    While we sat together there,
How the white vests of the chorus
    Seemed to wave up a live air!
How the cothurns trod majestic
    Down the deep iambic lines,
And the rolling anapæstic
    Curled like vapor over shrines!

Oh, our Æschylus, the thunderous,
    How he drove the bolted breath
Through the cloud, to wedge it ponderous
    In the gnarlèd oak beneath!
Oh, our Sophocles, the royal,
    Who was born to monarch's place,
And who made the whole world loyal,
    Less by kingly power than grace!

Our Euripides, the human,
    With his droppings of warm tears,
And his touches of things common
    Till they rose to touch the spheres!

Our Theocritus, our Bion,
  And our Pindar's shining goals!—
These were cup-bearers undying,
  Of the wine that's meant for souls.
                    —Elizabeth Barrett Browning.

————◆————

14.

ODE ON A GRECIAN URN.

Thou still unravished bride of quietness!
  Thou foster-child of Silence and slow Time,
Sylvan historian, who canst thus express
  A flowery tale more sweetly than our rhyme,
What leaf-fringed legend haunts about thy shape
  Of deities or mortals, or of both,
    In Tempe or the dales of Arcady?
  What men or gods are these? what maidens loath?
What mad pursuit?   What struggle to escape?
    What pipes and timbrels?   What wild ecstasy?

Heard melodies are sweet, but those unheard
  Are sweeter; therefore, ye soft pipes, play on;
Not to the sensual ear, but, more endeared,
  Pipe to the spirit ditties of no tone;
Fair youth beneath the trees, thou canst not leave
  Thy song, nor ever can those trees be bare;
    Bold Lover, never, never canst thou kiss,
Though winning near the goal—yet, do not grieve;
    She cannot fade, though thou hast not thy bliss,
  For ever wilt thou love, and she be fair!

Ah, happy, happy boughs! that cannot shed
   Your leaves, nor ever bid the Spring adieu;
And, happy melodist, unwearièd,
   For ever piping songs for ever new;
More happy love! more happy, happy love!
   For ever warm and still to be enjoyed,
     For ever panting and for ever young;
All breathing human passion far above,
   That leaves a heart high sorrowful and cloyed,
     A burning forehead, and a parching tongue,

Who are these coming to the sacrifice?
   To what green altar, O mysterious priest,
Lead'st thou that heifer lowing at the skies,
   And all her silken flanks with garlands drest?
What little town by river or sea-shore,
   Or mountain-built with peaceful citadel,
     Is emptied of its folk, this pious morn?
And, little town, thy streets for evermore
   Will silent be; and not a soul to tell
     Why thou art desolate, can e'er return.

O Attic shape! Fair attitude! with brede
   Of marble men and maidens overwrought,
With forest branches and the trodden weed;
   Thou, silent form! dost tease us out of thought
As doth eternity: Cold Pastoral!
   When old age shall this generation waste,
     Thou shalt remain, in midst of other woe
Than ours, a friend to man, to whom thou say'st,
" Beauty is truth, truth beauty," — that is all
     Ye know on earth, and all ye need to know.

            —JOHN KEATS.

15.

INVOCATION TO THE SPIRIT OF ACHILLES.

BEAUTIFUL shadow
　　Of Thetis's boy!
Who sleeps in the meadow
　　Whose grass grows o'er Troy:
From the red earth, like Adam,
　　Thy likeness I shape,
As the being who made him,
　　Whose actions I ape.
Thou clay, be all glowing,
　　Till the rose in his cheek
Be as fair as, when blowing,
　　It wears its first streak!
Ye violets, I scatter,
　　Now turn into eyes!
And thou, sunshiny water,
　　Of blood take the guise!
Let these hyacinth boughs
　　Be his long flowing hair,
And wave o'er his brows
　　As thou wavest in air!
Let his heart be this marble
　　I tear from the rock!
But his voice as the warble
　　Of birds on yon oak!
Let his flesh be the purest
　　Of mould, in which grew
The lily-root surest,
　　And drank the best dew!

Let his limbs be the lightest
  Which clay can compound,
And his aspect the brightest
  On earth to be found!
Elements, near me,
  Be mingled and stirr'd,
Know me, and hear me,
  And leap to my word!
Sunbeams, awaken
  This earth's animation!
'Tis done!   He hath taken
  His stand in creation!
                              —LORD BYRON.

—————◆—————

16.

CORINNA, FROM ATHENS, TO TANAGRA.

TANAGRA! think not I forget
  Thy beautifully-stonèd streets;
Be sure my memory bathes yet
  In dear Thermodon, and yet greets
The blithe and liberal Shepherd boy,
Whose sunny bosom swells with joy
When we accept his matted rushes
Upheaved with sylvan fruits; away he bounds and
    blushes.

I promise to bring back with me
  What thou with transport will receive,
The only proper gift for thee,
  Of which no mortal shall bereave

In later times thy mouldering walls,
Until the last old turret falls;
A crown, a crown from Athens won,
A crown no god can wear, beside Latona's son.

There may be cities who refuse
  To their own child the honors due,
And look ungently on the Muse;
  But ever shall those cities rue
The dry, unyielding, niggard breast,
Offering no nourishment, no rest,
To that young head which soon shall rise
Disdainfully, in might and glory, to the skies.

Sweetly where caverned Dirce flows
  Do white-armed maidens chaunt my lay,
Flapping the while with laurel-rose
  The honey-gathering tribes away.;
And sweetly, sweetly, Attic tongues
Lisp your Corinna's early songs;
To her with feet more graceful come
The verses that have dwelt in kindred breasts at home.

Oh, let thy children lean aslant
  Against the tender mother's knee,
And gaze into her face, and want
  To know what magic there can be
In words that urge some eyes to dance,
While others as in holy trance
Look up to heaven; be such my praise!
Why linger? I must haste, or lose the Delphic bays.

— WALTER SAVAGE LANDOR.

17.

ARETHUSA.

ARETHUSA arose
From her couch of snows
In the Acroceraunian mountains, —
From cloud and from crag,
With many a jag,
Shepherding her bright fountains.
She leapt down the rocks
With her rainbow locks
Streaming among the streams;
Her steps paved with green
The downward ravine
Which slopes to the western gleams:
And gliding and springing,
She went, ever singing,
In murmurs as soft as sleep;
The Earth seemed to love her,
And Heaven smiled above her,
As she lingered towards the deep.

Then Alpheus bold,
On his glacier cold,
With his trident the mountains strook
And opened a chasm
In the rocks; — with the spasm
All Erymanthus shook.
And the black south wind
It concealed behind
The urns of the silent snow,
And earthquake and thunder
Did rend in sunder
The bars of the springs below.

The beard and the hair
Of the River-god were
Seen through the torrent's sweep,
As he followed the light
Of the fleet nymph's flight
To the brink of the Dorian deep.

"Oh! save me! Oh! guide me!
And bid the deep hide me!
For he grasps me now by the hair!"
The loud Ocean heard,
To its blue depth stirred,
And divided at her prayer;
And under the water
The Earth's white daughter
Fled like a sunny beam,
Behind her descended,
Her billows unblended
With the brackish Dorian stream.
Like a gloomy stain
On the emerald main,
Alpheus rushed behind, —
As an eagle pursuing
A dove to its ruin
Down the streams of the cloudy wind.

Under the bowers
Where the Ocean Powers
Sit on their pearlèd thrones;
Through the coral woods
Of the weltering floods;
Over heaps of unvalued stones;

Through the dim beams
Which amid the streams
Weave a network of colored light;
And under the caves
Where the shadowy waves
Are as green as the forest's night;
Outspeeding the shark,
And the swordfish dark,—
Under the ocean foam,
And up through the rifts
Of the mountain clifts,
They passed to their Dorian home.

And now from their fountains
In Enna's mountains,
Down one vale where the morning basks,
Like friends once parted
Grown single-hearted,
They ply their watery tasks.
At sunrise they leap
From their cradles steep
In the cave of the shelving hill;
At noontide they flow
Through the woods below
And the meadows of asphodel;
And at night they sleep
In the rocking deep
Beneath the Ortygian shore;
Like the spirits that lie
In the azure sky,
When they love but live no more.

—Percy Bysshe Shelley.

18.

THE GARDEN OF PROSERPINE.

HERE, where the world is quiet;
　Here, where all trouble seems
Dead winds' and spent waves' riot
　In doubtful dreams of dreams;
I watch the green field growing
For reaping folk and sowing,
For harvest-time and mowing,
　A sleepy world of streams.

I am tired of tears and laughter,
　And men that laugh and weep;
Of what may come hereafter
　For men that sow to reap;
I am weary of days and hours,
Blown buds of barren flowers,
Desires and dreams and powers,
　And everything but sleep.

Here life has death for neighbor,
　And far from eye or ear
Wan waves and wet winds labor,
　Weak ships and spirits steer;
They drive adrift, and whither
They wot not who make thither;
But no such winds blow hither,
　And no such things grow here.

No growth of moor or coppice,
　No heather-flower or vine,
But bloomless buds of poppies,
　Green grapes of Proserpine,

Pale beds of blowing rushes
Where no leaf blooms or blushes
Save this whereout she crushes
    For dead men deadly wine.

Pale, without name or number,
    In fruitless fields of corn,
They bow themselves and slumber
    All night till light is born;
And like a soul belated,
In hell and heaven unmated,
By cloud and mist abated
    Comes out of darkness morn.

Though one were strong as seven,
    He too with death shall dwell,
Nor wake with wings in heaven,
    Nor weep for pains in hell;
Though one were fair as roses,
His beauty clouds and closes;
And well though love reposes
    In the end it is not well.

Pale, beyond porch and portal,
    Crowned with calm leaves, she stands
Who gathers all things mortal
    With cold immortal hands;
Her languid lips are sweeter
Than love's who fears to greet her
To men that mix and meet her
    From many times and lands.

She waits for each and other,
  She waits for all men born ;
Forgets the earth her mother,
  The life of fruits and corn ;
And spring and seed and swallow
Take wing for her, and follow
Where summer song rings hollow
  And flowers are put to scorn.

There go the loves that wither,
  The old loves with wearier wings ;
And all dead years draw thither,
  And all disastrous things ;
Dead dreams of days forsaken,
Blind buds that snows have shaken,
Wild leaves that winds have taken,
  Red strays of ruined springs.

We are not sure of sorrow,
  And joy was never sure ;
To-day will die to-morrow ;
  Time stoops to no man's lure ;
And love, grown faint and fretful,
With lips but half-regretful
Sighs, and with eyes forgetful
  Weeps that no loves endure.

From too much love of living,
  From hope and fear set free,
We thank with brief thanksgiving
  Whatever gods may be

That ño life lives for ever;
That dead men rise up never;
That even the weariest river
 Winds somewhere safe to sea.

Then star nor sun shall waken,
 Nor any change of light;
Nor sound of waters shaken,
 Nor any sound or sight:
Nor wintry leaves nor vernal,
Nor days nor things diurnal;
Only the sleep eternal
 In an eternal night.
     —A. C. SWINBURNE.

19.

ITYLUS.

SWALLOW, my sister, O sister swallow,
 How can thine heart be full of the spring?
 A thousand summers are over and dead.
What hast thou found in the spring to follow?
 What hast thou found in thy heart to sing?
 What wilt thou do when the summer is shed?

O swallow, sister, O fair swift swallow,
 Why wilt thou fly after spring to the south,
 The soft south whither thine heart is set?
Shall not the grief of the old time follow?
 Shall not the song thereof cleave to thy mouth?
 Hast thou forgotten erc I forget?

Sister, my sister, O fleet sweet swallow,
  Thy way is long to the sun and the south ;
   · But I, fulfilled of my heart's desire,
Shedding my song upon height, upon hollow,
  From tawny body and sweet small mouth,
   Feed the heart of the night with fire.

I, the nightingale, all spring through,
  O swallow, sister, O changing swallow,
   All spring through till the spring be done,
Clothed with the light of the night on the dew,
  Sing, while the hours and the wild birds follow,
   Take flight and follow and find the sun.

Sister, my sister, O soft light swallow,
  Though all things feast in the spring's guest-chamber,
   How hast thou heart to be glad thereof yet ?
For where thou fliest I shall not follow,
  Till life forget and death remember,
   Till thou remember and I forget.

Swallow, my sister, O singing swallow,
  I know not how thou hast heart to sing.
   Hast thou the heart ?   Is it all past over ?
Thy lord the summer is good to follow,
  And fair the feet of thy lover the spring :
   But what wilt thou say to the spring thy lover ?

O swallow, sister, O fleeting swallow,
  My heart in me is a molten ember,
   And over my head the waves have met.
But thou would'st tarry or I would follow,
  Could I forget or thou remember,
   Couldst thou remember and I forget.

O sweet stray sister, O shifting swallow,
　The heart's division divideth us.
　　Thy heart is light as a leaf of a tree;
But mine goes forth among sea-gulfs hollow
　To the place of the slaying of Itylus,
　　The feast of Daulis, the Thracian sea.

O swallow, sister, O rapid swallow,
　I pray thee sing not a little space.
　　Are not the roofs and the lintels wet?
The woven web that was plain to follow,
　The small slain body, the flower-like face,
　　Can I remember if thou forget?

O sister, sister, thy first-begotten!
　The hands that cling and the feet that follow,
　　The voice of the child's blood crying yet
Who hath remembered me? who hath forgotten?
　Thou hast forgotten, O summer swallow,
　　But the world shall end when I forget.

— A. C. Swinburne.

20.

BYRON'S LAST POEM.

'Tis time this heart should be unmoved,
　Since others it hath ceased to move:
Yet, though I cannot be beloved,
　　Still let me love!

My days are in the yellow leaf;
　The flowers and fruits of love are gone;
The worm, the canker, and the grief
　　Are mine alone!

The fire that on my bosom preys
　　Is lone as some volcanic isle ;
No torch is kindled at its blaze —
　　　　A funeral pile.

The hope, the fear, the jealous care,
　　The exalted portion of the pain
And power of love, I cannot share,
　　　　But wear the chain.

But 'tis not thus — and 'tis not here —
　　Such thoughts should shake my soul, nor *now*,
Where glory decks the hero's bier,
　　　　Or binds his brow.

The sword, the banner, and the field,
　　Glory and Greece, around me see !
The Spartan, borne upon his shield,
　　　　Was not more free.

Awake ! (not Greece — she *is* awake !)
　　Awake, my spirit !　Think through whom
Thy life-blood tracks its parent lake,
　　　　And then strike home !

Tread those reviving passions down,
　　Unworthy manhood ! — unto thee
Indifferent should the smile or frown
　　　　Of beauty be.

If thou regret'st thy youth, why live?
  The land of honorable death
Is here:—up to the field, and give
  Away thy breath!

Seek out—less often sought than found—
  A soldier's grave, for thee the best;
Then look around, and choose thy ground,
  And take thy rest.
—LORD BYRON.

* * *

21.

TO THE MUSES.

WHETHER on Ida's shady brow,
  Or in the chambers of the East,
The chambers of the Sun, that now
  From ancient melody have ceased;
Whether in heaven ye wander fair,
  Or the green corners of the earth,
Or the blue regions of the air
  Where the melodious winds have birth;

Whether on crystal rocks ye rove
  Beneath the bosom of the sea,
Wandering in many a coral grove,
  Fair Nine, forsaking Poetry;
How have you left the ancient love
  That bards of old enjoyed in you!
The languid strings do scarcely move,
  The sound is forced, the notes are few!
—WILLIAM BLAKE.

NOTES.

NO. 10. KUBLA KHAN. Coleridge says that this poem came to him in a dream, as he was sleeping one day in a chair. As soon as he awoke he seized a pen and wrote thus far, when he was interrupted by a visitor. He was never able to recall the rest of the dream. It was probably suggested by a passage in Purchas's travels, which he was reading.

NO. 11. TO A LADY, WITH A GUITAR. See the sonnet by William Drummond, entitled *To his Lute*.

Ariel, Miranda, Prince Ferdinand, Prospero. Characters in Shakespeare's drama of *The Tempest*, which see.

NO. 12. DAVID PLAYING BEFORE SAUL. From Browning's tragedy of *Saul*. See 1 Samuel, xvi. 23.

NO. 13. STANZAS FROM "WINE OF CYPRUS." See Classical Dictionary for the numerous proper names mentioned in these verses.

NO. 14. ODE ON A GRECIAN URN. "We do not know in the whole field of English poetry a more exquisite piece of fancy than this, which supposes a moment of early Greek life, with its buoyant gaiety and all its simple incidents, transferred to the surface of the Urn and there arrested forever." — *Miss A. B. Edwards*.

NO. 15. TO THE SPIRIT OF ACHILLES. From the drama entitled *The Deformed Transformed*, 1824.

NO. 16. CORINNA, FROM ATHENS, TO TANAGRA. From Landor's *Imaginary Conversations*. Corinna was a woman of Tanagra, (a town near Thebes,) who five times won the prize of poetry from Pindar.

NO. 17. ARETHUSA. For the myth of Arethusa, see Classical Dictionary. See also the references to Arethusa in *The Book of Elegies*.

NO. 19. ITYLUS. See note on *Philomel*, page 65. Also the poem on *The Nightingale* by Richard Barnfield, page 47.

NO. 20. BYRON'S LAST POEM. "These lines, written in Greece, and only three months before his death, are the last which Byron wrote, and, in their earlier stanzas at least, about the truest." — *Trench*.

INDEX OF AUTHORS.